CHICKEN

ALSO BY LYNN CROSBIE

Fiction
Where Did You Sleep Last Night
Life Is About Losing Everything
Dorothy L'Amour
Paul's Case

Poetry
The Corpses of the Future
Liar
Queen Rat

CHICKEN

LYNN CROSBIE

ANANSI

Published in Canada in 2018 and the USA in 2018 by House of Anansi Press Inc.
www.houseofanansi.com

House of Anansi Press is committed to protecting our natural environment.
As part of our efforts, the interior of this book is printed on paper that contains
100% post-consumer recycled fibres, is acid-free, and is processed chlorine-free.

22 21 20 19 18   1 2 3 4 5

Library and Archives Canada Cataloguing in Publication

Crosbie, Lynn, 1963–, author
Chicken / Lynn Crosbie.

Issued in print and electronic formats.
ISBN 978-1-4870-0286-2 (softcover). — ISBN 978-1-4870-0287-9
(EPUB). — ISBN 978-1-4870-0288-6 (Kindle)

I. Title.

PS8555.R61166C45 2018   C813'.54   C2017-904747-7
C2017-904748-5

Library of Congress Control Number: 2017953509

Cover design: Alysia Shewchuk
Text design and typesetting: Sara Loos

Canada Council
for the Arts
Conseil des Arts
du Canada

ONTARIO ARTS COUNCIL
CONSEIL DES ARTS DE L'ONTARIO
an Ontario government agency
un organisme du gouvernement de l'Ontario

We acknowledge for their financial support of our publishing program
the Canada Council for the Arts, the Ontario Arts Council, and the Government of
Canada through the Canada Book Fund.

Printed and bound in Canada

RECYCLED
Paper made from
recycled material
FSC® C103567

For Francis,
Sailor, Belly, *Hero* —
Sweet love of mine.

The real glory is being knocked to your knees and then coming back. That's real glory. That's the essence of it.
—Vince Lombardi

I am writing as an ugly one for the ugly ones.
—Virginie Despentes

THE TUXEDO, a Tom Ford Windsor with satin peak lapels, is lying on the bed.

Scattered over this limp wool-cashmere raiment is a selection of silk socks, garters, a red moiré cummerbund, and unmatched sapphire cufflinks—one the blue limbus of my eyes she serenaded, the other pink: her coarse cat's tongue, the petunia soles of her cat's feet.

I poke my finger through one of the Milanese buttonholes, sit, and watch the night begin to souse the windows.

There is time.

This is the story of Annabel and me. Of my downfall and rise, my fall and—do I rise again?

That would be telling.

Annabel once said, prophetically, that one of us would end up killing the other.

She said it with a smile, as if it didn't matter.

As if everything was plain as sundown.

1

Sundown in all the gold and copper, warm earth and rosy bronze of her skin, warm and cooling when she tumbles away, wild and cat-soft is how I best remember and this is for her.

ONE

PARNELL WILDE, LOS ANGELES, 2017
I BELIEVE IN YOU AND ME

I HAVE NOT shaved, or showered for that matter, in well over a week.

I do not like to leave my sofa bed, which is so laden with crumbs it feels like the beach by the Dead Sea, a rough, shadowy expanse trimming the water that once held me up like Disco Jesus—hair longish and feathered, clean-shaven and granite-jawed.

But the sickness is in charge, not me.

I manage to get up and order two bottles of Thunderbird and a carton of American Legends from Pink Dot.

"Throw in some ramen noodles and cheese puffs," I say. "Pack of gum, a comb."

I remember that my clothes have been decaying in the washing machine for two days, get dressed, and go to the laundry room.

A nice-looking young couple is folding bright, fluffy items as I scoop my pilly, rank-smelling load into a cardboard box.

Then the guy says, "Wait a second, wait a second."

No, I think. *Please.*

"Hey, I know you," he says, and approaches me. His girl-friend hangs back, scrutinizing the pillowcase I have slit and worn as a tank top; my shredded Hulk pants and woven plastic sandals.

"Man, I *love* your movies."

"Seriously," he says, as his girlfriend takes a genuinely horrifying picture of us.

He looks like a boy-band singer and I a conjunctivitis-eyed fiend by his side.

Expressing alarm at the lateness of the hour, I excuse myself, spilling my mini-pack of Ariel powder, and at the door I hear her say, "Are you *sure* that was someone famous?"

"Yes," he says, sounding deflated.

"Damn," he says, and spits on the floor. "I feel like I need a fucking bath."

I shudder as I scud home, just in time for my delivery — *O it's no world for an old man any longer.*

I feel dirty, yet strangely invigorated by my fan.

And I too will cauterize the bad memories in the tub: the memory of the couple; and of Barry, the superintendent, shouting as he mops up all the soap flakes and spit.

My fault my fault.

I will ritualize my ruin — holy bar of Linda soap, smell-ing of the blessed Filipina wrapper-girl's abundant black ponytail, holy the rough cloth and rusted water that dark-ens as I descend into its embrace.

You are still a star, the orchid flecks of soap remind me as they simulate the aurora borealis, fighting through the smog to be seen. *You still glimmer!*

I take a long drink of the blood of the Beloved Son. I drink from alpha to omega, and the heavy sea holds me fast. It rocks me to sleep.

I DREAM OF the éminence grise. He is a ghost who moves through me, telling me to avenge the girl so that I might purge and burn away his foul crimes.

I sit up straight, chilled, and rack my mind. *Hamlet*—I had dreamed of the play, with the words and meaning distorted.

I begin reciting, in a deep, orotund voice: "Swear—"

Rabi, the child who lives alone downstairs, turns up his Shafiq Mureed records.

I hold the washcloth over my face as a muffler and climb out of the ice-cold tub.

This was no dream.

This is what happens when you fall from a great height and crash.

I stop, and stand, frozen to the spot.

There was a small white jackrabbit in the dream, with a blood-red stripe down her back.

She handed me a flask, and a mouthful of cold, clear water helped me stand up and clear off the carrion birds.

After she springs away, I see the writing on the flask.

LOVE ME, it says.

I put on a pair of mephitic flannel pajamas and pat them down. The words, loose and silver, are in the breast pocket and I cling to them anxiously as I climb into bed.

They are gone in the morning but my life, my monstrous life, is the same.

Though tinged somehow, circled in faint pink, like something remotely desirable in a catalogue.

Like the sun breaking over the desert before it begins to boil and burn, it is strained cherries, it is new flesh, it is a perfume called Sugared Grace the girl I was sweet on in my youth once sprayed over her wrists, her throat, and the soft, downy insides of her tenderly open knees.

ONCE WOKEN, I cannot sleep.

I pour myself a cup of the noxious wine and pull out my fancy new Mead notebook. Its hard cover is orange, covered with what appear to be four chorus lines of limber maggots.

I write,

> With each passing day, with each fresh injury, fall, and abject humiliation, I am more and more certain that the God I pray to, near-constantly, is more on side with, say, the sadistic rapists in *Straw Dogs* than the innocent mathematician and his wife. Yes, He will put the bad men in bear traps in Hell, but that's not soon enough and I cannot shake the feeling He enjoys the brute elegance of the conquerors, while agitating their victims as if salting a pig's ear.

Later, I will run a line through these words, afraid of what He plans to do to me next. Write, "SORRY, YOUR MAJESTY," in block letters.

Crawl back into bed and think: I cannot shake Him, however I rant and rave.

He loved me once.

Loved me like a hurricane, the twelve-string guitar avows before a murder of drums.

WHEN *ULTRAVIOLENCE*, DIRECTED by the legendary Lamont Kray, was released in 1976, I awoke and found myself famous.

The film is quite a bit like *A Clockwork Orange*. Kray was furious to have lost the book rights to Stanley Kubrick years earlier, and is said to have muscled Anthony Burgess into permitting him to borrow freely from the novel at no cost.

But, to his credit, the film is not an imitation of Kubrick's. Rather, as the critic Torrence Walker observed in the *Evening Standard*, "*Ultraviolence* is an aesthetic sequel of sorts, which provides an even closer look at crime's luscious perversity, qualities the filmmaker joins in brute isogamy."

On top of this, Kray was given to brag, *his* young star had six inches on McDowell — and a better, stronger body and a sculptural Greek nose.

I had to plead with Kray to remove the tag line "More Blood, Less Ugly" from the posters, but was secretly delighted in assuming, and changing, Alex DeLarge's role, giving it more élan, more allure — and far more cruelty.

My life opens on a hinge. Before and after Kray, I mean.

After: I was too notorious to breathe, and often found myself pressed against walls, thinking, like an abused animal, *I don't feel safe, I don't feel safe*. I became a dragnet for love, the love of shadows and darkness, from all corners;

love that I courted, craved, and, of course, detested for its obvious inconstancy.

I have a contact sheet of photographs from that year, photographs that still show up online, accompanied by shattering new remarks.

"He used to be so gorgeous," or, devastatingly, "My God, what happened?"

In these shots, taken by Richard Avedon, I am wearing milk-white jeans, a heavy leather belt with a big brass buckle, and nothing else.

I smile. I frown. I say, with my large, heavy-lidded eyes, *Come hither*.

Women tell me often that they fell asleep staring at these pictures, wishing, convulsively, they were the daisy Avedon had me hold and pull apart from shot to shot.

The photographs are published in *Esquire* and mean, according to my new manager, that I have arrived.

He is a barracuda who has scripts sent over in the trembling hands of toothsome young girls.

I have a sybarite decorate my Kensington apartment and hire a realtor to start scouting homes in Los Angeles with my girlfriend, a deliciously fat-assed and very serious actress.

I drop the girlfriend the day after we arrive. She threatens to throw herself off the HOLLYWOOD sign and I am thrilled by my fatal allure.

My nights become what I can only remember as a montage, set to "Will It Go Round in Circles," of sexual misconduct, pyramids of cocaine, tumblers of potent tequila, and badly executed conga lines.

My reviewers proclaim that I possess "luminosity," "astonishing grace," and "sly, intelligent malevolence."

Yet everything reverts to my beauty. My dishevelled, pekoe-colored hair, tall, tawny body, and saucer-sized, jade-green eyes are pored and slavered over. One female interviewer meets me at my home, seizes the cuff of my shirt, and puts it into her mouth, her eyes closed and weeping.

I am poised to become a huge star, an *American star*— and, for a short time, it looks like I will be.

Vincent Canby, in the *New York Times*, states: "Parnell Wilde's Sid is a devastating icon and image of modern sexuality. More bestial than Brando's Stanley Kowalski, but just as alluring, he informs us, in a few feline strokes, that Plath's Fascist wants more adoration—and so fatally charming, so hotly charged is his performance, we are compelled to give the damned creature what he wants."

I clip this review carelessly, thinking it is the first of many more to come.

A new wave of prominent directors, including Scorsese, Coppola, and Friedkin—all *enfants terribles*—rushes me, wanting to work with an actor as lethal as their films.

My agent and I sort through offers, foolishly rejecting all but the highest paying.

IN A SHORT piece in *Time*, I appear in a glossy shag and beige turtleneck, and am cited as saying, "It's good to be on top." I am looking at this rimpled bit of arrogance now, which is sitting beneath my can of Colt 45.

I am sixty-seven years old today.

I am paunchy and balding; bloated, with crazed eyebrows and a nose that looks part radish, part road map.

And I am, incidentally, losing my mind.

Asphyxiation, bullets, choking, Drano, exsanguination—
these are the ways I may kill myself. The alphabet game
keeps my brain in some sort of shape.

My new manager, a bottom-feeder called Krishna, has
sent me a card and a box of Little Debbie Pecan Spinwheels:
I am eating them in bed and chasing them with the booze
I gave up ten years ago.

As I drink and swallow golden paste, I look at the letter
again.

> Dear Mr. Wilde,
>
> We are ZIP, a small yet thriving advertising agency.
> And we would like you — a classic badass — to
> appear as the Chickman Chicken mascot in a
> cool and hilarious commercial, introducing their
> new line of spicy chicken breasts. The pirate-
> chicken costume is a lot of fun, and the pay, we
> are afraid, is more of an *honorarium*. (Sorry, man,
> we tried to get you more.)

Krishna has forwarded the chicken suit as well, a massive,
beaked horror loaded with bile-yellow feathers.

I step into it and take a few steps around my apartment,
an outright dump in Koreatown near the Line Hotel.

The music below starts thumping. I had been pecking
and dancing: I had no idea.

I stand stock-still, then slowly return to bed. Drink from
my sippy cup of Dewar's and shake, disgorging fluff.

Things are going to get better, I tell myself faintly, just as
my lights and power surge off. The landlord knocks at the

door for what feels like hours, and then leaves an ominous-looking envelope.

I am, to come clean, flat broke. Together, my pension check and residuals (for an ancient Old Spice ad that occasionally airs in Peru) barely cover the occasional shockingly vile prostitute, let alone the rent on a bachelor apartment in Hollywood.

I will get up and shower, I decide, then go see Krishna.

I see myself walking briskly along Sunset, drinking a black coffee and feeling the old magic move through my veins like drain cleaner.

I will reclaim my life, I vow, deep into the belly of the sweat-soaked pillow, lashed by the rope-twisted brown polyester sheet.

There, I reread the letter slipped under my London apartment's door back in 1976. The pink paper has scalloped edges, soaked impressively in Baccarat's Les Larmes Sacrées de Thebes.

"PARNELL, MY DARLING," it begins, in perfect rotund cursive.

> I am writing you from my office on Lombard Street, where I work for a Very Important Man, who pinches me black and blue each day.
>
> And I am slipping my Budding Pink–painted fingers into my pink slit, thinking of you, in that movie.
>
> You are divinely cruel.
>
> You have dark animal's eyes and a luscious, feral mouth I can imagine tearing into my flesh and leaving beautiful rouge-red wounds.

I feel handfuls of your long, fleecy hair in my hands as you, as you.

My fat, hateful boss just called for me and I rejoiced in telling him, "I'm coming!"

Perhaps we will meet.

Perhaps you will loosen your heavy belt and, as my tongue travels the line of hair below your belly, strike me until I am your bleeding bride.

Until then,

There is a signature I am still unable to interpret.

I never met her, but this letter reminds me of that time and more. The pretty pink secretary's quiet tumult and barbaric love, I caused that. *Me*, I think, flashing on a chain of welts on her creamy back as I thrash my way out of the sheets and light a cigarette.

After smelling the letter again, I mate it with the Canby review, my MJB Video card, expired driver's license, and a picture of a fat, elderly poodle — I'd lifted the beribboned dog on Beverly Boulevard and was headed toward my car when an enraged old woman snatched her away, yelling, "Thief!"

We fought and she ran, dropping her cheap handbag.

I grabbed her cash and the dog's picture out of the bag, then dropped it into a mailbox.

The words *you are divinely cruel* whispered in my ear as I fled, stopped, and coughed, in a tubercular way, into my handkerchief.

"THIS CAN'T BE happening," I have taken to repeating like an inverse mantra, clapping my hands for emphasis.

Krishna, increasingly sullen, gets me a few voice-over jobs and an audition for "Dorothy's Dad" in a reboot of *The Golden Girls*.

"But Dorothy is sixty-five!" I tell my agent, who says, "Aren't you, what, late seventies?"

I drive toward the little studio in Mar Vista, spiking my stick shift with an unusually large marshmallow.

The car stops at a gas station and will not start.

My car is a '66 Arcadian Blue Mustang convertible, syphilitic with rust, its bat-black roof in tatters. I get out and work on it with a wire hanger and a selection of similar tools, then get back in and bang my head against the steering wheel, which squeals in unison with me.

I stare at myself in the rear-view mirror, motion over a custodian.

"I am the Creature from the Black Lagoon," I say. "Hideous. Doomed."

He is a wiry little Asian guy in a gray sweatshirt, with a shaved head and a tiny rat-tail.

"The fuck?" he says, scratching his RASCAL tattoo.

"Should I do this audition and debase myself further?" I ask, snatching up a ballpoint pen and writing "Rascal" on my own hand.

The guy stares at me, then laughs.

"Get the fuck outta here, bangobros," he says.

I fire up the car, text Krishna that I have a sprawling, possibly precancerous mole on my face, and drive off, waving. I feel almost good as I cruise along, smoking and listening to "White Rabbit." At a red light, I wink at a pretty blonde in a mohair sweater.

"Eat shit," the blonde mouths, peeling off and leaving me stalled at the light.

I get out of the car, ignoring the honking, shouting, and worse. Kick my baby's flanks, and she bursts into life.

I am flushed with triumph. When I am almost home, I buy a large bottle and a handful of scratchers.

Cigarettes too, and a lighter emblazoned with the words LIVE FREE RIDE FREE.

I LIE IN bed with my haul and, as I get more and more blissfully wasted, start remembering such beautiful things: a carpet of lotus blossoms, the soaring notes of Elgar's *Sea Pictures*, underwater empires I —

There is a muffled crash and a small gasp.

I am, I see, stark naked. I quickly shrug on my robe and walk toward the living room holding an aluminum bat.

IN A HEAP on the floor beside my nubby, oatmeal-coloured sofa: a young girl, hair stuffed into a watch cap, her long, skinny body hidden beneath layers of shapeless black garments.

Her face is plain, and free of makeup, her sloe eyes magnified by ugly red pebble glasses.

Her feet are bare; I see faint scars on one of her small ears, another below her maxillary sinus.

She is holding a notebook, which I pull from her and examine.

"FOUND HIM," reads the last entry. And *"SOON, I WILL—"*

Her dark, wolf-gold eyes flash as she snatches the book from my hands.

She smiles and I am swiftly repelled by a mouth full of metal.

"Why have you come here?" I ask, and lean against the wall.

She stands, scratching her scalp.

"I wanted to meet you," she says. "I fell asleep on the couch and woke up picking bedbugs out of my hair."

"You're Parnell Wilde, aren't you? I am such a big fan—"

"Please," I say, and I am filled with self-loathing. My intoxicated dreams have turned into terrors. "I don't want you or anyone to see me like this."

I start to nudge her to the door, nervously. What if she's crazy; what if she is here to hurt me?

She crosses her arms, and does not budge.

"Damn," she says. "You're so old now."

Christ. I was only twenty-seven when I made the film, what does she expect?

"I am going to have to ask you to leave," I say, pallid with misery.

Who is she, really?

"I'm an admirer," she says. "And I want to fix you."

She takes my hand and, resisting weakly, I let her.

We sit together in the small club chair and through the caged window watch the sky grow darker.

"What's in it for you?"

"Everything," she says.

"How did you find me?"

"I was driving by and saw you leave," she says. "I bribed the landlord by paying your rent, and—"

The lights spring on. The refrigerator groans.

"—paid your utilities as well."

"Why look for me?"

I watch her face screw up: she could flatter me, but does not.

"I'm obsessed with *Ultraviolence*," she says, but her voice is unsteady. "I make short films—well, videos for now. I want to make a sequel, in a short form or as a series, I'm not sure. I just finished a workshop with Tanya Hamilton. She thinks I should try."

She flushes with pride. I nod, never having heard of Tanya Hamilton.

"I'd write and star in it with you. Well, not you the way you look now."

She blushes.

"Sorry," she says, staring at her feet.

"Don't worry about it," I say, inflating with anger. "The way *you* look now would drive viewers to spike their beverages with cyanide and praise the Reverend Jim Jones."

"So maybe you can fix me," she says.

"Get me a pair of pliers and some scissors," I say, and she laughs.

"I can still see you under all those ruins," she says, peering closely.

Then the gangly, gazelle-elegant girl touches my face lightly, coaxing some of my youth and beauty back to the surface.

She is pleased: her long, burnished fingers meet and make a spire.

"There he is," she says.

I get up and start emptying the bags of groceries she has left on the counter. Starving and bewildered, I push a pie crust into my mouth.

"Why don't you leave me alone?" I say, as raw pastry flies from my mouth in queasy moonbeams.

I sink to the sofa, my shoulders heaving.

She opens her phone and plays something called "Everything Will Be Alright," by the Killers. "A little old school," she says, "but listen."

I do. And, vacantly, I believe, even though I know there will be many more catastrophes, humiliations, and horrors to come.

She dances around the room and, as she sways, her cap falls off and a sea of champagne-coloured waves fall, breaking at her waist.

She hides her hair again, keeps moving, and I stand still, watching.

Watching the criminal who claims to care for me; whose story is ludicrous; who is so ugly she looks like she is in costume.

But she is more than a little bit cute.

She is a girl in my living room dancing barefoot.

It is enough.

Some time later, I buy the biggest can of Raid I can afford and spray its delectable perfume everywhere, taking deep, delighted breaths.

ANNABEL — HER NAME is Annabel Wrath, she tells me — lives in Laurel Canyon. She is twenty-one and has a doctorate in film studies, she says, stuffing her mouth with Entenmann's flower-shaped frosted donuts.

"I make micro-films," she says. "Some work as cinepoems; others are video essays. I worked with Tony Zhou for a while."

More blank staring from me.

"Video is too simple a term, however. Tony says every frame is a painting, or should be, and that is the effect I try to achieve."

I am instantly bored and impatient.

"Every frame is in a frame," I say, being wilfully obtuse. I hate cinema theory, beyond the fantastic Roman assessment system of thumbs up or down.

"Why don't you just make your movie without me?" I say.

She stares at me, perplexed. "Because you *are* the movie. You're a famous fucking movie star, what's wrong with you?"

"In my last movie, an animated one, I played a piece of lost luggage named Gogo."

She laughs, stops when she hears me sigh.

"I saw *Gone Gogo*," she says. "There were moments—"

I wave off her faint praise, light a cigarette, and open the small bottle of Cutty Sark I find in one of the grocery bags.

"I'm done," I say.

"No, you need confidence," she says. "A way back to who you are. I was filming you before, as you walked toward me. But I stopped, it was too—"

"Too risqué?" I say, hopefully.

"Too goddamned sad," she says, showing me a fast clip of a lumpy old man wringing his hands like a prodigious fly: me.

"I'm sorry," she says. "One day we'll look back at this footage and laugh."

She gets up and heads for the door.

"Wait," I say, but I have no idea how to induce her to stay.

"We're just getting started," she says. "You'll get better and better and I'll make hot little movies of you that get everyone excited, and then—"

"What about the way you look?" I say coldly, watching her throat work like an anaconda on an entire donut.

"Worry about yourself, you dirty old bastard," she says, meeting my iciness with a goddamned avalanche.

She releases her hair again, spits her braces out, and smiles.

I get a massive erection, my first in I can't say how long.

"My, my," she says, taking it all in before slipping into the hall and stomping away in hideous army boots.

As I pocket her comical braces, I stare at my bulging robe and feel, deep within the repulsive dirt and trash that occupy my heart, a green seedling nose out.

O bold, dauntless thing!

AFTER ANNABEL LEAVES, I venture to the corner and scrounge through my pockets, hoping to grab some beer, a racing form, and a cigar.

I find a hundred-dollar bill and a glassine bag of adhesive gold stars.

I rattle off my list, and Angel, the usually despicable man at the K-Town bodega, smiles at me, baring his grill.

"You got some pussy," he says, and I am too shocked to answer.

He slides everything I want into a paper bag and hands it to me.

"For you, big star, free," he says, and retrieves an old shot of me in a loincloth, hunting a werewolf.

I sign it "To Angel, my friend at 'The Movies'" and walk home in a bouncy sort of way.

I need to call my bookie. A horse named Lady Annabel is running today.

Right after, I score a big bottle of Black Label, which rustles down my throat like fire honey as I listen to my Survivor tape, evangelizing "Eye of the Tiger" as if it were the Apostles' Creed.

I AM BARELY conscious, holding my phone and lightly kissing it.

"Who holds such mysteries?" I ask its porthole, then, somewhat hopefully, hold it to my ear.

Annabel has added herself as a contact. The photograph is a close-up of her smile. *Heavenly wine and roses*, it whispers to me. Her number spells out YOUR FUTURE like a punk-rock miracle.

And she lives on Wonderland.

"Lady of the canyon," I sing, creakily, and fall back on my suddenly dear sofa.

The phone rings as I am writing, writing in my sleep: my fingers move rapidly across the sofa's green wide-wale corduroy, iterating "the polemical nature of genius *as observed* not exp—"

Is it her?

I am hopeful but guarded: the bill collectors have become ruthless.

"Sit godless before the religious something of the telephone," I recite, desperately searching for my glasses.

Ultimately, I adopt my standard defense, the voice of a sad and brainsick old woman.

"Who moved the lard and what is their name, Precious?" I begin, only to be stricken by Annabel's voice, less a sound than a smell and shape, genies secreting cyprine that squeezes through the silver rectangle at the phone's slender base bottom.

"Are you still up?" she asks, a laugh percolating beneath her sugared words.

I see that it is nine. I have slept through dinner. My Annabel sandwiches—crustless pinwheels of PB & J and buttered watercress rounds—and a bottle of cherry, plum, and pomegranate rosé are waiting in the stuffed fridge; the room is dark with sky. When sparklets of dust shoot past, I make a wish.

"Of course I'm still up," I say, and shake away the clouds.

I light a cigarette and finger-comb my eyebrows, expecting some banter about hot dates and midnight assignations.

Instead, sleepy Annabel says such terrible things.

She went to see *Ultraviolence* when she was just thirteen and many of the boys in the theater she sneaked into were dressed like me and cheered during the infamous, singularly violent rape scene.

"I almost threw up," she whispers.

I say nothing. There is nothing to say.

"And I *did* throw up after you—"

I cover my head with the pillowcase. Wait.

"After he raped me."

She hangs up.

Liberating my head, I sit up, look in the mirror, and my stomach turns.

"WHAT?"

I answer the phone, which is wedged beneath the mattress, and feel my head clamp and start making molds of the words *brutal headache*

"It's chicken day," Krishna says. "The Golden Hags passed, by the way. I'm on my way. Get dressed."

I have a faint, persistent memory of Annabel calling the night before, but the details are hazy.

It was bad, though. I know that much.

I shuffle to the bathroom, piss like a stallion, and scratch my ass. Notice a decent pile of money, my winnings from the race, on the end table, and shimmering footprints everywhere.

I pull on the chicken costume: it is like being embraced by grim death.

Carelessly, I add the belt and scabbard, the Jolly Roger bib.

Krishna laughs when I answer the door, and I start to slam it shut.

"Come on," he says. "It's funny. People like to see villains—"

"Humiliated?"

"Let's go," he says. "These chicken fuckers don't like to be kept waiting."

WE TAKE MY car.

"Nice ride," Krishna says, hiding his face with his ball cap.

I frown, then imagine he is dead, which pleases me.

We drive to the office on Sunset, extruding feathers and blasting the only one of my cassette tapes Krishna can stomach: *Orgasmatron*.

When we get inside, we go right to the washroom-slash-changing room.

Krishna adjusts the head of the costume. I can see his tapered fingers through the grille in the neck that conceals my own smushed head.

We walk into the boardroom, which quickly fills with muted wool suits and bold, sassy scarves.

"Do the line," Krishna says.

"These are the most chickeny chick chick breasts," I begin to recite, sonorously, while gasping in short, tearful bursts.

"That's not it!" someone says peevishly.

I try and try as the anonymous voices flip from irritated to enraged.

"Avast!" I say. "These fiery breasts are *chicktastically* cherrific." At last there is a small round of applause.

Krishna slaps me hard on the back and says, "Chicktastic!"

A calamity of feathers rises through the bars of my cage.

"I told you I'd make you money, old man," Krishna says. "My ride is here, I gotta bounce."

On the ceiling-mounted camera, I am churning against a wall in the rear corner of the empty room.

I am having an episode of some kind: I clutch my heart.

The suits are gone and I am alone; there is no one to help me.

Fitfully, I gather my clothes and shoes, and make my way to the car. It takes forever to squeeze through the door. I am damp and anxious and passersby start to gather, pointing their phones and yelling, "Crazy chicken man!"

As they laugh and take pictures, I recite her name like an orison: *Annabel, Annabel,* and she appears.

She is less hideous today in a quilted one-piece orange jumpsuit, the same boots, and a balaclava. Her body, somewhat on display, intrigues me.

"I called that weasel agent of yours and he told me you'd be here," she says, withdrawing a pearl-handled revolver and training it on the crowd.

"I told him I was Joan Collins," she says, and laughs.

Crouching, she tells those gathered to drop their phones, walk away, and never speak of me again.

She stands and says, "Dance," aiming at their feet until they bust a few moves, pissing themselves with fear as she laughs.

Firing into the sky, she tells them to run and they do.

Annabel steps on the discarded phones, twisting a comely ankle until each one bursts, then kicks them onto the road and gets into the car with me.

I turn on the radio. Suddenly I am scared of her, and piqued as well. I don't want to be a damsel in distress.

"I was shooting blanks," she says and, as "Lazarus" plays, as the suffering man rustles that he is in danger, Annabel beheads then holds me.

"Never again," she says, and I lower my face to hide the fat, juicy tears coursing over my cheeks.

The feathers fly harder and are now exalted: they are a covenant between us.

"You need to be strong," she says.

Her benevolent hands smooth the shame and fear from my face and as I hold her, I squeeze, as if what is perfect inside her — I imagine a hot, white circle — will light up, that she will light up, pink and all the sun inside her, streaming.

I step outside and she peels off the rest of my costume, kicks off her boots.

Naked, I feel distressed and safe all at once.

In the new moonlight, I hold the chicken head, which is funny to me now.

Annabel. I hold her so tightly she is almost aloft. She is my last chance, and I know it.

"I have watched so many men marching to their deaths," I perorate. "Myself among them: *for an illusion and a little bit of fame.*"

She claps. "My lord," she says.

"Wait," I say. "Why did you call me last night?"

"To say goodnight," she says, and kisses me.

Unafraid, I stand bare and free, holding my luscious knight errant.

The blur of dark coats, green scarves, streams of blue wool that rush past us are the sea; the girl is safety and daring. I kneel and kiss her spotless, ice-cold feet.

"YOU TOLD ME that I raped you," I say.

We are in the back seat of my car: I was going to round second base, but stopped, distraught.

"I made a mistake," she says. "I was dreaming and thought you were Sid."

I hold her face in my hands and sing "Duchess."

"That's pretty," she says, plaintively.

Is she waving me forward? I start for second.

She blows the whistle.

It's all right and more than enough to kiss and breathe her young girl's face.

For as long as I am allowed this grace.
Anxiously, I adjure,
Put all the love back in me.

TWO

PARNELL AND ANNABEL, KOREATOWN, 2017
HORRORSHOW & LUSCIOUS GLORY

I HAVE NO idea how she got me home.

I wake up, sick, sweating, and swinish, on a new percale pillowcase printed with daisies.

I have a faint memory of her filling buckets with scalding water and scrubbing my linoleum floors, my grimy windows, and every scuzzy surface in the place. Of her managing not only to clean but brighten the hovel.

After overhearing a string of hushed exchanges between her and Rabi, I get up to see little kitchen curtains alive with happy sunflowers, a bright rag rug that hides the floor, and jars of snapdragons on the sills. The three-legged kitchen table decked out in a pale pink-and-blue-striped cloth.

I am speechless: I write her a note on a piece of cardboard torn from a takeaway box I pluck from the trash bin, thanking her. I say that she made me a palace, and hand it to her, all wobbly and lachrymose.

"I liked doing it," she says. "I like *you*."

She excuses herself: I listen to her in the bath, splashing and singing "Bound 2." She comes out wearing a towel turban, foggy glasses, and my Sulka robe, a moth-eaten remnant of better days.

Gathers her clothes and tosses them in her giant carry-all—a pink vinyl circle with a smiley face and looped strap.

I act cool, like the *Magnificat* that is her humility and grace is just something nice.

"Hey, thanks," is all I can manage. She is pure light and I am lost without my shadows, yet overjoyed to see them go.

"I left you a treat," she says, and dresses in huge jeans and a Snoopy sweater.

Long after she is gone I am still walking around my place, lightly touching everything—smelling, staring. There is an apple pie baking in the freshly scrubbed, ice-white stove, a fat cake of rosemary soap on the sparkling washroom sink.

I remove the pie and, as it cools, wash myself until I squeak. Discover a long, embroidered robe on the wash-room door's gleaming hook: on it, two dragons stand on their hind legs and kiss, making wild, swirling fire.

And I remember: she left her glasses on the damp towels, snapped into two pieces.

This is becoming the best striptease of my life, I think, and—*Bam!*—I am smitten, stupid with adoration, breathing her in and out, the most vivid of dangers, less a threat than a dare—

Be careful and stay in the light, rodent.

I will.

AS I PUT off falling asleep—the new violet-sprigged sheets are so crisp and fragrant, the pillows soft and springy—I think of Annabel, her sweetsoppy smell, Bambi eyes, and bouncy walk; how she sat in my lap and, when I apologized again for living in such a tip, said—

"No one is perfect."

I touch her warm skin, curious, and she deflates.

"I'm so sorry," she says.

"For what?"

"Never mind. It's over," she says, and the light of Florence fills the room, curving at the corners of the frame and waking me.

Annabel has rescued me, I realize, like a valiant firefighter, from the burning bag of shit that is my life.

Opening a worthless checkbook, I begin a journal. In it, I imagine her naked, and gasping for me. I am in the middle of writing a long, reverent fantasy about riding a barded destrier to save her from a fiery beast, about the fawn-colored inflorescence between her legs, about each swollen filament, when I hear a muffled chime.

I grope at the covers, trying to locate the sound, and seize the new iPhone my son sent me; it was loaded with his music, music that I deleted immediately.

It is a text, holding the image of me with a longsword, in plate armor. How did she—?

MY OTHER CHILD had given me the same phone—her old one—for Father's Day, its face smashed to bits.

"It still works, Dad," she told me once I'd liberated it from its festive wrapping and wearily pushed it away.

Afterwards, I would use it to take a picture of a pot of gardenias I was trying to grow on the windowsill, and see an album called "Venice, Ronnie."

The first photograph in the album: a nude of my daughter on all fours, naked but for a head harness, a ball gag, a rope, and a spreader bar.

I closed it, deleted the album one shot at a time, then walked the streets of Venice asking every man who passed me, "Ronnie?"

When one wiry guy in leather pants, a fur blazer, and a tube top said, "What?" I beat the shit out of him.

I beat him so bad my hand quails when it rains, rains his indecent blood, and I am surprised, not unhappily, to want to go roaming again.

"Who is Ronnie?" I ask Pudge, calling her from a pay phone on Lincoln, and she shrieks and hangs up.

"Who is Ronnie?" I ask the ocean, and it barfs up half a seal with white zigzags in its tender gray skin, a shredded beach ball, and a little treasure chest filled with doubloons I pawn for enough liquor to make me forget all of it, even the phone lying on the bottom of the Pacific playing "Twinkle" to a besotted vampire squid.

MY RELATIONSHIP WITH Christine — Pudge is the unfortunate childhood nickname she never lost — has always been fraught, or "sick and harmful," as she so often writes as a salutation in the rare greeting cards she sends me.

Pudge is a tantrum-thrower, a blame-layer, a loud and unpleasant monstress who cannot seem to shake the idea I am withholding something.

Money, primarily.

Love, probably, though she never says so.

My daughter is an exceedingly unattractive young woman with a large, turnip-shaped nose, cruel lips, and long, thread-fine, buff-colored hair. She is a morbidly obese sugar addict who is, to use the argot of AA, powerless over herself.

Chunky as a kid, though solidly, sweetly so; adolescence deformed her beyond recognition. Almost overnight, the child I thought I knew was swallowed whole. Suddenly, she was comprised of gelatinous shapes and lurid red distortions, all of her: even her forearms were baggy trunks, specked with deep clefts and cut with the livid red marks that covered her skin in massive sectors.

I would find her in the kitchen late at night, buttering bread, then soaking it in syrup, squeeze caramel, and chocolate, and dousing it with handfuls of raw unrefined sugar.

She would eat until her lips bled like another savory food, then poke her fat fingers into jelly rolls and suck out their deep garnet centers; pour bright pink Peeps into her mouth chased by cherry cola; stack sugar cookies into triple-deckers and shove them into her raw, churning mouth.

I try to ignore her. The sight of her confuses and disgusts me.

One day I see her fresh from a shower with two large towels pinned together and tied around her body, applying white ointment to her chafed thighs and wincing.

Our eyes meet in the mirror.

She sees my revulsion and I see her face change, irrevocably: watch it set into a look of stoic endurance, eyes unfocused and distant, jaw still and hard.

I step forward and stop.

She closes the door.

I decide to visit the skinniest bitch I know, a friend of my wife's who performs raunchy lap dances for dollar bills and lets me piss on her in the shower.

In ten minutes I am asking her, "Who's a stick-shaped slut?" as she swallows my balls like the queen of the jholawalas.

AFTER THE DIVORCE, my daughter stayed in Beverly Hills with Allegra, my ex-wife.

Allegra and I had come to loathe each other with whatever passion we had left. Prior to our overdue fissure, she and Pudge were becoming meaner by the day, which barely fazed me, so preoccupied was I with leaving.

I went on a terrific bender the night I moved out, foolishly called my wife and told her to forget any legal wrangling and "keep everything, I'm moving onwards and upwards."

She did, including all of the Kray film money. *That* hurt.

The little bit I was able to scrounge from the divorce I converted into women, liquor, and drugs: dear powdery flesh of Christ!

I LOOK AT Pudge's email, mildly curious since she so rarely communicates with me.

"See attachment," my daughter has written, eloquently.

I find one of my pairs of glasses and poke the screen until a video appears.

There I am, repulsive and inhuman, holding a skein of chicken feathers and saying, "My angel."

This is what I'd said to Annabel when she arrived at the commercial shoot, and it is she who has uploaded the tiny movie she has called *Swain* to something called Dailymotion.

It takes some time and some spiked instant coffee to discover that she is, it seems to me, insanely popular, with hundreds of thousands of followers on this site and on the many links I stab at.

Her avatar confuses me: it is an otherworldly model, coolly naked and carrying a spotted fawn.

One of the comments about me says, "We need to cure old age."

Another says, "Isn't that the old guy from *Ultraviolence*? The one who gets kicked to death by Sid?"

I *am* Sid. Or I was.

I resign myself to the truth of DiRtyBastid187's words: I am the old guy.

I feel beaten and tap out an impulsive response to Pudge.

"My new girlfriend made this. Isn't she pretty?"

She writes back like lightning, "That's Annabel Wrath, she's an experimental filmmaker. She goes out with Will Harford. Sorry to blow your fantasy."

Will Harford is a famous actor, whose charismatic ugliness assaults me from magazines at the bodega almost daily.

He is tall, dark, and emaciated, and dresses like an undertaker.

He played one, a psychopath, in a recent Oscar-winning film.

Fuck me.

As I absorb this blow, I see the little brat has ended her note with a happy face and an utterly horrifying photograph of me taken as I was squatting in my kitchen, trying to catch an enormous cockroach, the one and only time she visited me.

I am coronary event–colored and sweating: the bug is actually lying on its side, bored.

"P.S.," she writes. "Send this to your girlfriend?"

I am about to send her a picture of Godzilla with YOU in the subject line, but can't. She's just sad, I remind myself.

When Pudge was four, she made me a picture of her dad going off to work in a plumed hat, musketeer suit, and gun. She has painted herself watching from the doorway in a sunny yellow dress. Her eyes are hearts and hearts flock around her, some alighting on the word *love*, which she has painted in pretty red script beneath the two of us.

I still have the painting, folded up in an eight-by-ten envelope containing my valuables — now including my DIY journal and a strand of living Veuve Clicquot hair.

MY CRUSH DEEPENS in spite of Annabel's boyfriend, whom I find online and stare at, sick with jealousy.

I find a clip from an interview with him that mentions me!

A pretty girl, poignantly oblivious to the tatty bra strap that has fallen from her shoulder, has just asked Harford a question. He smiles.

"*Influenced by Parnell Wilde?*" he responds, as if this is an astonishing suggestion. "Maybe, in the vaguest possible way, but there's been loads of bad guys since him, and far better, I might add."

The girl smiles and nods as he stares into the distance, gently stroking his tall, product-loaded hairdo.

I loathe him.

And I give up—but not on *CHANCE*.

I write the word in my new journal, a pad of blue Post-its I swiped off a pharmacist's counter. When I can afford it, I fill out the prescription for a fentanyl patch a crooked doctor in El Sereno wrote me, with repeats. I gave him, in exchange, a hundred dollars and a picture of Heather Locklear I'd ripped out of a magazine and signed, with many kisses, "To Doc Marcus, who wettens me."

And, when I can afford it, I spend at least a day and night floating and songwriting. My first, promising lyric reads, "The girl with the fizzy-colored hair is everywhere / with her kick-ass ways and apron on / Cellini eyes and legs *to there*."

This gets affixed to my dashboard.

I am crushing hard, distracted and flooring it. When I reach a phenomenal eighty miles per hour, I gather the attention of a cop and, because I am so stoned, think I am wheeling through space.

When he asks for my license and registration, I say, "Nice ass," to get his attention, then press the sticky note to his chest.

I get his attention. And a black eye.

When he finally peels off the paper, he skims it and says, "Not bad, old-timer."

"Oh, that?" I say. "I wrote it in like—"

He has left, but when? Judging by the enraged cortège behind me on Olympic, I'd say an hour ago.

They are so angry. I must soothe them.

I strip, get out of the car, and dance.

My reviews are mixed. I listen most attentively to "Move your saggy ass before I shoot you," and do just that.

Someone, her voice high and euphonious, yells, "Parnell Wilde!" She claps and whistles; sounds I carry with me in my invisible jetpack as I flee the scene, coursing through palms, nipping at fish, and crashing, inevitably, on the less coily and damp end of my sofa.

AFTER THE MONDO-LETTERED CHANCE, I write that Annabel and I shall "revise and repair" each other. However crazy, or impossible, it seems.

"Love each other?" I write, in letters like tiny swarming cell cultures I am tweezing one by one.

The landlord bangs at my door.

"What the fuck do you want, you hairless cunt?" I say, moving to the door in a fury and opening it in time to see him scurrying away.

I catch a glimpse of myself in the mirror, big and scowling, and it occurs to me I have something Harford doesn't.

I'm not weak.

I spend the rest of the night making a sign for Annabel's and my new enterprise.

STARTING OVER, I write with a chisel on a scrap of wood snatched from the street, gouging in two birds ascending the letters.

I varnish it and wrap it in some old paper Angel gives me, kiddie stuff, clowns and knives.

One day I will buy a fine tuxedo, classy as fuck, and drape Annabel's sable-colored skin in pearls and priceless stones, proving to her that she could be a very attractive lady with a bit of work.

This day is just cell detritus, floating in my eyes. But, however small and fleetingly I behold it, it is clear that my new life is real and only beginning.

"Come and see me?" I write in the comment box below her video, signing my request, "Chicken."

She says yes, she says yes!

I START WRITING short romantic manifestos. One-line urgencies like "The only thing stopping us is *us*."

When I have accumulated a large number of these, and when I am parlously drunk one night, I go to Hollywood and Vine and recite them, dressed in a violet frock coat and spangled black slacks I find in a box on the curb.

I want people to know of my oratory power.

I am circled and told to stop.

"Your woman will leave you," one man says. His wife, a furious behemoth, says, "We're in from Omaha. Just sing 'Purple Rain,' motherfucker."

I do.

I sing it badly, but with such pain that the woman drops her phone and cries. She takes my hand and sings the chorus with me, her face a wet black rose.

ANNABEL TEXTS ME:

The masquerade is over

What is she talking about?

She knocks, and I am worried. What if she is a whiskered selkie? Or the dreaded Ligahoo?

She is not.

The tall, slender lady I admit is a luna moth in miles of white crepe. She has black-cherry lips and black lashes like folding fans; her lustrous hair is pinned up with sweet alyssum. Her ears are pierced to the apex; a ruby glows above her dark, lush mouth.

I stare, transfixed.

And remember that I have chosen to dress in denim overalls and a melon-green shirt I think brings out my eyes.

Denim overalls.

She rakes her eyes over this outfit, over my tan suede Clarks desert boots, light-blue socks, and red paisley neckerchief.

And Annabel's lip curls, fractionally more as she opens my present, which she tosses, barely unwrapped, on the little table by the door.

"Come in," I say, and try to guide her to the sofa, where two cold Genesee Cream Ales await.

"I thought you could hang the sign in your office," I say, and stop. She isn't listening; she is lightly whistling, so very like a nightingale, standing by the open window, drawing in fresh air.

I feel less nervous than miserable. She is so beautiful, it is terrible.

She is that model holding the deer: I flash on her holding a repugnant star-nosed mole — me — as it loudly relieves itself.

It's fine, it's fine, I think. I am a movie star! Who is she?

Composing myself, I tell her that I have been working on some inspirational writing, and move closer, touching her arm.

She removes my hand and excuses herself, while I quake, thinking I have left the toilet bowl freckled with my posterior anguish; that the towels reek of me, that the sink still cups the blood I spat into it late last night trying to extract a black molar with Rabi's needle-nose pliers—

I hear my dresser being opened. What could she be looking for? There is nothing to steal.

She returns with an old photo album: a ribbon-bound rectangle with magnified snowflakes on its laminated cover.

"These are your kids?" she says, rudely leafing through the professional portraits Allegra insisted we have done each Christmas.

Her finger is jabbing my son's face.

It is a picture little Pudge took of him dressed in red velvet and a black bowler hat, setting fire to the tree.

My wife told everyone it was staged but no, no, there were firemen and lies and blackened presents and yet still she claimed he was "just playing around."

"I will beat you to death," I said to him that day.

I take the book away and tell her I am not much for looking backwards.

She is so desirable that I ignore her misconduct, sidle up to her, and say, "Is it getting hot in here, or is just me?"— then laugh like an idiot.

Annabel frowns. "Look," she says. "I want us to work together, but this feels like a date, and it's too much, too soon. Also, I don't date guys like you," she says, and I cringe.

What, ugly old bastards?

And where had I heard that first bit before? Oh yes, *I'm* the one who has said as much to more girls than I can remember: wanting to pursue but never be pursued, getting bored when my overtures worked.

I'm angry to be trapped in my obvious crush. *And* overalls.

I stand up and dissever my journal. Face her.

"I was inspired by you," I say. "I thought I — I thought we were going to change. But only you did: why, why did you come here in the first place?"

I am shaken and tear-damp, and at this moment a bumblebee heads straight for me, droning its murderous intent.

I panic and run in circles as Annabel lights one of my cigarettes and uses its smoke to guide the little fatso out the door.

Mortified, I turn away, my shoulders moving up and down.

"Oh fuck it," she says, and suddenly she is behind me, snapping my overall straps until I turn around and then she is kissing me, deeply, and digging her pearly nails into my back.

"I love my present," she says, and smiles. "Buzz."

She hands me my beer and we both drain our cans in long swallows.

Squashing hers, she presses her palm to my cheek, leaving a pink mark that will spread all over, softening me.

"I came here as myself because I trust you," she says. "That's saying a lot. Please. Give me some time. It's complicated."

"That's supposed to be my line."

"Yes, and this is yours too," she says, rudely forcing her hand between my legs and rubbing, roughly, until I am excited and mad.

"You'd better go," I say.

She looks at my tented pants and laughs: "Again?"

"I'll see you later," she says, blowing me a kiss. I catch it and jam it into the bib of my overalls.

I have to remind her to take the stupid plaque, which she sticks into the slit of her big feathered purse.

Long after she has gone, I discover a photograph missing from my album—she can have them all.

For there is the smell of oakmoss and May rose; there are feathers enough for the delirious end of a cockfight.

I AM FEELING scared and hopeful the next morning when her email appears:

> I'm going to Rome with Will. I need to work on my screenplay and book.
>
> I behaved badly last night. I want to change. With you.
>
> I hung the plaque over my desk, thank you.
>
> I will see you when I'm back, and will be sending witchy things your way, some by mail and some, well—
>
> *Attendere vostro specchio!*
>
> AnWr Xo

DOES ANNABEL CHANGE her mind, and get off the plane? Does she appear, as I read her message, to offer me a bite of her long neck?

No, no, no.

It just rains goddamn hell forever.

She's gone, gone with him. I must have been insane thinking she and I—

I shake off a memory of my hand, hovering near her like a fat, skittish lapdog.

Turn the phone off, and check my mail. Find among the final-notice bills an embossed invitation to a gala at the Biltmore's Gold Room.

I see that the gala is tonight. It has been a month, easily, since I opened the mailbox.

This is something, I think.

I pull my one good suit and shirt from the wardrobe and hang them by hot running water in the bathroom. Shave carefully, and shake the last of my Drakkar Noir onto my palms, my face, and my balls. Then sit on the bed, in my undershirt and shorts, until night falls.

When I arrive at the party, the host, a famous bene-factress named Mrs. Show, frowns and snaps her fingers. Her assistant nervously scans the guest list and finds me. Mrs. Show lets a smile slowly ascend her polymeric skin.

"*Darling* Parnell, so very good to see you," she says, and as she walks away, I see her savagely crossing my name off the list.

I swallow hard, find the bar. There are a few pretty girls there, drinking apple martinis.

I start to tell them one of my best stories, about Sir John Gielgud and an amphetamine-crazed squirrel, when the short one interrupts with a sullen "Who?"

This is their cue to turn on their heels and leave.

I keep a look of fake confidence in my eyes and start to plot my exit. Jason Velour, a hot director, approaches me and starts to rave about *Ultraviolence*.

"—and when you tell the girl it might not be too repul-sive to violate her!" he is saying when I interrupt.

"Do you have any work?"

I sound like a migrant tobacco picker.

"Oh. Ah, no. Things are crazy right now. But call me, absolutely, and we'll talk." He winks at his seven-foot-tall girlfriend, and scribbles on a dirty napkin he hands to me with a slap of my shoulder.

"This guy is *the best*," he says, and disappears into the crowd.

I pluck a pimiento from the napkin, thrilled by my daring, and look at the number.

310-555-1212.

And this is how well things are going: I turn my phone on and try it.

I AM STANDING in the corner of the room, by the open bar, having a rowdy conversation with no one.

I press the phone to my ear with one hand and use the other to signal for a double Nicaraguan Twilight, then pour the deep-violet drink down my feverish throat.

"I *told* Finchy they weren't Scottish delicacies!" I am shouting as the bartender summons over a fastidious man with a short, curly wiglet who tells me I'm cut off.

"Please ask him to leave," an ancient dowager says. *Allegedly* I rifled through her purse while she talked to her walker, a miserable young man in a too-large baby-blue tux.

"I was on my way," I say, leaving in a huff after snagging a slender bottle of cognac. When I get outside, I feel my heart contract. This is something new: I slide slowly down and plant my ass on the sidewalk.

I have several twenty-dollar bills and a gold pillbox in my pocket.

I'm rich!

A girl whose legs look like skyscrapers walks past in a cloud of 24 Faubourg.

"Hello, my lovely," I say, discreetly hiding my frayed cuffs and the new, jagged tear on my slacks.

"Creep," she says, picking up her colt's pace.

"I'm not crying," I say to myself as the sky opens and issues forth, lacerating my face.

I get up somehow and aim myself at the valet, who is stepping gingerly out of my car.

"You take it easy, man," he says, and gives me a short squeeze.

I put the pillbox in his palm and drive away.

There is some goodness in the world, I think as I zigzag home.

At a crosswalk, a chubby pimp flicks his cigar onto the seat beside me, starting one hell of a fire.

"Bitch, watch out," he says, brushing ash from his ankle-length zebra coat.

But ugliness always prevails, I realize as I do the unthinkable and walk home — and by home, I mean my local bar, Cindy Club, where at least one older lady believes I'm something special.

"Thanks for waiting up," I say to Siobhan. She jumps up, yanks at her tube dress, and gives me a wet, smoky kiss.

SIOBHAN IS A former actress, a year or so younger than I. In the right light, she is quite pretty, and tonight I decide to take her home with me.

We take her car to my place and the minute I close the door, she gets on her knees and eases my limp dick from my fly.

It just sits there in her orange-tanned hand like a sea slug.

She licks and rubs it, grazes it with her teeth, and finally yells at it, "Get hard, for Christ's sake!"

I return it to safety and zip up.

"It happens," she sighs, peeling her dress off and walking to my bed in her large, buttressed bra and support hose.

I want her to leave so badly.

I drain the rest of the cognac — Bache Gabrielsen Hors d'Age — in a single draw.

"What about me?" Siobhan says, and I think she means the bottle.

But no. She has spread her legs and exposed the slit in her beige underpants: all I can see is gray bush and crumpled labia.

"I'll be right back," I say.

I run to the door, slam it, and keep running.

I hear her follow: she is calling my name as I lie under a balcony by the parking lot, gripped with blind panic.

"*Fine*, you fucker," she says, and I hear her go inside and quickly come back out. I see her marker-mended heels two feet from my hiding place.

Her voice catches as she tells me never to call her again, which is when I sit up involuntarily, cracking my head.

Her footsteps stop, then resume.

I stay put, enjoying my view of a wedge of deep blue sky and a glitter of stars.

I think of Annabel in my bathtub, how her pussy must have looked like an apricot, with a thin slit at its center.

I go inside and to bed, where I abuse myself, howling with pleasure and abominable loneliness as I release white spume onto the mattress.

IN THE MIDDLE of the night, I wake up sweating.

I had forgotten being arrested.

On my way to the bar, I'd seen a grimy blank star-shaped tile on the Hollywood Walk of Fame.

It is perfection, I decide.

It is located at Vine and Cahuenga, right beside that of another monster, Bela Lugosi; his star is dressed with tiny bat wings and framed by old vials of morphine.

I rush into a souvenir shop and lift a Sharpie, a packet of Kleenex, and a bottle of Windex, then take off my shirt and get on my hands and knees to scrub the tile. I have just lettered my name on it when red lights illuminate this fraught exercise.

It is too awful to talk about: the cops' amused faces when I finally produce my sagging, cowboy-stitched wallet, the radio call — "What's the numerical code for fastidious old drunk?" — and then my clumsy attempt to button my soiled shirt.

"Whatever happened to respect?" I had called after the little cop with the handlebar mustache.

He stroked it as he told me to ask myself that very question.

The little sage.

A NEW DAY.

I pass a nearly bald deodorant under my arms, stick my head under the tap, dress in a deep-yellow shirt, brown slacks, and tan loafers.

"You look like a hot dog," Rabi says when I step into the hall.

He's wearing a gingham dress, tap shoes, and a knit taqiyah: he pushes past me, carrying a box of mice dressed for a relay race.

I am meeting my daughter at SEAS Café, a beige, institutional place she likes "because none of my classmates ever come here."

At twenty-eight, after innumerable failed ventures, she has returned to school—she now wishes to become a dental hygienist.

As I approach her, I see she is wearing pink scrubs, that her damp hair is tied back with a length of blue floss.

She had wanted me to meet someone—her Oral Hygiene instructor, it turns out, an ill-conceived fix-up.

"I told her to forget it: she's too old for you," she says, glumly shaking a cannonade of sugar into her fudge latte. "She's your age," she says, sinking into the chipboard booth. I pay her tab and walk her to her dorm; attempt to ignore her roommate, who is napping in her underwear and nothing more.

I look at my whalelike daughter, whose eyes look a bit like mine. Mine, which were compared by one exuberant reviewer to "Hiroshige's sea in *Sudden Shower over Shin-Ohashi Bridge and Atake.*"

And I grab her and smell her head, which is always salty and filled with sun, like a little beach.

"How did things get so bad between us?" I say, handing her a tuition check that is going to bounce.

"You left us," she says, nudging me to the door and closing it.

As I walk down the hall, I see *Ultraviolence* posters in three rooms.

In the film, I beat a college dean half to death and raped his wife while whistling the theme from *For a Few Dollars More*.

The music escapes my lips as I hit the stairs.

The woman who played the dean's wife was thirty-five at the time. I fucked her. I almost go back and tell Pudge, but I am suddenly limp with exhaustion.

I sit for a while on the steps, and am eventually shaken awake by the janitor, who recognizes me from *Kill Your Face!*, a straight-to-video movie I made in the 1980s.

"That was so scary, man," he says.

He has no idea.

PUDGE IS VERY wrong.

There was an Arabic actress and activist I met through Kray.

Fatima: a maker of smiley-faced breakfasts, the owner of lithe, solid legs, a gifted cellist, and the fifty-eight-year-old mistress of dirty, thrilling talk.

She left me, she said, because her husband "didn't deserve to be hurt."

But for a short while, she called me her *Chérie* each time I rode between her sleek, sandalwood-soaked thighs; she let me comb her lustrous dark hair and wear her long pealing necklace. Craning her head on her lovely neck, she would talk about things I didn't understand in words that sounded like rain freckling a tin roof.

The many men at her funeral kissed her white tombstone, leaving imprints.

The kisses remain. On occasion, I visit the marble grave with lotus blossoms. I still fall to my knees the way I did the day her husband, who never knew, called to tell me about the car accident and her neck broken horribly, the neck of my mare.

Kray came to the funeral with me, and, as her ivory casket was lowered into the grave, asked, "Did you bang her?"

"Yes," I said quietly, and he laughed.

"Oedipussy," he said.

I THOUGHT OF Kray as a bastard and a genius.

When he signed me up for *Ultraviolence*, I smoked some hash and went to see *Exterior*, Kray's first film, in a nearly empty theater on Regent Street.

It is, on one hand, a barely comprehensible story about a space cavalry led by a messianic stallion who communicates with the past by racing past the stars for a gifted astronomer.

On the other hand, *Exterior* is an almost painfully beautiful, Promethean study of what film *could be*, divorced of linear narrative, consensual logic, and the prevalent metanorms regarding structure and meaning.

When X, the holy stallion, is spurred to his death by a sadistic chimpanzee, I throw my hard, sugared popcorn into the air and, as if physics do not apply to the Locust Theatre, it rises to form a glowing nebula that I and the others pray to, fervently.

I say another prayer for Kray to save me.

The small shrouded woman three seats to my left stares at me and, with some difficulty, pulls what appears to be a golden stick from her heart. "More tears are shed over answered prayers than unanswered ones," she says.

I am so stoned, I know none of this is happening. Not really.

All the same, I have a glass of wine with the saint, Teresa, and stroke her wimple, dreamily.

"It's all coming true," I say, and she murmurs her assent

Weeping, she says, "Yes, everything you want."

I AM THINKING of Fatima, of Teresa, and of Kray's movie as I coax the engine to turn over.

"Purr for me, precious," I say, stroking her dash and patting her gently.

Nothing.

After *Exterior*, I see another of Kray's early films, a black-and-white adaptation of *The Miracle of the Rose* starring Warren Beatty as Harcamone and Catherine Deneuve as Jean Genet.

I recalled the scandal around the film; its own tag line was "What sort of madman would adapt *Jean Genet?*"

I bring Flora, my girlfriend, with me, and am so mesmerized I forget to squeeze her ass or insist that yes, of course she is prettier than Deneuve.

My hand falls out of hers and covers my mouth.

Even now, I cannot bring myself to speak of how he managed to persuade me that extreme criminality and ravishing beauty are one and the same; that both reveal themselves slowly, as roses do, to be exquisite fatalities not suited to live once captured and enslaved.

Divine monsters in leg irons; a mutilated *rose des vents* molesting a buttonhole!

I look up at the end of the credits and Flora is gone, FUK U written on a candy wrapper beneath her seat.

I don't care. I love it, I love it all.

I see everything he has done, five movies, each of them a strange jewel commissioned by a greedy, mad, and brilliant king for his heavy, listing crown.

Ultraviolence will be the largest gem, part sea urchin, part pink diamond, and I—

My car starts, and as I slowly reverse, Pudge's roommate, who has thrown on a dress, runs toward me.

"MR. WILDE? CAN we talk?"

Has Pudge been sleep-violent again? I steel myself.

"Yes," I say, weakly.

She is Cat, in a charmless yellow frock, and her boyfriend, Cotton, she says, who does odd jobs and is older, has *created* a screenplay.

"Oh," I say, not at all happy, but relieved my strange daughter has not punched her while snoring and yelling the selection of deeply offensive German phrases she picked up during a student-exchange program in Munich.

"Is the screenplay in your—" I want to say "bag," but she has none.

"No, we are going to improvise. Cotton works best that way. But the plot's all up in his head," she says, knocking her skull to make sure I understand what this piece of his anatomy looks like. "It's about a home invasion, a terror film, a real mindfuck. You'd be the old man who—"

"Invades the house?"

"No." She laughs. "You'd be the victim."

"How much?"

"We're broke. But we can give you, like, two hundred dollars now, and offer you some of the revenue. It's pretty obvious you need to make a comeback. This could be your *Wrestler*," she says.

"Or my *Beaver*," I say, thinking of Mel Gibson, a slimmer, more respectable version of me.

"We start shooting in the next two weeks," she says. "Cotton thinks we can do your scenes in a day. What do you think?"

She looks so hopeful, it gets to me. And who knows? Maybe Cat is right. What I do know is that if I don't get my second act soon, I'm done for. I'd thought Annabel would change me, but—

Better not to think of her. I imagine her choking on pasta puttanesca, and let Harford save her.

"I'll do it," I tell her. Cat kisses my cheek, hands me some bills, and climbs out of the car.

She waves at me as I twist the key again: the Lady is wide awake.

"*O dulce doncella*," I say as I maneuver onto Sunset, thinking about what it might be like to be a star again.

PER VIA AEREA. ESPRESSO.
Via Vittorio Veneto, 125, 00187 Roma, Italy, #786

Dearest,

I spend my days filming: the light is like Hollywood, beatified. Enclosed is some *stregoneria*:

drink it at midnight, when my wolves are calling.

AnWr Xo

She has sent me a vial of sunshine. I drink it that night and, after I have driven to the Hills, it hits and I run wild with golden dogs until morning.

I CALL KRISHNA as I drive, interrupting him occasionally to curse poky old drivers and young ones with death wishes.

"I got you Fan Expo," he says.

This is a notorious low point for actors: sordid events usually held in cruddy basements filled with crazy-eyed fans in costume.

"You can walk away with a couple of grand, cash," he says. "Just for being the guy who slept with Darth Vader."

I did. In *Star Wars SexyBack*, the most despised in the series and the by-product of an insane, drug-addicted director whose child groom wrote the screenplay.

"There's a ticket to New Jersey under your door. You leave in a week."

Why not, I think. I could cover some bad checks and possibly spend some time in New York.

When I get home, I see Krishna has started packing for me. He is clearly happy to get me out of town and away from him.

The last time I asked about new parts, he said, "I can't hear you. We must have a bad connection."

I was standing right there.

BEFORE EXPO, I shoot *House of Crazy* with Cat and Cotton.

All of my scenes take place in a warehouse space modified to look like a typical suburban home.

These modifications include a GOD BLESS THIS MESS needlepoint pillow, a plaid sofa, and a stereo console that leaks Meat Loaf ballads all day.

They blew Cat's book allowance at a thrift shop and cannot afford to hire any more actors. My wife is a mop.

Cotton divines my lines, then feeds them to me.

I say things like, "You'll never get away with this," and "Hey, that really hurt."

I am spit on by Cotton's friend, a kid in a snowflake-patterned balaclava, menaced with an axe and a chainsaw, and doused in ketchup and flames.

"I am slain!" is my final line, recited as I stagger to the bucket and embrace the mop.

"Oh, shit, this looks so good," Cotton says.

He is filming the movie on his phone and will have to edit out the several calls he takes and his "Panda" text tone.

He "drops it" fast, emailing me the link to YouTube in less than a week.

I watch all forty-five minutes of it on my own phone.

My face never moves.

I wrap the phone in a paper towel, then another, and place it carefully in the crisper beside an untouched, viridescent onion.

Then I lie on my belly and fall asleep.

"Why?" I ask God. He is sitting beside me on a small raft in the sea, throwing vegetable chum at a desultory shark.

"Be patient," He says.

I swim away, and He calls after me.

"I love you like a son," He says, and laughs His ass off.

"Thank you," I say, and wake up.

The bedding is shredded. I find a shark's tooth in my pillowcase.

The phone makes noises. I mummify it more densely and whisper, "It's a funeral. Show some decency."

I am leaving for New Jersey in a few hours.

I lower my head and say, "He was not a good man, nor was he evil."

IT IS TIME to accept my failure with humility, and to endure.

To endure is all!

I take a bus to the airport, make a detour, and, on the plane, learn that Annabel Wrath's boyfriend is also appearing at Fan Expo.

How wonderful.

My seat is directly beside the rank, stinking toilet, and a frightened woman who keeps spelling BOMB with peanuts on her drink tray.

I rattle the *Star-Ledger* and learn that Harford is making a documentary about fan conventions that he calls "a poignant look at the American underbelly."

Creep, I think, yawning.

I tear strips from the paper, make a few cranes, and wonder if she'll be there.

A drunk guy in the seat kitty-corner to mine interrupts my reverie by leaning back and telling me, "You look really nice."

I stare at my reflection in the window and see that the crown of my skull is covered with new, Folgers-brown hair;

that the thick crease between my eyes has vanished into a silvery line.

Enchantress, I think, remembering that when we met she said that she would change me.

I try to lean back but cannot: I have forgotten I am in the back row.

Instead, I toast my seat companion with the Crown Royal I slipped on board in a contact-lens fluid container.

"Cheers, darling," I say, and hastily she reassembles her peanuts to say CHARMED AM SURE.

I keep making cranes. I have 666 to go and need all the good luck I can get.

THE CROWNE PLAZA HOTEL hall is agreeable enough but we, the stars, are relegated to the basement.

I meet people all day, if fewer than Leatherface and Burt Ward, who are seated next to me.

And I pocket a fair bit of cash, mostly for signing *Ultraviolence* posters and arcane *Star Wars* memorabilia.

At noon, Malcolm McDowell is seated beside me. He is small and angry and at one point yells at a distressed, middle-aged woman in a ballgown, "I don't want to read your fucking fan letter, just give me the cookies!" He yanks a package of Oreos from the lady's gift bag, stuffs several into his mouth, and looks at me.

"Fans, amirite?" he says, spraying me with chocolate crumbs.

Strange men and women try to kiss me and I am asked repeatedly if I am single. After a while this starts to feel good, it is so utterly unlike my life.

And when I look up, there she is, dressed as someone she says is Jill Valentine: tight black rubber shirt and fatigues, head-to-toe body armor, long hair braided under a Yankees cap.

"You're adorable," I say, reaching nervously for her hand, still wary after our little date.

She flicks her braid off her shoulder.

"I got dragged back from Milan for this," she says.

Just then, a fat man in sandals slaps down a sheet of paper.

"Sign it," he says.

I ask for the money and he is incredulous.

"What the fuck for?"

My Valentine spins and elbows him in the face, takes him down, and, using his prone body for elevation, kisses me.

"You smell like cheap cigarettes," she says, and films me for a while as I write, laboriously, on photographs of myself in a hot tub with Darth Vader.

"WHAT'S THE BOOK about?" I ask Annabel. "And the movie?" She, Harford, and I are in Atlantic City, having lethal zombies at Martell's Tiki Bar on the boardwalk.

"They're very similar," she says. "The book is about *Ultraviolence* as a sequel or coda to *A Clockwork Orange*. It's an examination of the ways in which ideas regarding sex and gender are attached to new ways of thinking about the usual binaries, female weakness, male predation. And the film will—"

Harford is obviously bored. He finishes his mai tai, whispers something to Annabel, and wanders off toward the water.

I look up and the Tiki Cam has captured him and a hula dancer in a clinch below an orange-neon palm tree.

"What did he say?" I ask Annabel to distract her.

"Oh," she says, coloring. "He has a fairly big part in it, can you believe it? So he thinks I should be more discreet."

I press a little green sword to my wrist, feel a rush of fatigue and desolation.

"And that talking about it is more tedious than shopping for pantyhose."

"It's not," I tell her, taking all of her in: the crown of plumeria flowers, grass miniskirt and pink combat boots; her pink macramé bikini top.

"Come with me," I say impulsively.

I steer her to the ocean's shore and together we release the cranes.

We make wish after wish and she buries the last two in her hair, where I envy them.

"Why do you like him?" I ask, crossly.

"What's not to like?" she says. "He's good-looking, he's successful. He's you, forty years ago."

My eyes narrow and she turns away: I slap her ass, hard, and run my hands up and down its glossy rounds, pulling her to me.

"What is happening?" she says, finally, pulling away and breathing hard.

"More to come," I say, and lead her back to the table. We sit, and she opens my hand with the cocktail sword.

"Much more," she says.

Harford returns. He yawns and dumps sugar on the table.

Annabel resumes: "The book is," she says, "completely academic. I may use it as a prop in the film, maybe a weapon."

"I could make a cameo," I say, adjusting my plastic lei.

"Why would you do that?" Harford says.

"Because he stars in the original movie," says Annabel, embarrassed for both of us.

The ocean roars, pitching seals and giant whales into the air and sucking them back into its black velvet mouth. Our mai tais catch fire and I drink mine hungrily, exhaling tangerine flames.

Harford opens his big mouth, a wonder of white coral teeth and codfish lips.

"Right, fuck, sorry," he says, speciously. "You're the *Weekend at Bernie's* guy. That was surprisingly funny. Didn't we just watch that on Netflix, Bells?"

He wraps a hairless, inked arm around her and she shrinks into him, nods.

"Yes. I'm the dead man," I say, draining my drink and wishing, desperately, that I were.

DRINK IN MODERATION. Quit smoking.

These are the first items on the self-improvement list I start the morning of the second and last day of the expo.

"Exercise every third day?" I write as a group of exotics swarm my booth.

"We saw you on Annabel Wrath's web site," a young man with illustrated arms says, and the others nod, coolly.

"Is she making a movie about you?" he asks.

"How the fuck should I know?" I say, recalling that people were afraid of me once.

"Yeah," he says, and the kids stay at my side, alternately intimidating and astonishing people all day.

One of them shows me her web site. Underneath a nicely composed picture of me, taken I know not when, she has written, "Feed me truffles in bed, darling."

Does she mean that I am a truffle-sniffing pig?

When Annabel comes by, wearing a black suit and heels and pulling a pink suitcase behind her, my heart sinks. She will never kiss me again, I think, noticing for the first time a diamond engagement ring the size of a papaya ripening on her left hand.

My new entourage goes crazy, taking pictures and firing questions at her about a film she has made called *Dead Kids Rising*, a documentary short about a satanic cult's seizure of poorly disposed biomedical waste.

"Are you shooting one with him?" a multiply pierced girl says, snapping her fingers at me.

"Of course," Annabel says.

Her own impressive collection of piercings is not visible — last night, she told me that she was letting them grow over.

"*Everyone* is tribal now," she had said, parting her hair to reveal three intricate scars. "But I'll leave two available for some serious ice," she said, and winked.

She is wearing big silver hoops today that roll forward as she does something extraordinary: she stands on her toes and kisses me again, letting her candy-pink tongue laze on mine as she emits a small sigh.

"He's my inspiration — for everything hot," she says, rubbing her mouth with a hand that comes away cardinal.

"Look at my YouTube," she says. "He's all over me. Now leave us be, please. I'm trying to say goodbye. *Memorably*."

To me she says, "I do want to shoot you some more. Can we talk when I'm back in L.A.?"

"Of course," I say, my voice rickety. I write out my number and the email address that Pudge maliciously assigned me: DeadManWalking@hotmail.com.

Annabel laughs and tucks the slip of paper into her bra.

"You're a demon," I say, crossing and uncrossing my legs.

"And you, child, are looking good," she says, blowing me a final kiss as she turns on those shining heels, a kiss that comes in like a drone and lands on my smooth cheek, painting it the sun-dappled colors of a new plum.

ON THE PLANE I get a good seat. I'm bumped to first class when the ticket agent recognizes me from *Ripper the Male Stripper*, a straight-to-video film I made many years ago. In it, I play a sex criminal and faded dancer: the women at the club throw rotten apples as I crawl offstage, my serrated feelers aslant.

"Do you remember when you were killing that whore and the *bobbies* showed up?" he says, drawing heart-shaped amendments on my ticket.

"I do," I say, politely. We pose for a selfie, a term I learned through brute force this weekend; I board early and am surprised when the attractive stewardess winks at me.

Annabel brings me luck, I decide, as I recline to a near-prone position and signal for *one* Scotch, with soda water and ice.

Surreptitiously I pull out my compact — yes, I have a compact — and gape. I look ten years younger, at least.

My eyes are clear and vivid, my skin lined, but not gouged, and all of the dissolute red has vanished.

My hair has stopped growing in, but it is longer, darker, and shaped into a cool widow's peak.

I look around: the seat beside me is empty; the couple across the aisle is asleep. Then I peel up my shirt.

I don't have a six-pack, but my barrel belly has been deflated and is lightly scored, like the top of a loaf of challah.

Emboldened, I am grabbing my round, firm ass as the winky stewardess approaches and asks if there is anything I need.

"*Anything,*" she repeats, and I tell her to bring me a glass of still water.

"This tastes like motor oil," I say, pushing my drink at her and slipping on a pair of white Totokaelo sunglasses I have discovered in the magazine pouch.

I look out the circular window until she leaves.

She is attractive but I swear.

I could do better.

"YOU LOOK FUCKING sick," Krishna says grudgingly when he picks me up at the airport.

I make him stop at LAX 24/7 Locker Rentals, and a gas station.

I bring my bag with me.

When I am fastened into his Lexus, he angrily demands his cut from Fan Expo.

I look him over, thinking of all the disgraceful auditions he sent me to, of the money he swindled me out of when I was drunk and depressed, of the Twitter page he set up to make a fool of me.

Sample tweet:

Sad to hear of the death of my good friend
#RichardBurbage. Heaven shall be on fire tonight,
my excellent peer!

And:

After consuming twenty capsules of #Senokot
I'll be live-tweeting the arrival of some exceptionally soft stool. Join me, friends.

In a rare moment of concern, Pudge succeeded in
having the page taken down after complaining militantly
about several appalling jokes about "a Mexican gal and
her burro."

I stare at Krishna intently. He is a little weasel, nothing
more. Holding out a jittery hand—he has been doing fat
lines off the dashboard as he drives—he says, "Fifty percent," and snaps his fingers.

"How about zero percent and you're fucking fired."

He starts yelling and I tap my jacket, clearly holstered.
I checked the gun on my way out of town: I have been
looking forward to this.

"Goddamn, you're full of surprises," he says, and then
shuts up until I am home, where I punch him in the throat.
"Tweet that," I say, slamming the car door.

I call William Morris and ask for Jerry Gallo, who is not
there.

"Have him call me," I say, strip naked, and strut around.

An email arrives and when I click on the link in the message, a film starts. It's a WRATH production and it's gathering likes by the second. Jumpy and dark, it is set to an

industrial punk soundtrack Annabel has produced and played on, using flash-scenes from *Ultraviolence*. In one, she saws a violin as I pistol-whip a cop to the ground.

My life is changing, I think, and hum like a splendid insect in mid-flight.

JERRY CALLS BACK.

This is huge.

I tell him I am looking for new representation, and he agrees to meet me at the Chateau Marmont to talk.

He is my former agent, one of the many people who worked for me and decamped after my disastrous falling-out with Kray.

He has not retired because he makes too much fucking money and is supporting four ex-wives, a new one, and ten kids that he knows of.

I go and bang on Rabi's door.

The boy answers: he is smoking a cheroot and wearing a long black velvet robe.

"What you want, *abbu?*"

"I need clothes. You always look chic. Strange, yes, but chic. Would you—"

"Hang on."

I peer through the latched door and see a number of boxes overflowing with fabric, plaster figurines, model ships, sea glass, diadems, and more. A swarm of pale-blue budgies drifts by, and Rabi hands me an old bumblebee-striped I. Magnin bag.

"Had this stuff a while now, doesn't fit me," he says, down-playing his largesse.

I thank him and go back to my apartment: put on a white linen shirt, black peg-legs, black suspenders—which I wear loose—and blue suede brothel creepers. Everything fits.

Anxiously I approach the long mirror on my closet door and see Sid looking back at me. Well, Sid's father, I suppose, but just as mean and cool.

"That witch got you moving," Rabi says from the landing when I step into the hall. "Don't fuck this up," he says, feeding one of the birds on his shoulder a cherry from his lips.

They kiss.

I STOP BY the bodega and Angel is fully agitated.

"My man, Parnell," he says loudly, so the nodding junkies and lottery fiends can hear him.

He hands me the *National Enquirer*. An old shot of me with Pudge, then a little girl, walking through Griffith Park, occupies a square in the bottom-right corner of the front cover.

The headline reads, "Movie Star Parnell Wilde Caught Cheating with Will Harford's Girlfriend!"

I rifle through the pages and find a shot of Harford spitting at the photographer, and another of Annabel kissing me at Fan Expo.

Oh, so this is why Jerry is meeting me.

Regardless, the story is extremely flattering. Never mind they call me "elderly" in the caption; I look virile and deadly.

Annabel looks sublime.

"*Chupa mi pinga, mamacita!*" is what Angel says about her, frowning when I hand him a bottle of Perrier.

"Don't talk about her that way," I say, staring him down. I win and he rolls the water in a few copies of the tabloid.

"My man, the *coño* magnet!" he says, holding his hand up for a slap.

I leave him hanging, and the atmosphere charges in a way I have never felt in this store.

I feel envy, and respect.

ANNABEL CALLS ME one night, obviously drunk, the line crackling as she moves from branch to branch of the Chandelier Tree, an infamous, garish beauty on West Silver Lake. She is back from I have no idea where.

"Have you trespassed?" I ask, and she tells me she is a good friend of the makeup artist who owns the property.

I drive over and pick her out above the lambent eyes and shining mouth of a reclining tabby.

I climb to her.

Her face is a Turner of purple storms cut with black ships, with a sluice of red dawn; Ruskin scurrying to write it, in the distance.

She says, abruptly, "Will thinks I'm a dumb cunt who can't fuck."

I fold my hatred into my heart and let it take deep, rapacious root.

"And I can't," she says, crying now. "I can't."

She is glowing among the golden branches.

I carry her home and, after rapidly changing the sheets, pillowcases, and coverlet, put her in bed. Using a small comb, I untangle her hair and tell her, "Of course you can, you can do anything."

She smiles as she drifts off and I throw myself against her side, and sleep too.

Annabel is gone in the morning; my room is filled with tiny Chinese lanterns.

The note, brief as usual, says, "Soon." It is written on my hand, the hand that lay on her hip as we slept and still tingles.

What splendid shocks await you!

"PARNELL, DARLING," JERRY says, standing to greet me.

It is early spring and hot as hell: we sit outside.

"I may have something for you," he says, covertly eyeing my outfit as if trying to decide if I am absurd.

When the young waitress touches me repeatedly as we order and stammers when speaking to me, Jerry tells me I look sensational.

"Kray wants to film a sequel to *Ultraviolence* with you and Lana Del Rey," he says. "The working title is *Deadly Nightshade*. You would play Sid again. He's old and ravaged, hell-bent on revenge against the younger players who have crowded him out."

I nod coolly. This is my big shot.

"Let me think about it."

Excusing myself, I go to the washroom, kneel in one of the stalls, and vomit lacy bile. After I get up and wash my tear-stained face, I swallow some mints from a dish by the sink. They taste bitter, like — like what?

The attendant brushes my shoulders and I turn and hold him, sobbing soundlessly.

"There, there," the warm, wintry man says. "Try to remember that this is your life and no one else's."

I thank him and offer him cash that he waves off.

The problem is, I can't.

I can't remember a single time my life was mine, barring several brief encounters with an elusive girl likely just toying with me like a spoiled, fleshy cat.

"I'll do it," I say, approaching the table to sit down. Jerry's unctuous smile makes me sick all over again.

"BUT WHAT ABOUT my movie?"

Annabel has returned, banging at my door at 3 a.m. and wanting a drink. So I have one with her—my first in days.

She is unhappy and tense.

"Will broke up with me when he saw the *Enquirer*," she says. "He was angry enough about me asking you to feed me truffles in bed."

"I'm sorry," I say, although I am not. I am filled with joy.

"He smashed all the plates. He called me a—"

I hold up my hand; I cannot listen to this.

"I can't blame him, I guess. I wanted to fuck you that day at the convention center, in front of everyone. I fantasized about you the whole time I was in Italy, even in those awful overalls."

I keep a straight face but my heart is doing backflips.

Annabel is sitting cross-legged on my bed: a sunbeam, moiling with dust motes, glances her face.

I am in white pajamas; she is wearing a sheer magenta-colored sari and sandals. Her hair is a perfumed mass of helices pierced with a yellow pencil.

"I missed this place," she says. "The sadness emanating from everything is so wrenching."

"That note you handed me. *You made me a palace.*"

She smiles, remembering.

I watch, afraid to move or talk in case she flies off again.

She does not. She pats the bed beside her and beckons me with a crooked finger.

"I have to warn you," she says. "I don't like sex, I mean, it doesn't get me off."

I join her, shake my head, and think of myself as I was, once.

Which leads me to pounce on her and open her dress with a firm rip. Her smile disappears and her pupils dilate. I undress, hand her the switchblade from the end table, and flip her on top of me.

Her hands tremble.

She presses the knife open and holds its sharp edge to my throat, drawing a few beads of blood.

"I'm sorry," she says.

"You aren't. *Don't stop.*"

She holds the knife more firmly, and uses her other hand to squeeze my balls.

I lie perfectly still and tell her, "Say it."

"No," she says, letting her hair cover her face.

"Say it."

"Fuck me," she says in an orange, then black streak, moving with me, slowing down to slap or scratch me. "Fuck me hard."

She fits herself over my cock's wicked curve, the curve that hits the cross drawn deep inside her, that hits and hits it until she is soaking wet and radiant: she makes high-pitched, unreal noises that the birds answer, with songs of love and pain.

I am sleeping when she leaves but I catch a glimpse of her face, alight with something muscular, but soft.

FIRST TIME, she has written on the bathroom mirror in plum-black lipstick.

I read her exultant words and feel her closing around me, strangling me in short, brute intervals.

ANNABEL UPLOADS A film to Vimeo and then, spreading her bet, to the rest of her sites after midnight.

Blessed with Beauty and Rage is a Super 8 of her and me moving languidly beneath my blankets. It is set to Pretty Yende singing "Violetta Aria," run through Appalachian mandolins and what sounds like a cement mixer. At the end of it, she raises the blade victoriously and spectral O's pour from her mouth.

Within an hour, I hear from everyone I know and many I don't, mostly on the Twitter page she has set up for me, its banner reading simply, "Parnell Wilde: Actor, Killer."

"He's still so hot," writes @Gina69, using up her character limit with heart-eyed emojis.

This is the general tenor of the responses, leaving aside the occasional troll—such as my own daughter, who writes, "This is FAKE," only to be attacked by a geek-genius who says he can prove it isn't and does.

I get thousands of followers that night, and in the morning Jerry calls with offer after offer.

If you could see what she looked like, when she bent back and the light hit the knife—

I say yes to every interview, every party, every script-read. Jerry advances me some money and expedites an AmEx

Platinum Card: I spend a fair bit on a good suit and shoes, buttery shirts and ties, and fine hosiery.

And a shining surprise.

I wear my new clothes to Little Tart and hold my hand up when cameras start clattering.

I pick up and discard handbags, perfume, and shoes for Annabel. I want to give her something remarkable.

My Briar Rose will wonder all day, as it turns out, whether just one branch will appear at the hotel she stays at anonymously when she and Harford have split.

Where she will look at herself in the mirror and be consumed with fear and revulsion.

I almost ruin everything.

Then I am inspired.

WHEN I REVISIT our wild night, the thought of my sagging chest, tassels of fleecy hair, and uncut, shanty-mick cock torment me.

I am scared she is remembering me with disgust. I need to remind her that I have far more to offer than he does.

Thinking of him provides my inspiration.

I shop for a few items and get into my car.

On my way to the Hills, I get a text from Annabel.

A cute baby bird flaps around the words "miss u."

When I park, I see she has sent me an email, and attached to it is another short film, this one called *Verity*.

I decide to watch it later. Quickly, I text back:

Miss you more super-busy talk soon.

There. I am certain I sound desirable: aloof and confident.

I arrive at the luxury condo building wearing a thick stick-on mustache and plaid cap, and walk into the foyer holding a bouquet of flowers.

"Delivery for Mr. Harford," I say to the porcelain doll behind the desk. She waves me forward and keeps waving: she is drying her jewel-encrusted claws.

When he answers the door, I shove the bouquet in his face and knee him in the balls.

As he lies on the floor groaning, I jump up and land on his chest, kneeling there while punching his face savagely.

"Parnell Wilde," he says, before passing out.

I wash up in his sink, rinsing my bloody hands under a gold dolphin faucet.

I kick him, and when he opens one limp eye I say, "Leave her alone or I'll kill you."

His eye leaks and I kick him again.

"Understand?"

He nods. His cuts are firegold, leaking sticky shiraz. I lick my lips, wanting to taste what I have done.

"She wanted it," he says, and when I once again aim my foot at his face, he pulls out his phone and scrabbles for a video.

"Look," he says. "Look."

On the screen, Annabel is being slapped by a repulsively nude Harford. She starts to undress, her face a stone.

"More," she says. "Harder."

He hits her with a frying pan and she laughs.

"*Yes*," she says. "Make me feel something. Anything."

He stops the video. "Psycho," he says. "Take her."

"I will," I say.

I am pleased by my beloved's coldness, and I laugh in a new way—that is, the old way. The sound Kray seized on, having heard my amusement after decimating someone in a bar fight.

I rifle through Harford's things as he lies unconscious, then sail down the stairs whistling a different song.

"Me and Jesus the Pimp in a '79 Granada Last Night."

WHEN I GET home, I look around for a minute and grab my envelope of valuables now containing a Roman postcard and floriferous bits and pieces of Annabel. I book it with the few good clothes I have, jammed into two WinCo shopping bags.

I check into the Roosevelt and try calling Annabel.

Then I text her.

And email her.

I am feeling fine in my terry robe and slippers, with my slicked-back hair and lightly browned skin.

I click on the TV: Harford is everywhere.

As is Annabel, crying and saying, "Who would do this?" as the reporter—a black woman with dreads and a power suit—holds her hand and murmurs to her.

I cycle through the channels faster and faster. News of "this senseless beating" is everywhere.

A reporter accosts Harford as he is being wheeled into an ambulance on a stretcher.

"Who did this to you?"

He looks afraid.

"Sid," he says. "Some motherfucker named Sid."

I feel so good! My knuckles sing; from the rocks they sing each to each. I change into a black sweater and jeans I took from Harford's closet, along with a pair of his meticulously distressed engineer's boots. I comb my darker-brown hair back, slick, and call Annabel. She answers so demurely, I feel desperate for her.

"Come to me," I say.

I pace the room drinking Bollinger from the bottle. I tilt my head, remembering, and feel Harford's blood warm on my flesh as if I have savaged the sun. I am picking at one or two stray, dried drops when Annabel knocks. I open the door and, exquisitely dishevelled and frail, she falls into my arms.

"*Daddy*," she says, and I like it.

"IT'S MY FAULT," she says.

Annabel is enclosed in a black cashmere wrap, deep in a red wingback chair like a perfect gemstone shining from its velvet-draped box.

"I'm all tangled up," she says, morosely.

This is intolerable. I thought she would be grateful, that she would look at me and know my rough kindness.

"Get up," I say, and she does, dropping the wrap to the floor. "Now get the ropes and the gun."

She flicks through the desk drawer, her face changing in degrees from remorseful to rapt.

She wheels around, trains the gun at me.

"Get undressed," she says, and I do.

She orders me to lie down and ties me to the bedposts securely.

Undresses bit by bit, walks over, and sits on my face while holding the gun to my temple.

I get her off until she falls back, exhausted.

She raps my skull with the gun to punish me and then unties me.

We roll toward each other. She cries over Harford and I remember her wet lips skimming my teeth and the new, louder noises she made, like an engine starting. I press my hard cock against her thigh and cradle her head, saying, "There, there."

Then she takes me in her mouth, swallows, and chokes.

She slips away again as I sleep, dreaming of a miniature world where only she and I live, wearing coconut and grass apparel and singing Hawaiian cowboy songs.

"We are changing each other," her note says.

Changing! I roll over and glance into my compact: Chanel, brand new.

My devil's eyes possess clarity and definition; my nose is refined.

I close my fantastic eyes, and feel Annabel everywhere.

Her little feet have left impressions in the carpet, a trail of shapely pins, of seed pearls strung above them; her behind: two perfectly melon-shaped dents in the mattress. Her silvery charmeuse bra, its spheres still chiming, is slung from the bedpost: I hear the *primum mobile*, doubled. Her sounds linger and catch on the heavy drapery; the air is filled with clouds of her Mitsouko perfume.

I fall deeply asleep as these billows rain tiny pears of lemon wash, of pink pressed powder, and the red, sugared meat of her cunt, where dwarf fish swim through salty plankton.

I GET A text in the morning with kisses and a link to another film, this one called *Big Daddy*.

The sex seems more graphic, more disturbing. Seen through a yellow filter, the two-minute video shows Annabel hitting me with the gun while Beethoven's *Sonata Pathétique* plays on a scratchy old record.

My arms look corded and strong as I hold her meaty hips; the fast shot of my still, intent face is all shadows and planes.

I admire myself some more and call room service for a carafe of coffee and a bowl of fruit, then slip into my robe.

Jerry calls and says, "Keep doing whatever it is you're doing to that girl. I'm sifting through hundreds of offers for movies, interviews, and commercials. Good stuff too, no more chickens."

I put the phone down. How does he know? The ad never ran: Annabel had a couple of her criminal fans steal the master footage and rough up the Chickman CEO.

Returning it to my ear, I laugh and say, "Where did you hear about that?"

"Let's just say I have my ways. And that I'm hanging on to it as a little insurance policy."

Krishna has sold me out, I realize, already considering our next encounter.

The near-fatal assault is a *fait accompli*.

The aesthetician has arrived and is soaking my feet in a lavender brew.

"Insurance," I say, calmly. "Do you mean like the old pictures I have of you sticking your tongue down a fourteen-year-old girl's throat?"

It's a risk, but the pictures could easily exist: Jerry used to throw the best and the most debauched parties.

"Let's go through the offers," he says, briskly.

"After you get rid of your policy."

"What policy?" he asks, and I know that I've won.

"Paint them a white," I say to the girl kneeling before me.

"Like the moon on a pure black night," she says, separating and kneading my frothy toes.

"Sure, like that," I say, lighting a contraband cigarette.

"Miss you," I type to Annabel. And, "Good movie."

"Can we just talk tonight?" she zaps back, and I groan.

"OK," I write, even though I feel she is cheating me.

"Other foot, Handsome," says the girl, and I check out her cursive-w ass. It bobs as she works, which barely excites me.

What has become of me?

Instead I think of Harford, of the crack that is bone on bone, then the soft yielding, blood like a fountain being fed in pieces.

Vengeance is mine, I think, and feel a chill finger on my spine.

"Leave," I tell the girl.

She packs up her case, exits.

And a voice says, "You are wrong my, my, my—"

Christ cannot bring Himself to say *my child* and tries a few synonyms: my kid, my boy, finally settling on "my ravening wolf." He preaches this phrase from the shore of Capernaum until soft white-bellied orcas pile up like cordwood, their souls unhooking happily.

We may now live without fear, they say.

Without shame, without humiliation.

I was in StarWorld this winter, and I had the shakes. A very assertive bat assailed me as I handed the cashier —a pudgy boy with a rabbinical beard and high-water jeans — a signed picture, admittedly soiled, of me in *Hamlet*, a London production that received very fine notices.

He is chatting up a cute teenaged girl and is angry to be interrupted.

He sizes me up, flicks the picture back at me. "Look around, has-been," he says, and I glance at all of the new stars I do not recognize.

"Take your dirty picture and fuck off," he says, and the girl laughs shrilly, and so I memorize him and the winter's flaw is expelled!

I will tell an airier version of what happened at the store to Jimmy Kimmel tonight and laugh, and he will negative-advertise them enough to send the cashier right into my arms.

And there lies the blade: what I did not hear as I walked, half-mad, away.

Away from what he never said as I lay on the sidewalk inflamed by vermin, before they came for me again, that is.

Now cracks a noble heart: never has anyone taken the blame.

ANNABEL APPEARS IN jeans, running shoes, and a big, hooded sweatshirt that covers her hair.

I am wearing a new navy suit with a pale-blue shirt and matching pocket square.

I feel absurd.

"I see," I tell her, and leave the room, to change into sweatpants and the HOLLYWEIRD T-shirt I have found in the back of the drawer.

"Better?" I say, coming back to the living room, where she is lying on the sofa, drinking mini-bar bourbon and popping candied almonds into her mouth.

"Yeah, you look great," she says, ignoring me.

"What did you want to talk about?"

"Nothing in particular," she says, emptying the bag. "These are the notes for my screenplay, and this is the final draft of my book."

I move beside her and weigh them in my hands.

She jumps up, visibly agitated. "Will refuses to talk to me. When I asked why, he told me to ask you."

"He must be brain-damaged from the attack, the poor kid."

I open the book in the middle:

Reading Kubrick's fragmented, agonized women — the milk dispensers, tables, lashes, teeth, and garish wigs — as misogyny is a dangerous misprision. As with Kray's deployment of fingernails, heels, and the infamous blow-up doll, this death-camp detritus supports the idea that women are in peril; that the feminized, made-up Alex and Sid are de facto women themselves —

"Women?" I say, remembering myself in the film, pouring a tumbler of milk as two girls snaked up my naked body.

"Well, symbolically," she says. "Remember in *Clockwork* when Billy Boy tells his gang to get Alex, or *her*?"

Her skin has broken out; she has put on a pair of glasses that are taped together at the bridge and is standing behind me, animated and as homely as I have ever seen her.

"Kubrick and Kray sympathized with the oppressed: the women of their generation were in danger. Well, we still are in danger. But—"

"Why don't we have a little nap?" I say.

She is furious.

"You hate me like this, don't you? This is who I am. This is me in high school, this is still me." She is breathing hard.

"I don't understand," I say, frightened.

"No, because I remade myself, just like you should have, after Kray."

What does she mean? I see myself young enough still to be growing. This boy says, "Never tell."

Tell what? I pull, I pull the T-shirt off: I seem to be having a heart attack. I throw up inside of it and curl into a ball.

"I don't know what you mean," I say mildly and see my mother, on one of her good nights, hovering over me with a crocheted blanket, smelling of cold vermouth.

I WAKE UP attached to lines and a pole.

Annabel is asleep on a hard chair beside me, with all her papers and a plush teddy bear wearing a GET WELL SOON sweater and a bright red cap.

As she sleeps, I convince the nurse to give me my phone and I watch *Verity*.

It is black and white: in it, four teenage girls are smoking and dangling their legs in a kiddie pool.

They are all very pretty, including the hefty one with thick glasses and braids, who never looks up.

Three boys ride up on bikes, and I feel nervous, I am not sure why.

"Hi, girls," the oldest one says. "You," he says maliciously to the hefty girl.

The girls squeal and splash water at the boys, who join them.

They stop eventually, but this one boy won't let up.

He douses the same girl's shirt and pulls her hair.

"Stop it," one of the girls says, but she is batting her eyes as well.

The screen goes black, and returns in vivid color.

"Go hang around with your own friends," he says, shoving her face into the water. "The other animals."

She manages to pull her head up and howl.

Everyone else takes off, but the older boy lingers a bit, watching her, amused.

"Leave me alone," she says. "Please?"

He throws a lawn flamingo he has wrenched from the grass at her, and it cuts her face.

His friends call and he finally lopes away.

She stumbles to her feet and walks up to the lens. Wipes the blood from her face and says, "It is my thirteenth birthday. This is my party."

She must have then thrown the camera onto the grass by the pool: the last shot shows an inflated giraffe drifting up to the lens and sticking to the sound of a girl's grim, miserable crying.

I delete it. I can't ever see this again.

"No one cares about me," Annabel soughs in her sleep.

Tripping more alarms, I get up and lift her into my arms.

"I care about you," I say. She doesn't answer, but holds me tight as I walk the room, soothing her and myself.

I screw the surprise pair of marquise-cut diamond earrings into her delicate lobes. They are four-petalled flowers. She feels their necrotic white centers and soft platinum tips.

"You didn't have to, I wasn't hinting," she says nervously, meaning the day she teased me about *serious ice*.

I ignore her objections and say, "You are my invaluable cure," and we cry a bit and the orderly follows the alarms and I tell him everything is all right.

That my heart has been cured by a duchess.

"Amen," he says as he reconnects me and kindly says nothing about the girl in my arms I won't let go.

"PARNELL WILDE IN Heart Attack Drama!"

So rages the *Star*, which Annabel brought me along with a pile of cards, a bouquet of balloons, and loads of flowers from well-wishers.

I hate it all. The smell is disgusting, the cards toxic with insincerity.

"Very recently," I say, "I'd have been on the county hospital payphone, begging my daughter to bring me a pair of socks."

Annabel leaps the bars and arranges herself next to me. "I would have come," she says.

"You might have," I say, softening, as she whispers "movie star" in my ear, and picks at the knots holding my robe closed.

She slams the curtain shut, making the rings rattle, and strips.

I am wearing a catheter: alarms sound.

She is up like a shot and rolls under my bed when the nurse with the spiky mole bursts in, asking what I have done and jamming the stick back into my urethra so roughly I cry out.

Hearing this, Annabel cuts the nurse's ankle, nicking her Achilles tendon; crawls toward and kisses me quickly, before sprinting off.

"I'll be back tonight," she calls out from the hallway, and I place my hand between my legs and try to think of unpleasant things.

That mole. The little cop. Siobhan's undergarment. Annabel, topless, her breasts full and firm, spilling over the frilly edge of her pink satin bra. No, no.

I ask the medic who is working on the nurse, and to whom I have denied knowing Annabel — "Just some crazy fan, I guess" — to remove the catheter again.

It releases with a pop, and I say, "Keep it out."

I hold on to an elimination jug and let myself remember every spot of Annabel, including the three heart-shaped beauty marks on her ankle, shoulder, and lip.

WHEN I AM returned home by town car, I take one look at the Elsinore, my splintered, puce apartment complex, and demand to be taken somewhere else.

My phone pings and it is my daughter, leaving the following, thoughtful text: "Heard you were sick, sucks. I need my tuition money, btw."

Delete!

I want a place of my own. The driver, Dante, who is clearly stoned, is agreeable, and stops at several places for rent. I settle on a tiny house in Malibu, a short drive from the ocean.

He even signs the paperwork for me.

I give him the keys to my Mustang and a vague description of where I abandoned it. "She needs a bit of love, but the old lady's got style and speed," I tell him.

His brother is a mechanic. He tells me about repainting the car "in the *dolce stil novo*," with speedy silver details, while methodically popping orange gelcaps.

Dante gets me inside the furnished house and kisses me goodbye, promising to visit.

Annabel was gone when they discharged me. No note this time, no text or email.

I check her social media sites, and none has been updated. Love is pouring in, however, for *Catheter Cutie*, which consists of a shot of her hand inside my robe that blows up into a grid of thousands of the same shot, as she sings "I Will Always Love You" in an operatic soprano that crumbles, during the verses, into raw, almost feral, growls.

I sit cautiously on the massive bed, and rest my head against its pink quilted headboard. The house had belonged to a pop star who swiftly milked the last drop from her only hit, the insufferably insincere "Mad Girls."

This song is also the doorbell chime, and pipes through the house ceaselessly: I will soon find its source and take a sledgehammer to those "Mad girls, bad girls, you feel me, bitch?"

But first, I need to find Annabel.

Between calls to her voice mail, I phone Rabi and send him shots of the essentially barren house. I have furniture and electronics, but it looks featureless, like a large-scale variation on my miserable apartment.

He pulls up in a panel van a few hours later with a crew of big kids. They hang lamps and huge paintings, unroll modern Afghan rugs covered in rifles and ammo, and throw bright faux furs on every surface.

Rabi arranges the smaller objects—goldfish luxuriating in big, glass globes, plaster divinities, dioramas of famous murder scenes, beaded curtains, and pillows screened with Black Panthers.

And he places one of the best pieces, a seven-foot-tall stone angel—tinted with *bleu des Anciens*—by my bed. "In case you're jonesing for her," he says.

I hand him all the cash I have, and he refuses it.

Standing on a chintz ottoman, he looks me in the eye and says, "Don't forget who she is, and what she did."

Then he whistles for his crew, who are smoking by the pool and drinking banana daiquiris.

He lets me tip them, and I do. Extravagantly.

One of them pulls out the *Enquirer* picture of me and Annabel and says, shyly, "This you?"

I say that it is and he whistles.

"Where she at?" he says, and I tell him I don't know.

"Find her," he says.

I swear that I will.

I poke around for voice memos on my phone and find "Serenade, Annabel." Lie back and listen to her warble,

Green eyes ringed in blue, the world captured by a Delft lasso.

Play it again. It is so awful, it is the *algorithm for perfection*, I sigh, before singing along.

JERRY HAS ME do small, significant roles for money and prestige before TOP SECRET KRAY SEQUEL begins shooting. Kray and I have yet to speak in any form, which is both suspenseful and soothing.

When my first new film appears, I am singled out for stealing scenes and for "muscling my way to where I belong."

My management team tells me to be modest yet assured in interviews.

Jerry calls in favor after favor.

I talk to Howard Stern about my early retirement, a euphemism that he seizes on: "Do you mean your total, humiliating failure?" he says.

I am deflated, but he quickly spins my decadent years into my having been "king of the big '70s bush," drops a few starlets' names, and declares that I am well-hung—which I am, legendarily so.

I do a few local TV morning shows, and Jerry manages to get me Fallon.

I play a game with him that involves me guessing, blindfolded, what ladies' garment he is wearing. I am applauded for saying "an edible G-string."

This appearance leads to bigger requests, which we decide to put on hold until the Kray film is done.

We agree to one *Vanity Fair* shoot: a one-page shot of me in a torn Sex Pistols T-shirt, artfully lacerated jeans, and motorcycle boots, pointing a gun at the camera beneath the words SID VICIOUS. The accompanying paragraphs, pure fluff, call me "hotter than ever and back with a vengeance."

I look insane; the photograph is unreal in its nasty perfection. Yet I am more like the man in the picture every day.

I wonder if I am delusional, and take a walk through Cherry Park. I see a young lady down by the river, toasty-tanned, with a cumulonimbus cloud of rich amber hair.

"Hey," I say, sounding cool while apprehensively clenching my gut.

"Hey *yourself*, sugar," she says, and winks. Her boyfriend catches up to her, and she walks away with him but turns her head back and smiles.

And that smile—

Like the gates of heaven swinging wide open and all the angels inside singing, "In the club."

FIRST I GET a little haughty, then a lot, then mean: at first only to people who have it coming.

I happen to meet the girl from the car, for example, the one who told me to eat shit when I looked at her. She is reading for a walk-on in an HBO crime series; I have a guest role as a refined butcher and law professor. The suits want my character to recur. Coolly, I say I'll think about it, and when the girl walks in and smiles at me, hard, I write NO on the script in front of me and pass it down the line. "Next!" the director says, and I look at the girl and laugh when she bursts into tears.

I become vain. I visit surgeons, a hair specialist, and a cosmetic dentist who renders my teeth opaline. I have my own nutritionist, hairdresser, makeup artist, personal trainer, and stylist. Jerry is taking a calculated risk: Kray never fails.

I am being groomed to win an Academy Award. The team has even located my Palme d'Or for *Ultraviolence*, in the pawnshop by Cindy Club.

It is hard to tell anymore what magic Annabel has unleashed, and what is happening because of a run of good luck.

One morning, after I turn on the TV and see her and Harford checking into the Four Seasons, I tell myself that she is simply a nice girl whose kiss and whose little videos kick-started my comeback.

I should write her a thank-you letter, I think as I sit in my Jacuzzi, listening to the coyotes howling.

They are almost as hungry, as deeply incensed, as I am: "Dear Annabel, Best of luck and do remember that I enjoyed our meetings."

This is the letter I write her later this night, the polished one I complete after crumpling at least five drafts. On the brush-calligraphy envelope I have sent to her hotel, I pick out the words HATE YOU with a straight pin in Braille.

I meet new women every day now. I am fine.

I'm *fine*, I cry underwater, fighting the overwhelming urge to stay there, my lungs burning, my eyes huge with despair, the sickly yellow of the recessed sun.

THE NEXT MORNING, I awake and shout.

Where the fuck am I?

An egg-shaped man in purple livery walks into my bedroom carrying a standing tray bearing coffee, rolls, fruit, juice, and a selection of papers.

Someone has hired me a butler.

"I am Charles," he says, and nods at the bell beside the sugar bowl. "Ring if you need me. I'll be cleaning your master bath. You'll be able to eat off the floor," he assures me, and disappears.

Among the papers is a Four Seasons envelope that I open, shaking.

"My darling," it begins.

> I'm not surprised you hate me. Will is like a sickness with me. When he hurts me, I feel that only he can make it better, like venom & anti-venom ☹.
>
> Anyways, I know that I am just a step on your way back, and I should leave now before you leave me.
>
> Weak, I know. I made another movie about us. You know where to find it.
>
> Xo A

"I love you so much it hurts," she has written, and crossed out, in the margin.

I watch *Cannabel*, a hazy love story in which she takes small bites of my body as I sleep in hospital. She cries when someone knocks at the door and leaves singing "Cherish," in a low, thunder-dappled voice.

I've had enough. The dramatic entrances and exits, the broken promises, the mere existence of her cretinous boyfriend, and her willingness to be demeaned by him.

"Find a new leading man," I text her. "And try to protect yourself, JFC!"

It makes me sick, sending this.

I end up crawling back under the covers and when Charles returns with my pressed clothes and pictures of the spotless bathroom, I tell him that I am going to fire him any second.

"I shall wait in suspense," he says, and leaves me be.

I feel Annabel with me in my bed, walking her fingers down my chest and snap, beneath the elastic of my pajama bottoms.

She is swallowing me with her dark throat, with her tight, aromatic asshole.

"Are you sure?" I ask, and she responds by arching her back and moving toward me, taking me in inch by inch until I explode, until she soaks my crooked fingers and squalls — her hot, salty storm spraying us both.

This happened, once: my God, *the power of beauty*. All alone, I nurture my melancholy like the tender shoot of a black flower.

But I hear her crying, I hear it above the brisk house-cleaning and suddenly raging wind, I call for her and she doesn't answer.

I cover my ears to drown her out and somewhere under the same cool, Egyptian sheets, my girl —

A girl I am crazy about is choking, she is crying so much. She can't show anyone my text so she deletes it, throws the phone against the wall and breaks it.

"I'm trying to sleep," says her boyfriend, who came to bed at 6 a.m. calling her unspeakable names. "I'm sick of you," he says, raising his hand, and her nose bleeds, meeting her tears and mucous.

I see all of this and do not move. I barely breathe until Charles carries me into the verbena-scented tub and scrubs me from head to toe, murmuring, "There, there," as my own face seeps like hers into a hot washcloth.

Women's faces are carved into the granite walls of the washroom. The sinks are womanly forms in a curvy ped-estal with shapely legs.

She is everywhere; she is all in pieces.

"Forget her," a small, mean voice insists, and I do, until I am clothed, and for some time after, driving my bottle-green Jaguar along hairpin turns and as fast as fucking lightning halfway to Mexico.

I HEAR TWO things on the radio that make me spin the car around and race back.

One: Harford has eloped with a French film star named Hedy Conasse.

Two: Annabel, "Harford's former lady love," is in intensive care at Cedars-Sinai, my recent habitat.

One report says she has been assaulted: I pull onto the shoulder and find the story online.

"Allegedly, Miss Wrath was assaulted by Mr. Harford in his home. The fight ended, bystanders report, when he tried to throw her through his living-room window to her death."

I call someone I fear and despise.

He listens to my imprecation. Hangs up.

Harford's plane crashes over the Pacific, killing him, his new bride, the pilot, and several hangers-on.

The pilot is revealed to have been drunk out of his mind: the black box has recorded him talking to his co-pilot, a glass of vodka with poor navigation skills.

But still. Did he arrange this? I asked only that he have someone shoot out his tires. Something, but not this.

"May God bless you," I say to the infinitesimal remains of the dead, the flocking on gull's wings, the small shimmer in the blue glass of the sea.

I get back on the road. It is her turn to hurt, and to want — want me — I hope, as my reservations about her are reconstituted and leave the car like a pale tendril of exhaust.

I FRESHEN UP in the hospital bathroom, combing back my hair, smoothing my striped sleeves, and checking out my worn blue jeans and the engineer's boots.

I buy her flowers in small clay pots, two heart-shaped balloons, and a box of truffles, and add to this haul a copy of *Nightwood*, the new *Guns & Ammo*, some loungewear, marabou slippers, toiletries, perfume, and a cashmere robe I have quickly shopped for on the way.

And the bear in the sweater we call Tubby: he rests on top of a shopping bag in a dapper new cap and scarf.

I evade the nurses and slip into her room, which is barren of cards or flowers.

Quickly I set up a nice tableau, slipping the same kind orderly from my own residence here a few hundred-dollar bills to fill the windowsills with tulips, bright gerbera daisies, and a selection of forged, cheerful notes.

I sit beside her and hold her hand, evading the PICC line. Her face makes me cry, which wakes her.

"It was an accident," she says dreamily, swatting at her morphine dispenser.

"I fought back," she says with frail pride. "I don't remember much of anything, though."

She tries to smile. The smile dies halfway up. She slaps her hands over her face. "I remember everything. I hurt so much. He said things too, things I never want — What will I do if he calls?" she says as I hold her carefully, smelling the marrow and peppermint that emanate from her little fiddlehead ear.

It occurs to me she doesn't know about his marriage.

Or death.

"I won't let you take his calls or see him anymore," I say. "You are mine, and I'll fight him if I have to."

"I am yours?" she says shyly, and shrinks into her pillows.

"Yes, and we are going to begin from the beginning: I want to know about you, and I will tell you things about me I have never told a soul."

"Like what?"

"Like we are the same, you and I."

I kiss her, and her smashed face begins to reassemble. It is as if I am watching rugged caterpillars push their way into their glorious wings.

A nurse walks in when her transformation is well underway.

Shocked, she asks, "Are you the plastic surgeon?"

"Yes, and I am also Miss Wrath's hairdresser," I say as I brush the mats from her hair and coax it into lustrous waves.

"You're a witch?" Annabel says, quietly.

"No, and neither are you. This is adoration, that's all, and that is everything."

"I need to work on her body," I say to the nurse, and she opens and closes her mouth. Leaves.

I call Dante, who collects us in a prom limo, half a block long and appliance-white.

When she is home and changed, I ravish the prettiest girl in the world until she sings in plainsong then polyphony, prying apart the bars of the staves until she reaches, then sticks to me with her own succulent goo and ravenous lips: "Let's stay together," she says from a heart-racing height.

"You are the one who always leaves," I say, and we crash as she rakes my back until it opens into fine red stalks.

I fall asleep and find her reading something on her phone when I wake.

This will destroy her. I hold my breath reflexively, to prepare for her exit.

"That actor died," she says. "The one in the new Desiree Akhavan movie."

"Are you all right?" I say cautiously.

"No. A lot of people died in the crash, the poor things: he even had a wife."

"So why are you laughing?"

"I'm just so happy," she says, slipping into my shirt with me, so our hearts may speak privately.

"Tell me everything about you," I say.

She pops my buttons, rummages through one of the hospital bags, and sprays herself from a glass DeVilbiss atomizer. Runs her long, candy-striped fingernails through the rope of amethysts she wears over her pink-and-blue nightgown and asks me to find her a pair of her diamanté gripper socks.

"He liked me barefoot," she says, and grimaces, a revisionist Cendrillon.

So do I, I think and, sensing my little dolor, Annabel says, "*You* can see them naked anytime," and I kiss her toes, arches, heels as they disappear into their fuzzy shells.

"I started making movies when I was a kid," she says, and stops. "Do you really want to hear all this?"

I feel the heat between her legs meet mine and burn.

I do.

ANNABEL, NÉE CAROLINA Rivera, grew up in Toledo, Ohio, in an apartment with her single mother, a ruthless claims collector who never spoke about her birth father except to call him a "pasty-faced liar" and a "ghost."

Beautiful and almost mute, her mother worked long hours and spent the rest of her time taking long baths, smoking, and listening to jazz or, when she was feeling bitter, bachata on the radio. Annabel holed up in her room with books and movies whenever she was home, which was seldom.

On her ninth birthday, she found a pink video camera in the park and started shooting everything she saw.

She would work on the films after school. Kelly, the AV man, hunched-over and squirrelly, showed her how to edit, score, and upload them; he taught her effects, lighting, and sound. The short films became popular online very quickly: they were weird and edgy; she was still a kid.

She had to let Kelly hold her hand now and then, and once, perch on the very edge of his lap as he stroked the arms of the chair and said, "Pussy, my little pussy."

When she puked on him, he was genuinely remorseful: he got her sugar water and ice and gave her a twenty-dollar bill, which she refers to, sardonically, as "the first time I made money hooking."

ANNABEL IS THIRTEEN years old when she gets her first break.

She is advanced to the eleventh grade after winning a prestigious nationwide arts competition for seniors, for her essay "Alex in Wonderland: DeLarge and Frightening Girl in Stanley Kubrick's *A Clockwork Orange*." Her principal asks her, timidly, to redact the section on Kray, whose work he feels "is quite a bit like pornography, isn't it?"

When she meets the judges, who convene to award her a comically oversized check, they are aghast to meet a short, thick girl in a romper, her hair combed like segmented farmland, with elastic-tethered haystacks on each plot.

When they try to take the prize away, she calmly asks to speak to an advocate. "And a cop."

She then extemporizes, succinctly, her thesis about Alex/Alice: the Humpty Dumpty–smashed *eggiwegs*, the auto-erotic hanging of Alice—a man in drag, the many time-pieces, the Cheshire Cat–lady, the white rabbit liquefied or gendered as milk, the EAT ME card on the hospital gift basket, the—

The panel has heard enough.

"Well, *this* looks sexy," the lady educator in seamed stockings and a sausage casing–tight suit says as they pose for a single photograph and then flee, leaving Annabel wearing her heavy medal and beaming, alone.

She has never won anything, not even good grades. Her long, ponderous essays are returned to her unread with thin, penciled comments like "Didn't read, too long," or once, in flaming red, "Get outside once in a while with the other children."

Barely liked, she can't even stake out choice loser turf like the corner of the teachers' lounge or the long table in the library where the ugly algebra hounds and stinking biology mavens gather, mocking their popular classmates who would, they were certain, "wind up selling burgers to my kids one day!"

She hates them more than the oblivious, the bullies, and the pompously hateful. Obsessed with style even then, she admires the way these kids look, walk, talk. Like they are dying of a mysterious illness that makes them speak slowly and unintelligibly; that makes them move as if underwater; that requires them to wear gown-loose, flowing, and bandage-tight garments.

She tries to walk as they do, slowly, but she is electric with possibilities. She wears the medal to school and runs down the hall. It bumps against her, and one kid, the only nice one in the world, says, "That's so cool." She thanks him, then repeats his name — Damian, Damian, Damian — until it lies among the promises etched in longhand on her brain.

I will spare some and torture others, she thinks, and runs outside, skipping the rest of the day to cash the check.

She buys an important pair of shoes at Dillard's, lilac-colored Prada kitten heels with wide T-straps and silver buckles.

A perfect black dress: simple, elegant, and short, that she will wear all her life, coal-heavy mascara, diamanté powder, grape-purple lipstick, sheer nylons, a luscious gold bottle of Mitsouko.

Hits the Franklin Park Mall for a bag of books, an iPod, a leopard cape, a spiked belt, a sharp knife, and an enormous bag of sunflower seeds she eats, exclusively, for weeks and weeks until she is rail-thin.

And a new phone, from the back of a station wagon. It's practically free, but the clothes — there are more basic, yet essential, items in the bags — eat all of her check.

Just having these riches makes her feel as though she is on the threshold of beauty, the great illusion — so great that when she smiles at the young man at the electronics store, he becomes confused, and as he stammers and starts rifling through inventory, she deftly tosses a digital Nikon into her (new) violet purse while releasing her tightly wound hair, which springs out roaring like a lioness.

"I saw you," he whispers later, at her doorstep, but by then his hands are so enamored of, and all over, her plump, tight ass that he does not give one fuck.

THE MUSIC THAT Annabel liked the most as a teenager is Charlie Parker.

Then she tells me the rest, leaving a lot out because she finds the past painful and because I find anyone's past, including my own, mostly monotonous.

Female chanteuses and hardcore hip hop. This Lupe Fiasco song, and Joe Williams, A Tribe Called Quest, Sade Adu — more music she likes.

Here she is, stroking my back as though I am her plush, dreaming pet, and letting me in on some of her secrets.

In 2011, she grows rapidly to her full height, five foot eleven, and skins down to 127 pounds, a little heavy for the modelling assignments strangers thrust at her as she walks down the street.

These agents are willing to ignore her heft because of her electrifying beauty: her Angel Falls of hair, Aphrodite's face, and bordering-on-obscene body.

She turns all the shoot money into her films and tuition and works three days a week in a smock and a pink uniform, selling Mexican food out of a quilted silver truck. She also buys crates and crates of vinyl at thrift stores and church, lawn, and street sales. Her collection has a bit of everything, from Sahara blues to Nintendocore to Peking opera.

She makes soundtracks by sampling these and conversations she records in school or on the bus: everywhere she goes.

Her favorite collage is a live recording of Julio Iglesias's "Hey!" pouring over a drunk bus driver's tirade: "You think I'm driving any of you to the Rapture? No fuckin' way, beg your pardon, Jesus, but look at these animals."

"We have known such lonely pain," Iglesias sings, from a scratched record she divines from.

She films Soledad piping churro dough beside her, lost in a dream as sweet as the dulce she is squeezing onto the hot confections, her eyes half-closed and filled with a man's dark, delicious skin, his holy vows, and Annabel calls the movie *Deep-Fried Sacrament*.

"This should be a real movie," Soledad says when they project it onto the rear of the truck after work.

"Maybe," Annabel says.

"You start university soon, no?"

She tells her she is going be the only fifteen-year-old at Columbia.

"I'm sure you'll meet a bunch of freaks like you," her friend says, blowing powdered sugar at her like a kiss, her first real kiss.

SHE BLITZES THROUGH university, completing a Ph.D. at Harvard on "Psychosexual Pathology and Pleasure" in Kubrick's and Kray's films, and moves to Los Angeles.

Her mother has died by then, of breast cancer.

During her illness, they become close: she learns about her grandmother, her namesake, who was a *mujer fatale* and renowned mathematician, and that her father, "the goddamned son of a bitch," was a singer and "very handsome, like a painted saint."

Annabel held her mother's hand when the morphine hit and ran through her. "He took me salsa dancing every Saturday," she says. "Everyone watched us, whispered, *Míralos, son tan hermosos juntos!*"

She misses the man who left her, who was "not always bad," her skeletal mother confesses.

When she gets to Los Angeles, she sprinkles her mother's ashes on Miles Davis's star, her favorite next to John Coltrane, who's not there.

She longs for a love supreme.

She is an orphan, and is brooding over her fate when she meets Harford at Venue, the nightclub she works at between the modelling gigs she keeps secret.

He deflowers her on their third date: they go to Nobu, then to his place, where he undresses her and slow-claps.

"You are one serious piece of ass," he says, easing off his gold Toms, Nudie jeans, and floral Reyn Spooner shirt.

He is rail-thin yet yogurt-wobbly. She feels nothing.

After jamming a finger, then two, inside of her, he says, "You're not a virgin?"

"No," she says, and frowns. *Is she* a virgin?

Oblivious, he says, "Good," pulls her to her knees, and sticks his short, tuberish cock inside her for five strokes — she counts — groans, flips her over, and cums on her back as he pulls her hair.

"*Yes!*" he says, exultant. "Tell me you love my moves."

"I love them," she says.

She is unhappy about the way he treats her, but mystified. She has no experience, and maybe sex is supposed to be brief and listless.

He holds her; wraps his bony legs around her waist in a vise grip and starts snoring.

She looks at him as he sleeps. He is sexy enough, she thinks, as she discreetly swipes between her legs to get a little charge going.

"Oh my God, did you cum?" he says, waking up, and she says, "Yeah, I looked at you and it just happened."

"Sweet," he says, yawning, and tightening his hold.

When she interferes with herself, she thinks of the scene in *Ultraviolence* where Sid grabs a girl beside him at the cinema, forcing her head down.

All you see is her bouffant rising and falling; his angular face as still as a cobra's, poised to strike.

"SO WILL INTRODUCED me to the right people, I got tons of good gigs, made a lot of money, and now I can do whatever I want."

"Hey!"

I had fallen asleep, dreaming of a girl with stiff, teased hair giving me head.

"Sorry. Yes, it all sounds too good to be true. Other than your dalliance with Harford. So why does your face get tiny and pinched when you talk about your life? And why are your little films so grim?"

"Why were you living like garbage when we met?" she counters.

Then we both burst into tears: we are reserved by nature, but unfortunately prone to crying jags that often last, with breaks, for hours on end.

This is a bad one.

I stand up and bury my face in my hands; she falls to the floor, beating it with her fists.

"You're so mean," we say at the exact same time.

"I hate you," we say, and fade to whimpers.

I cannot but notice that the pearl buttons of her antique lace nightgown have popped open; that her breasts are actually heaving.

She, in turn, appears to be riveted by the inflated region of my jeans.

"Sex is supposed to be like this," she says some time later as she bends backwards, keeping me inside of her while resting her head on my ankles.

I twitch, which sets off a reaction that ends in a blast of fission.

"Yes," I say, feeling myself grow small and cold, but unable to pull out and leave the carnival, all of its barking and music and gunshots.

"I LEFT OUT the part where he — who he looked like — when he raped me," she says as I fall asleep, dimly aware of her difficulty phrasing these familiar words.

"Listen to my story," Annabel says. "I am in New York for the essay-award ceremony. That night, I walk through Central Park.

I see three boys.

The tall one, with hair to his shoulders, is attractive. He is slender and fair, dressed in a long black leather coat.

Although I have fallen to the ground and rolled myself into a ball, I see him through the lens of three girls in chiffon, singing.

I sing, 'then he kissed me,' from my burrow, and his small, strong friends laugh.

He lifts me up, opens a knife, and cuts away my shirt. Then he slices my tights from bottom to top and tosses them aside.

When his friends start to whistle, I realize they are re-enacting something I have seen before. I forget what it is, I am so petrified.

The first slap has knocked me senseless.

He pulls me into an underpass, slams me against its wall.

The rape is slow and painful: I am filled with shame and terror.

And something else —

Please, I say: I am only thirteen years old, a never-kissed virgin and a bookworm.

'Please. They always say that,' one of the small men says as the tall one moans, then, hearing footsteps, pushes me to the ground.

He takes aim and kicks me in the belly.

'I'll find you and kill you if you tell,' he says.

Then he kneels and says, 'You're not bad, you know. I bet you turn into a real beauty,' flashes a brilliant smile, and darts away.

It is years before I speak about what happened, and Christ! Look who I'm telling—

I have the boot print tattooed on my guts, above the words *ne obliviscaris*. You've seen it. It is an act of defiance," she says.

"Pain as sharp as the blade he buried in my throat; pain I will not let myself forget.

Later, as the nurse tweezes and swabs between my legs, I sing, 'I have been blessed with beauty and rage,' and her eyes roll above her mask.

Parnell, he looked like you!" she says, and crawls under the covers, rolling herself up like a pill bug.

"NOT YOU, NOT you," she murmurs, sleeping now, curled into a ball once more.

Then who? I think, having heard certain bleak fragments. It doesn't matter. I will find him.

I am preparing the waxen cerement in my pitch-black mind as she moans and cries out for him to stop.

"I will make this right," I say, and she whimpers, safe in my arms, as I make my cruel and pleasing plans.

MY PHONE RINGS in the middle of the night: Annabel, who is enjoying the morphine Dante lifted for her, is out cold, but I am less fortunate.

It is Kray, his sibilant voice still as familiar as my own.

"Come to my office tomorrow," he says. "I'll send a car."

I hang up, go downstairs and pour a glass of whiskey, drain it, and pour another.

I am lighting a cigarette when Annabel walks in: her face falls when she sees me.

"What?" I say, in a low, mean voice.

"I'm sorry," I call after her as she runs back upstairs, and I look out the window at the low-hanging belly of the sky.

"I was almost there," I say.

"Happy," I tell an indifferent lariat of stars.

THERE WILL BE no stories of my childhood, a horror show I don't wish to reprise.

Father, also decamped; alcoholic mother, hunger, neglect.

Down the road and past high red gates was a field of poppies.

When the flowers grew tall, and as the sun began to set, my old black dog, Darkling, would race though the poppies after rabbits, leaping high into the air to find them.

Misery has always stuck to me like a thistle, but the thought of Darkling poised high above the sea of crimson blooms still appears in sanguine dreams, as if we are both still hunting for concealed, succulent conquests.

In school I started acting, which gave me the chance to be anyone but myself.

Every day and every night I watched the tall ships sail in and out of the harbor.

When finally I do leave home, I pack a cardboard box with some bedding, clothes, and a photograph of my parents holding me in front of the church where I was baptized. They look dazed and frightened of the sun: I am slipping out of my mother's arms and my yellowy-white gown.

I am tall for my age, well over six feet, and look older than I am. Malnutrition and hard living have cut my cheekbones into blades and left smutty marks under my eyes.

I leave Liverpool for London and get to know the streets.

Eventually, I audition for RADA.

My audition consists of a single piercing shriek.

I FUCK MY way through half the company that year and seduce many more girls I meet at pubs, through friends, or on the street.

I have cultivated a look: long, loosely layered hair and a single diamond earring, given to me by an old lady—a fifty-year-old admirer I take to bed to thank.

Thank *you*, she keeps saying as I dress, as she fans her hot bush and takes a final swat at my ass, which she describes, in bed, as "two swollen Asian pears snug in their white netting."

I wear tight stovepipe jeans or leather pants with motorcycle boots or tobacco-colored Adidas, along with frilly vintage blouses I fasten over savaged undershirts with kilt pins, and a thigh-length, black plush coat with saucer-sized red buttons.

The men who try to copy me look ridiculous; I am just tall, thin, and athletic enough to pull the look off: the girls love this *neue garçon/frau* aesthetic.

Kray will copy my look outright for the part of Sid Delacroix in *Ultraviolence*, and take full credit, of course.

I don't much like looking at pictures from this time. I look so artlessly good it is physically painful. Particularly when compared to the elongated troll doll I see so often in the mirror.

I think of the girls instead.

Of an entire chorus line of my conquests, high-kicking on a vast stage and teasing me with their tiny ruffled pantaloons and quivering teardrop breasts.

FOR THE LONGEST time, I overlooked Lola, but one day notice her standing at the barre in a rehearsal room, her soft pink leg bent, her fair arms interlocked.

She is eighteen, a romantic who gravitates toward suicides and fairies but is too rosy and plump for these roles.

I develop an attachment to her, and she rescues me from the indescribable room I am renting, asking me to live with her in Chelsea, in a refurbished flat her parents bought her.

I knock her up the first week and she starts to show almost immediately.

We are kids ourselves, but game. The small guest room is painted pink and blue, with a beaming sun on its ceiling. We pick up odds and ends and fix them up: a crib, a chest of drawers, a changing table, and the tiniest clothing imaginable. I keep a truly pathetic sock — orange with black spiders — in my pocket at all times.

Lola goes off sex within a few months — feeling, she says, too tired, too irritable, too goddamned fat.

She is vivid and lovely, but will not hear of it.

One day her best friend, a tart called Heloise, comes around when she knows Lola is at the doctor's for a checkup, and flies at me like a bloodthirsty bat.

Not that it matters, as it turns out, but I think of Lola the whole time.

Of the first night I spent with my living Fragonard girl, rolling the bed into pie crust, filling it with burst sugared berries.

I AM ACTING in a play when it happens.

I come home to find Lola howling in bed like a sick cat, the sheets doused in blood. She has visited an abortionist, a highly unqualified one at that, who used old, unsterilized instruments and thrilled at her pain.

Her suitcases are standing in a neat row by the door with a note.

It says, "I will never forgive you. I killed Gabriel and he was old enough to feel it."

Gabriel is the name she had chosen.

I extend my hand, warily, and help her walk out the door, which she slams.

Shaking, I fold the night's playbill, then discard it: *The Duchess of Malfi*, my first real production.

I have only one line, but all eyes turned to me, glittering of my fame.

I sleep on our balcony, mummified in blankets. The baby waddles up to me wearing a single sock.

He is deep blue and mournful: a huge aspiration pulls him away as he reaches for me, as I cry out, "Don't leave me!" to this portly gallant I know I will miss for the rest of my life.

I AM ASKED to make a film with Sir Kenneth Welthorpe, an esteemed theater director, who has just procured the rights to Joe Orton's screenplay *Up Against It*.

I play Ian McTurk, a licentious cross-dresser and murderer.

Welthorpe, secretly enamored of me, lingers on my every gesture, and inserts a scene in which I undress to "Stray Cat Blues" as the virgin, Rowena — whom I am about to deflower — is seen mounting a wooden chair and heatedly slamming herself against its slats.

The film receives mixed reviews, but I am singled out for praise and panegyrics.

I also become the object of teen girls' sexual hysteria—and, critically, secure the professional attention of the legendary director Lamont Kray.

He asks for a meeting about a film project and I invite him over. But I am to pack, and must finish today, I am warned by Lola's raging father.

The project is *Ultraviolence*: "I keep envisioning you as the lead," he says, smiling enigmatically.

He is not mysterious to me. I know him, and what he sees when he looks at me.

I put my hand in my pocket and squeeze the orange sock.

"Can you make it all go away?" I ask this stout, impeccable man.

"It's gone," he says.

We walk out of the flat and I never return.

In two years, I am a star, living in a Los Angeles bungalow and plucking lemons from my own tree on the bedroom balcony beneath a muster of palms.

I am rich, tan as a stick, and Kray now calls me his "cash bull."

And here's where my story takes its first sickening turn.

HAVE YOU EVER woken up and felt dread pour into your stomach like hot magma?

Woken and covered your face with the sheets, you are so embarrassed and startled by the magnitude of how bad everything is?

I have. Still do.

After we finish touring with *Ultraviolence*, Kray asks me to make another movie with him, an adaptation of *Les Chants de Maldoror*.

"You would make a superb Maldoror," he says, showing me the storyboard for the scene in which the eponymous creep rapes and murders a boy.

When I am interviewed, at a later time, about working with Kray, I often recite the novel's warning to the reader:

> Unless he should bring to his reading a rigorous logic and a sustained mental effort at least as strong as his distrust, the lethal fumes of this book shall dissolve his soul as water does sugar.

And then laugh lightly, as if being playful.

Quailing with revulsion, I tell Kray it is time I branched out, and decline.

He says he regrets, but accepts, my decision.

And so his fervid crusade begins. He tars and feathers my name everywhere, indicating en masse—I learn through one loyal old friend—that to work with me is to work against him.

But I am young and arrogant. He will change his mind, I think. My talent will win out in the end, anyways.

It does not.

In addition to spreading fabricated stories of my villainy, Kray informs everyone I am a gay man—in far more ghastly language—who prefers the company of very young men: as in barely-adolescents.

Never mind that everyone I work with is gay. Their secrecy is steadfast, and my alleged proclivities make everyone sick.

I cannot defend myself against blind items, innuendo, and gossip.

The fall is fast and steep.

MY POSH AGENT quits, and my representation grows worse and worse. I have to resort to the Yellow Pages, and my pay scale plunges accordingly, as does the caliber of the work.

The chicken-hawk rumors die down when I am never seen doing anything but squiring my listless wife and frightful children around.

And crying brokenly on sidewalks or in traffic.

Enough gay men stand by me that I am able to get work, which is why there is a triangle branded on the underside of my wrist.

I make B movies — I am always cast as the villain — which, thankfully, very few people see.

And go back to the theater, but the plays are horrid: *Gorboduc* performed by men and women in diapers and paper crowns; an experimental work called *Mr. Dirty Man*, mounted by a women's collective who beat me half to death on opening night.

During *Titus Andronicus*, which runs several weeks at the Asylum, I get drunk and greet people I know, or wish to know, in the audience.

I am fired the night I sit on the stage's edge eating a large piece of cheese and playing vulgar games with a laser pointer.

I shoot TV pilots and guest appearances on increasingly unpopular, mean-spirited shows where I am asked to respond to such lines as "Hey, who invited stinky Grandpa?"

Changing tack, I make infomercials for a potato peeler that doubles as a universal remote, and for a male hair-loss product called Harvest, which is, essentially, a bag of seeds and dirt.

Then I write a memoir, with a ghost, naturally, called *I'm Still Here!* (I lobbied, unsuccessfully, to add *You Heartless Bastards*). It is remaindered the week it comes out.

Shortly after its release, I come across a second-hand copy in a shambolic Hollywood bookstore, painstakingly inscribed "To my dear daughter, from her devoted father." I slip it into my breast pocket, slink outside, and dry-heave by the entrance.

And this is where you found me, more or less.

In my tenth domicile or so, on my fifth car; entering my deplorable career as a chicken huckster.

Kray transfigures everything, like holy magic.

I try to remember this when the bile-hatch opens each morning, filling me with fear and other poisons.

WAS I DREAMING of Kray, my nauseous stomach wonders as I sit bolt upright and barf an *Exorcist*-green arc.

Annabel is on top of it. She has the bed stripped and changed in a flash as I brush my teeth and wash my par-boiled face, while assiduously avoiding my reflection.

She dresses me in clean white pajamas and pours me a Scotch, neat, in my old sippy cup.

"You were talking—well, screaming—in your sleep," she says, raking Zen lines in my hair.

"What did I say?" I ask her and tremble. *Not this, no.*

She pauses and looks at me sorrowfully.

"I couldn't make it out," she says, and if she is lying, I cannot tell.

I fall into the ring of her arms and dream of many bright toy dinosaurs circling a full-blown yellow rose.

Mon semblable, she murmurs as the room fills with music: "Keep Me in Your Heart."

"A song for you," she says.

A song about dying, I think. And the few bright sparks in life, an otherwise insufferably long, dark passage.

My likeness — what does she mean? — sings along as an aurora of bees dive-bomb the flower, drinking greedily of her inexhaustible sweetness.

As I swipe lightly at her open lips and rich hazel skin, at the straps of her filmy salmon-pink slip, sleep, in the guise of a ten-foot-tall T. Rex, plucks at, then swallows me whole.

Take me to your dreams, Annabel, my mango-bellied starling, sings.

The dinosaur, now small, hears her and claps his little hands.

"You were wrong," he roars. "He is not his *doom'd son's spirit*."

She nods, lifts him by the tail, and swallows him whole.

Annabel will watch over me for hours — but needlessly, as my dreams have become *Fantastic Voyage*.

Her blood is an 1865 Château Lafite with a complex flavor, something like willow-tree shavings stirred into a strongman's blood; and a clear, ruby appearance, legs to *here*.

And so I remain in her arms and deeper, inside of her splendid veins, euphoric and afraid of nothing until my phone alarm sounds and I, as Caliban, cry to dream again.

KRAY DAY is what I have written on the bathroom mirror with the eyeliner I apply each morning in strictest furtiveness.

I dress slowly and move even more so, thinking of the Bataan Death March and of rifle stocks jabbing me forward.

Kray's office is in Century City.

I sit on a soft white block as his Bardot look-alike secretary drifts around with bottles of water and a sympathetic smile.

"I've seen that video your girlfriend made, the sexy one. I get off on it," she says, rushing back to her desk as Kray's shadow enters the room.

"Please ignore this dumb bunny," he says fondly, and pats her head. "She gets off when sea turtles mate on the Discovery Channel."

"So what if I do?" she says, and pouts. I am tempted to crawl onto her lips and take a long cleansing nap.

Kray takes my elbow, and his hand is a glacier.

We sit in a room empty of everything but two hard-back chairs, an abbreviated desk, and his film posters.

"So, let's talk about the movie," I say, my legs crossing and uncrossing convulsively.

"No time for catching up?" he says, and smiles, revealing rows of tiny amber-colored teeth.

"No," I say, but I am paralyzed, lost in his stabbing gaze.

"You are still beautiful," he says, and leisurely reaches forward to cup my face in his great, rough paw.

I stare back at him helplessly.

This is how it starts all over again.

I DON'T REMEMBER leaving the office, or getting home.

Just that I sat in the living room drinking whiskey from a jar, with night falling on me like the cape of a count.

Or blanket, the blanket she shook over me while speaking softly in my ear: "Let me help you."

Words that I push away: "You don't know what you're talking about."

"But I do, I do," she says, as if she is marrying me; as if she is my new bride, she lifts a veil of light and kisses my lips.

Cold, medicinal lips like a plantain poultice: I fall asleep and wake up still wrapped in the blanket that is covered in a print of smiling bees. "Buzz" is what she most often calls me, my Annabel, who is gone.

I find her in the living room, in a fort made out of sofa pillows and a tablecloth.

She is lying on her side, her fingers splayed across her face.

I watch her adjusting Tubby, who has been conscripted to serve as a pillow, and burrowing in my old coat from the hard times: a carefully mended M-51 field jacket with ersatz red windmill buttons.

"My sweetheart," I say, and her eyes snap open.

"You have to talk to me," she says, shrugging off the coat. "We are so much more alike than you imagine, and—"

I don't want to hear this and halt her by covering her mouth and producing a black bullwhip I bought in West Hollywood.

She melts.

And lashes me hard enough to leave open, bleeding welts I know she'll repair with her first-aid kit.

Later.

She is my reverse cowgirl now, and I am starving for a taste of the golden pear that is her waist and hips, the supple stem of her refined neck.

"I'm sorry," I say, breathless and lowing, and she silences me with a flick of the whip—just a taste really—and I know I am off the hook, for now.

My cell rings at the worst possible time, and I throw it across the room.

"Who is Alexander?" she says when she retrieves it later on.

"My son. Remember his kiddie picture, the one where he's setting my house on fire? He's not named after the *Clockwork* Alex, though. It was my wife's father's name."

She is agitated, starts pacing.

"I'm a bad father, I know," I tell her, still reclining, not at all interested in the conversation, and fascinated by her from this angle.

"I should have mentioned him before. It's just—"

"What? What is it?"

"Oh, we don't get along. I can't imagine why he's calling."

"Call him," she says, throwing on a robe.

I do, unhappily, and he gets right to the point. Can I give his latest girlfriend a part in whatever I'm working on? he asks.

"No," I say, and Annabel grabs the phone.

"Your father is joking; of course he'll help you," she says.

He says, "You sound sexy, what's your name?" and she tells him and hangs up and goes outside and screams until she cannot speak and is spitting blood.

"Don't ask and I won't ask you," she says elliptically.

I see us colliding in a space accident that a Venusian anchorman reports in a series of shrill beeps and a single flat blast: my mouth opens and shuts as the distance between us lengthens.

We are in danger, I think miserably.

Baise-moi, she says, crying. I am so gentle she becomes furious and slaps me until my ears ring.

PUDGE CALLS. "ANNABEL Wrath is my age, Dad. And she's—"

"She's what?"

"Never mind," she says. "Call Mom right away. There's a very serious problem with the pool."

My strange daughter hangs up abruptly as I lie in the demolished fort, after cleaning my cuts with witch hazel; after waking Annabel with promises of coffee and admiring her sleep-creased backside making its way upstairs. Reluctantly I call Allegra and sort out the problem, which turns out to be "an unusual smell."

"I can't be alone in thinking it's coming from you," I say.

When her breathing becomes rapid, I promise to send over a handyman, laughing as I spoon coffee grounds into the press.

I FELL FOR Allegra Swan when she was giving me my first pedicure on Rodeo Drive, shortly after I arrived in America, flush and successful. This was not long before Kray's offer and revenge.

She teased me with thrilling views of her cleavage as she sanded my neglected feet, speaking in an irresistible Southern accent that she has fabricated, I will later discover, entirely.

I have just filmed my first American movie, *History Repeats Itself*, with the vivacious and equine Karen Allen.

I play my first significant good guy, in mutton-chop sideburns, a bald spot, and various rayon blouses. I am an archaeologist in love with a mummy played by Miss Allen, who devises a transparently impossible way of travelling back in time to meet her in her original form, trapping us both in ancient Egypt with no way back.

My high hopes of crossing over are dashed by a very large number of reviews stating that the movie is ludicrous, deadening, and, "if the title is true, a call to arms."

I turn to my aesthetician for comfort in my shock and shame, and soon discover she is not Allegra Swan, twenty-five, but Angie Sales, a thirty-seven-year-old barber from Staten Island.

She cries so pitifully when she confesses that I shrug and let it go. We drift together as my star fades; as it explodes, we manage to pass many unhappy years.

Just as I decide to move back to London and start again, she gets pregnant, first with Alexander, then with Christine, who is born only eleven months after her brother.

Her body changes and it disgusts me. Zigzags of maroon appear all over her poultry-white skin; her vagina could pass a pickup truck, and her breasts!

They are distended bulbs, also electrified with stretch marks, which leak through her clothes, wetting the bed and disgusting me at the dinner table.

"You're no bargain either," she tells me after I have rebuffed another of her crude advances (ball-cupping followed by stale, sloppy kisses). "Your ass stinks and your cock is never hard, your nose and ears are stuffed with hair, and you have a bag for a belly."

"Then let us not touch each other," I say, relieved and deeply offended. Allegra takes to sleeping in a separate bedroom, smoking and seething, writing what she calls an "explosive memoir."

I sneak a look at it one day. It is a pad of legal paper and on each page is a tear, glistening at the corner of one of her distinctive cornflower-blue eyes.

There are hundreds, captioned with times and dates, and that is all.

I am uneasy about her instability and creative virtuosity. I put the pad away; this Rachel's sea of weeping, the drowning of all she had hoped for, reached—

Only to lose.

I want to leave, but I am very partial to my children, and I stay with my wife because of them.

Pudge is kind, even to worms in the garden I am ready to strike with my spade, kind to me when I am hungover, patting my forehead with wet facecloths and resting one dimpled hand in mine.

And Alexander—

When my son was born, I was elated. We bonded at first sight: our eyes locked as I held him; he sighed deeply and stopped yowling, only to resume when the nurse or his own mother reached for him.

I saw in him a small, uncorrupted me. I saw another chance and something far bigger, beating everywhere like a telltale heart.

I envisioned his candy heart filling my own nearly barren heart with redolent messages: *Sweet Pea, Me & You, O Kid!*

He grew so quickly, in inverse proportion to my career.

By the time he was a sturdy, flaxen-haired three-year-old, I was working on a film that demarcates the moment at which my life went off the rails completely.

It was pitched to me as *Richàrd*, the story of a man in the grip of a "Kafkaesque loneliness," whose moonlighting at the city zoo has led him toward a tragic empathy with a rhinoceros slated to be euthanized.

My French-Canadian character, unable to save his friend, would lock himself in his vacated cage, becoming an exhibit himself.

It was a good and very moving script, and the director, Jaime Sommers, was a cherished old friend who had worked with me at RADA on a number of revenge tragedies, stories we liked for their emotional candor and highbrow gore.

But she was fired, and a hack with a megaphone and cowboy hat Western-stitched with the only name we knew him by — CHEESE — was brought in, who changed the title to *Nightmare in Tusktown*!

He changed my role too, making me a sort of a were-ungulate, lingering on scenes of my agonized transformations; on stops, mid-escape, to peer into women's bedrooms to watch them undress by night lights; and, for reasons best known to him, on a lengthy quarrel with the zookeeper about "the best anal bleach technicians. Right here in Tusktown!"

I was perpetually mortified and locked into an ironclad contract that did not preclude their lowering my pay as they pleased.

But being with Alexander made everything all right, including Allegra's company, for she doted on him also.

He had an outrageously bad temper and disposition, yet he had countless friends, friends I knew were bound to him by fear. I admired his magnetism and confidence.

The worse he got, the sweeter he was with us, with me especially, and so, like the great, damned *Rex*, I blinded myself.

When our pets went missing, when his teachers sent urgent letters, when he attacked little Pudge so often that we had to install a deadbolt on her door and a security camera, when he wrote *Devil* on his forehead with a heart over the "i," using a razorblade, when he turned twelve and started smoking and dropping acid—

It exhausts me to continue.

Still, he flew at me every night when I came home, asking me about my day and calling me so cool. He begged me to read to him from books he had obviously jacked, embarrassing pulp novels like *Tigress, Kill Baby*, and *Swamp Brat*.

And he kept his hand over mine at dinner, and whenever we sat near each other.

I liked him, I must have loved him, but that changed, irretrievably.

By the time he was thirteen, I had abandoned any pretense of being a respectable actor.

My job at the time was a recurring role (involving another transformation premise) on a comedy set in Transylvania, Louisiana, called *Night Shift on the Bayou.*

I played a hotel manager-slash-vampire who disappeared during the day, causing all sorts of problems for guests wanting to check in or find their cable listings.

My sidekick was a Cajun alligator named Beau, whose catchphrase was "You be cooyon."

Humiliating is not the word: Beau made more money than I did and, during a swamp scene, bit a half-moon out of my ass, leaving a livid scar.

Annabel's mouth alight on this scar, altering it into our linked initials, her tongue sliding into the crack of my

Alexander is fifteen when I come across him one night forcing a terrified girl down into the basement, her arms pinned behind her back, his hand jammed over her mouth.

She is Aisha, the twelve-year-old daughter of a cancer-stricken single father, a good neighborhood friend who has asked me to look out for her.

"What are you doing?" I say to him, pulling her away. She runs and she runs like Atalanta out the door and across the lawn.

His hand comes away wet with her blood: what has he done?

"Take it easy, Dracula," he says, and I snap for the first time.

I faintly recall kneeling on his chest and punching him until I have made a nice crater in his fucking face, the pulse of an ambulance's light in the trees, his shock, and the contempt in his eyes that has been there all along.

He tells the police officer that someone from school—"He was wearing a mask, a pig mask"—attacked him, and asks that I go with him to Central Booking.

I refuse and, just like that, cut off all communication.

I stay until he is sixteen, then tell him and my bitch wife that I'm out the door.

"I've done my time," I say. *"L'incident est clos!"* I snap, like Yves Montand, whom I vainly feel I have come to resemble.

He moves out, and does very well for himself.

He is currently the lead singer of a psychedelic punk band called Kraut: his hair is bleached white, his eyes altered to look pale blue, with vertical irises.

He tells the media we are tight and that my films are fucking dope, even the bad ones.

I don't want to think about him; memories trick and violate me.

I turn my face upward and stare at the unfinished ceiling—Annabel wants a skylight, I want a mural—and try to count the specks there while separating them into three categories: stain, bug, and mold.

But my son returns, like Catherine Earnshaw scratching at the window.

I get up, demolish the bathroom, pad downstairs and pour the last of the whiskey into a cup of cold coffee from the day before, and light a cigarette.

Girls still came home with him.

Lots of them.

Muffled screams, once, that I ended by firing a shotgun through his door. Two preteens scurried out; Alexander lay back, pleased.

"I'll kill you," I said, and he laughed out loud.

BEFORE I LEFT, two things happened.

One: I fucked the cleaning lady, Midge, whose visits we had reduced to once a week.

Midge looks like Popeye: short, squinty, and strong, with a huge cleft chin.

She curses like a sailor too, at the squalor she must tackle each visit: piles of sodden, reeking laundry; sinks teeming with stained, unscraped dishes; fungal tiles; toilets caked in shit and hemmed with viscous, bright yellow piss.

I come across her one day using a knife on the powder-room sink to extract rosettes of paste, blood, and phlegm.

Allegra does not do housework. Watching Midge excites me; she is so ruggedly sexual.

I place my hand meaningfully on her yellow glove: she is game.

Allegra swings open the door to find me teabagging her on the floor as she works my perineum with a toilet brush.

"How could you?" she says, then, "Pudge, look at what your father is doing to us!"

Midge and I spring up, dress in a flash, and face our inquisitors.

No one speaks.

Midge says at last, "For the record, this kinda heat starts *itself*."

Pudge and Allegra stare, appalled, and walk out, slamming the door.

I feel unclean and excited.

"Get them balls back here," Midge says, and we roll around like pigs in unseen manure until we are both squealing with pleasure.

I tip her extravagantly and she leaves her number on the wall with Lysol Power Foam.

Two uneasy weeks pass and Allegra returns.

She is not alone.

THE SECOND THING.

Enter Cal.

He is an unemployed glass-blower with a ponytail, earring, and panel van decorated with an airbrushed portrait of Allegra as Adele Bloch-Bauer. Low on funds, he is forced to use yellow instead of gold. She looks jaundiced and incontinent.

"I love her, man," he tells me, assuming a judo stance.

"Then by all means take her," I say.

Exit me, at last—too bad Cal leaves her by the cheap motel in Butte where they have been fighting for an entire week; that she, sheepishly, must call me for a bus ticket.

She returns to the house, huffy and disgraced; I move to a little place in Artesia, where Pudge visits me to stare at her phone, stream X-rated horror movies, and raid my cupboards.

I barely notice her except to grimace at the sight of her circus tent-sized jean dresses and purplish ankles jammed into yellow Crocs.

I date a different girl every night. "I'm so lonely," I tell each of them before asking them to leave.

"Let me help you," they say, and I think of something that Michael Jackson told me — or was it Jermaine? No, he was small, and perfect. I was blowing my head back with a celery-sized rail of coke —

"Girls don't want to take away my loneliness," Michael said. "They want to share it."

I never saw him again: isolation had folded him into a tiny bindle and inhaled him whole.

My son vanishes also.

He calls me now and then — Allegra gives him my details, repeatedly — and sometimes he sends me checks with fatuous notes in the memo line, like "Saw you in *The Wee Pubkeeper*. Super!"

It was a serious, though mawkish, movie in which I played a legless, vigorously Irish publican — I kneeled, miserable, for weeks.

Most often, he simply, evilly, writes, "Daddy, please treat yourself, you deserve it."

Psychopath, I seethe.

On the rare occasions that I answer his calls, I tell him I will rip up his checks and do.

I then tape them back together and empty entire shelves at Catalina Liquor.

Shame: drink enough and the word loses all meaning.

ANNABEL PRIES IT out of me.

It is midnight and she is bathing. I am rapturously cleaning her dusky shoulders, her prominent rib cage, and her convex belly with a rough, soapy little washcloth.

"This tattoo," I start to say, and she stands up, shaking like a dog as she steps out of the tub.

"Don't ask," she says. Groans and tells me.

"My girlfriend and I were drunk, and we wandered into some ancient parlor with crazy old boards. She got this cartoon tattoo that says KEEP ON TRUCKIN'. It covers her back, she won't go swimming."

"You dumb kids," I say fondly, I think. But all she hears, and she's not entirely wrong, is a pompous old man.

The fight is on.

We hurl insults at each other and shake with rage.

She pulls out her camera after she's dressed, which infuriates me.

"Why do you lie all the time?" she says in the background as the lens homes in on my pursed, sweating face.

"About what?"

I dodge and she follows me, never losing sight.

"Isn't this your son?" she says, holding up a photograph torn from a magazine.

It is one I have never seen. He is dressed as Sid from *Ultraviolence* and looks just like me.

"Yes," I say. "We're not close, you know that."

All at once, I remember my son's birth: his large head crowning as the delivery room fills with the smell of fear and shit.

"Do you want to meet him?" I say speciously, and she throws the camera at me.

I never see this film; she doesn't mention Alexander again until it all comes down, and when it does, she can't speak for fear of dying.

THREE

ANNABEL AND PARNELL,
PACIFIC PALISADES, 2017
THE WAR IN HEAVEN

ANNABEL AND I would come to refer to the night of our big brawl as the War in Heaven.

We fight for hours: crockery is shattered and a picture window; pieces of furniture become kindling; some of my good clothes are altered with bleach, scissors, and a Magic Marker.

And the bear, our fat little bear!

Just as I am holding manicure scissors to his now-rumpled GET WELL SOON sweater, Annabel yowls.

"Oh no, not Tubby!"

We are imbeciles regarding his welfare and company.

He spends half the week with her, in her purse, usually, on a bed of flannel squares she has sewn into a small quilt and matching pillow; during the other half, he rides in my car in a shoebox outfitted with a floccose lining, a shag pillow, and his travel gear: a coat and loose pajamas that Annabel made from a pattern and scraps of colorful, downy fabrics.

He also has a case containing several more garments, three additional hats, a pair of yellow rain boots, and six pairs of knitted socks.

His own nanoscale teddy bear, which we made together—drunk and cursing, then proud beyond reason at the amiable, misshapen result.

A tiny book about grizzly bears, a bowl and cup, a ring of keys.

And a framed picture of us, holding him from either paw.

Tubby sleeps with us separately and together, and has a high, gentle voice that has ended a lot of animosity between us.

"I'm so sorry," I say, to her, to the bear, as I quickly retrieve his robe and shower sandals and place him in the tub with his Chiclet-sized bar of soap and rolled-up square of Turkish towel.

She runs a few inches of water and we wash him with Q-tips, dry him off, dress him, and, exhausted, place him between us on the bed.

We sleep.

Her voice is a bird that has lost its way: "Are we a joke?"

"What do you mean?" I say, and reach for her hand.

"Look at us," she says sharply, flicking Tubby to the floor.

I move to get him and she stops me.

"It's a toy," she says. "Leave it be."

I retrieve him anyways, with a lot of elderly grunts and one bottomless wheeze.

"This toy is who we are and what we yearn for, made tangible," I say, and she writes a note on her phone. I see the words PW: REIFY.

"And it means as little or as much as we want it to mean. It means everything to me," I say, and tuck the little chap between our pillows before turning away from her.

I cannot stand the thought of her seeing me cry again.

Then again, she is crying, audibly.

She is so beguiling when she cries, as the entire world gathers in breathing, tensile drops and breaks, and the seas and forests rush in living lines along her miraculous face, and gusts of salt air rush from her quivering lips.

I, on the other hand, shout and honk, turn crimson and leak dense, viscous fluids that gather in the folds of my raw skin.

"Why?" I manage to say.

"I'm crying," she says, as she delicately tidies herself with a chiffon napkin, "because of what you said about love, about us. It was so beautiful," she says, and I light up. Secretly, I am fairly intimidated by her, and afraid she thinks I'm an idiot.

But Annabel wrote down something I said. The woman followed and venerated by more than a hundred thousand smart, cynical kids; the woman constantly singled out by the right magazines and papers as an unparalleled rising star in her field.

The woman I never said I loved, not ever.

I keep crying, as does she.

We cry into our dreams, dreams where we run and cannot escape the agony that awaits us; we cry until we are hoarse, roll back and hold each other on the sodden raft, raising the white flag that the pirates never fail to shoot at and burn.

THERE IS A call: Kray is ill—his doctors believe he has had a stroke—and shooting is postponed indefinitely.

This is after the War in Heaven and its concomitant terrors. We are inseparable, and have woken up wound together like snakes.

"I'm sorry," Annabel says, disingenuously.

I am free to work on her untitled film now.

"Oh, what a shame," I say, making a solicitous call to Kray's wife, Vivienne, and bounding downstairs to make French toast with fresh blueberries, singing, "Every 1's a winner, baby—"

As I stir the batter and hum, I think of what has changed between Annabel and me. Our affair feels so fragile, as though one harsh word would shatter it, and shatter us irrevocably.

She keeps her apartment because we concede that we are something of a Molotov cocktail together and prone to agitation.

That said, she uses it only to store clothes she has tired of and to retreat to during bouts of anger that never last longer than a day.

I put it out of my mind: as far as I'm concerned, we will live together forever. I have enchanting visions of us, of me, elderly and riding up a set of ornate stairs on a plump motorized chair as she, still beautiful, but silver now, waits for me.

There are more, there shall be a lifetime of such visions!

WE FIND A house in the Pacific Palisades, a billionaire's 3,500-square-foot cottage on countless acres of lush, fertile land where mustangs run free and painted birds perch on every tree.

There is a studio/office for her, and a den I can retreat to now and then to rest, as happy as I have ever been; happier than that.

We ventilate our life to include a small group of friends, oddballs that she has collected — antique poets, young gangsters, jaded, heartsick models, corpulent acrobats, and more.

The house is decorated, with pleasure, and we welcome strays: two dogs, a half-wolf, who scare everyone but us, and a litter of abandoned skunk cubs we tame and have de-scented after a few misfires.

Annabel cooks some nights, a strange, sherry-loaded mock–mock turtle soup — made with tomatoes, green peas, and amniote-shaped crackers — with fresh-baked bread; vegetable creole stew, swaying soufflés, and desserts dripping in chocolate that we eat on the slate roof, as it rains and rains, holding us fast.

Mostly, we order food in and project movies onto a sheet that we staple to the living-room wall. We lose our phones and fuck constantly to Moroccan love songs.

I email Pudge that I am going to Venezuela to play Rum Tum Tugger at the Caracas Athenaeum; Annabel sends a mass email saying she has joined me.

Occasionally, we dress in black, with large sunglasses and her hair in purdah below a white Hermès scarf. We visit MOCA and watch Arthur Jafa's *Love Is The Message, The Message Is Death*, standing against the back wall like violet-flowering jacaranda trees, still, our heads swaying toward each other, sending questions we answer by kissing passionately, and, being impudent, write TL;DW in the comment book.

We eat tofu dogs at Pink's and visit the planetarium. Very stoned, we name stars after each other and when one shoots by we squeak the same wish and say *If I tell you it won't come true*

We document and love our adventures, the drives to the ocean and desert, weekends in Catalina, Ojai, and Palm Springs, but what we love the most is being as close as possible, something that has caused us to be thrown out of two cinemas.

And a diner, almost.

She was telling me about visiting her mother's folks back home, and living, for a while, in the mountains with lambs, wearing nothing but a linen scrap, and I slapped a hundred-dollar bill on the table for the advancing waiter and slid from my booth to the ground, crazed with love, parted her legs and—

Made her come true, and me too—she slings silverware like the Great Throwdini, nailing someone.

We don't know who. When the cops show up, we have long since vanished in a cloud of smoke.

WE ARE ON our way to a puppet show–slash–play reading by some casual friends, people Annabel knows, and are wanting coffee.

"Starbucks?" I say.

She says no.

She tells me she had an idea in high school about why the shop was named after that *Moby Dick* character.

"Starbuck is a minor character, but near the end, he falls asleep and messes everything up," she says, animated now. "I always wondered if the Starbucks founders were making a joke, like if the eponymous sailor had drunk some coffee, he'd have stayed awake and, you know, *whale meat for everyone!*"

"I like that," I say admiringly. "Did you ever tell anyone?"

"I did," she says. "Some barista, who brushed me off and wrote *Bananaball* on my cup."

"Bitch," I say, frowning. "I'm glad we fucked on their kiddie changing station."

This excites her, and she starts teasing my fly and then loses her hand inside my jeans.

We pull over and fuck fast and rough.

Skip the show and hurry home, where my insatiable beast flips me onto the sofa while gnawing off my pants, leaving me gasping in socks and a too-short dress shirt.

But I am half-limp, distracted. Should I impress her coffee idea more vigorously to the Starbucks suits?

In such a way that they *have* to hear her out.

As if she can read my fiendish mind, she redoubles her efforts.

Eases open each shirt button, removes both socks while filling my ear with blandishments like "so sexy," "pussy burning," and "take me like a god."

Quietly, almost soundlessly, *to be enraged with a dumb thing seems blasphemous.*

I fold her open and hammer away until we are both hoarse and traction-burned and exhausted. I am reduced to pulling feebly at the sofa bed's bar until it springs open and, relieved, we crawl aboard, finding individual pillows and blankets at its stern.

"This can't last," I say.

I say this hours later, when she has managed to fuck me again in something like a hot trance, and I burst open and blossom.

"No," she says, squeezing all of our ravishing life inside her as time waits on the sidelines, smoking; watchful.

VOLTA, I WRITE on my palm with my dentist's pen the following day.

We sleep late, and after dinner we drive around, Annabel wanting to go to the ocean while I would rather park at the observatory and look at the stars.

We decide again to have coffee, to spike with whiskey later, and a bag of donuts.

"Let's go to both places and have picnics," she says, and we head over to Spudnuts on Figueroa.

We park, step outside, and start playfully grappling when two cops, fat and thin, stop us.

"Is she bothering you?" the fat one asks, and I smile.

"Always," I say, smiling, and suddenly she is pushed up against the cruiser as the thin one demands to see her ID.

What the fuck is happening?

I take a swing at him, and see the fat one hit Annabel with his baton. I hit him again, but this is different, I feel weak and enervated and I am cuffed and she is cuffed and Jerry bails us out. He scares the two cops with talk of lawsuits and the press and she and I never speak of it, although we should, and some time later their two bloated bodies are pulled out of Bell Creek, naked and mutilated.

"Crazy Cop Killer on the Loose," claims the *L.A. Times* in its lead story. "A surgical scalpel found two miles downstream, our reporter has learned, is thought to have removed segments of their flesh."

"There go Fat and Skinny," I remark, passing Annabel the paper that she looks at as though she is blind.

"This is a dangerous city," she says, and stretches. "I'm still craving a donut," she tells me, playfully chewing on my ear and teasing me until I drag my ass to Stan's and feed her bits of blackberry and raspberry and blueberry.

She cries when we kiss.

"I love how things work out in the end," she says.

I love all that blood, I remember the Night Stalker saying during his murder trial almost thirty years ago.

I felt disconcerted at the time and now — "I do too," I say.

ANNABEL'S BAD DREAMS persist.

She wakes and moves around the dark bedroom, eyes wide, arms outstretched.

"Please help me," she says, collapsing into me when I reach her.

I lead her to bed and within the hour she is up again, cowering in the shadows, clutching her nightgown at the neck and pleading.

I will get up and carry her several times before she falls asleep, clinging to me and praying on what appear to be rosary beads.

After a few days of this, I ask her to see someone.

She refuses angrily and that night sinks her teeth into my hand so deeply I tell her to take me to see a doctor.

Ashen, she drives me to an urgent-care clinic, her pale face framed by damp segments of long, snaky hair.

I let myself feel every bump of the ride, watch the pulsing lights, and place my wound in my mouth.

It is dangerous to be this happy: the blood ringing her mouth is the first sign that we are too far gone, too hungry and fearless.

It's just a flesh wound, we discover, and a badly bruised bone.

Later, at home, as she crawls on the floor, weeping for someone to save her, I get up. Cloaking my injured hand in a pillowcase, I pray for relief, just a morsel, and there is none.

MY NIGHTMARES FOLLOW suit.

The man in the bridal veil and morning suit is never far behind me. When I spin around to confront him, he becomes a raven and flies away.

"This won't hurt," he says, and I bury my face in the pillows. It hurts so much. The blood is his nourishment; it is the sea he plunges into and patrols, revealing only the apex of his black dorsal fin.

Annabel is sleeping.

"We were the Piccadilly Circus freaks," I tell her.

Runaways, addicts.

Some of my friends are rent boys, but I stick to crimes and shacking up with the occasional old lady.

The men won't leave me alone, though.

This one, a huge brute, tells me he'll give me a hundred quid for a few kisses.

"You're the prettiest thing I've ever seen," he says, and I believe him: just some kissing.

But he changes his mind and demands a blow job. I do the best I can; he cums all over me, then throws me out of his car, calling me a dirty little nance.

I go to one of the old ladies' places and say I have the flu. She runs a bath and tucks me in bed, sets me up with tea and juice.

I am so grateful I thank God.

Then the old bitch grabs my cock. I knock her out, rip the gold choker from her baggy neck, and hock it.

"I've always had bad luck," I tell Annabel. "You're better off without me."

Annabel yawns.

"What time is it? What did you just say?"

"It's late. Nothing at all."

I hold and pet her, feel her burrow under my arm like a little rabbit.

I am grateful she knows none of this. The story gets worse, I tell her. It's not for her.

"Are you worried I'll love you less?" she asks between slow, somnolent breaths. "Because I won't. I'll love you more, because you're brave and a survivor. And you are the prettiest thing I've ever seen," she says as the moonlight crowns her lustrous head. I kiss her limp hand and it wakens, grabs me, pulls me close.

"A miserable failure" is how one of my late reviews started: the critic was referring to me.

You were wrong.

To hold Annabel, to be filled with her, is to flourish; to know what joy is, a melody the miserable wind tries to pick out on taut catgut strings, failing every time.

WE TAKE OFF.

In London, I try to connect with old friends and colleagues, but most are dead or missing.

Jerry, however, ensures that we are invited to all the right parties and premieres. After our picture appears in the papers, Vivienne Kray personally invites us to the opening night of a retrospective of her husband's work at the Saatchi Gallery.

We see *Date with the Devil*, a noir about a bookie who keeps getting blackout drunk and waking up with Satan—a forked tail is coiled on the pillow beside him, a horrified glance reveals scorch marks on the sheets, and so on.

Not as complex as his later work, it is still visually stunning, and the ending, where the protagonist and the devil kiss, put on cowboy hats, and ride into a flaming sunset, is both modern and quaint at once.

Vivienne, a sculptress, is taken by Annabel: she presses her enormous Chanel cocktail ring on her after she admires it, and the two of them speak privately and with animation about the script, and about Kray.

"Are you sure?" says Annabel to a question I do not quite hear, and Vivienne tells her, "I'll place it in his hands myself."

"What?" I hazard, and the older woman, a congenital liar, says, "All in due time, darling Parnell, all in due time."

So I choke on my curiosity and hold out my arm for her withered, diamond-loaded arm to grasp, the opulent vulture.

She tells me that Kray is recovering *beautifully* and will be back soon, or so she hopes, blushing in a way that makes her skin mottle.

I tell her I am happy to hear the news and squeeze her like a python until she weeps.

"How very ugly you are," I murmur as I blot her tears, knowing she is deaf as a stone, and she readily allows my ministrations.

When we return to the Dorchester that evening, Annabel models the ring and a pair of sequined silver slippers as I lie on the bed.

We are very drunk.

"Fuck me," she says, biting her lip hard.

I take my time, nervous as a honeymoon girl, with kisses and nips and bites, all the time waiting to be tapped out.

But she remains reclined, circling me with her silver nails and crossing her stilt-legs over my back until I take the plunge.

And plunge and plunge until I am depleted and she is in tears.

"I'm sorry," she says, turning away.

"Darling," I say, holding out my hands.

In them is a nostalgic assortment of fine cutlery.

"Oh!" she says, spooning and forking me ecstatically until she is ready to climb aboard, waving the knives like six-shooters and coming loudly enough to wake the gentleman next door.

He raps on the wall between us and we hear, "Good heavens, old girl, where are your manners?"

Annabel falls off me, laughing, and I join her on the carpet, where she lands.

I join her in Persia, epicenter of the Parthian Empire, where the Tigris pours glossy square jewels and lilac water and Annabel's skin is an unbroken, silt-smooth ostracon.

WE TOUR THE continent.

She shops as if possessed and I buy travel guides and join groups of other old men on literary walking tours, usually led by scandalized spinsters.

"And here is the saucepan that Lord Byron's half-sister, *his lover*, employed to boil his diaries, the flabby bint, and there is the cock ring that Oscar Wilde fashioned in Reading Gaol."

The matron, who is clearly insane, is pointing at a napkin ring in the middle of Harrods.

The other old men gasp and take pictures. I text one to Annabel, who speeds back a shot of her in the changing room at Glamorous Amorous, modelling a pair of white scalloped knickers from Strumpet & Pink, gathered with white ribbons and affixed with a black taffeta bunny tail.

"Buy everything," I write back as our tour guide brandishes "the dull knife that Jane Eyre used to blind poor Mr. Rochester."

"Reader, I mutilated him," I say, and the other men grunt amiably.

But I am preoccupied looking at yet another of Annabel's lingerie shots; in this one, she is denuded of everything but plush cat's ears, blowing me a kiss.

"Cleopatra's Needle *pronto*," I text, leaving my group to marvel at John Donne's extensive collection of nude lipsticks.

Annabel waits in a long black coat that I open just enough to peer inside at a black bustier and stockings fringed with cherry-colored fluff and fringe before entering her without ceremony. We rock slowly and languidly as pictures are taken and the interminable rain begins.

"It's almost working," she says, gnashing into my neck, so I tear off her coat, and before we are arrested, Annabel howls into the lovesick wind, purpling the perfumed air with her amazed pleasure.

"We'll let you off just this one time," the officer says after cuffing and pushing us into the back of his squad car.

We have been recognized from any number of gossip columns and papers.

Annabel ignores him and, leaning forward, shouts through the open window.

"You are so alive," I say as she drops and rests against me, then, adorably, asks the cop to drive us to our hotel, which he does.

We are the happiest right now, I think, pushing a pin through the moment as it passes into memory and is leached of color and sound.

We fall into bed fully dressed.

She kicks me in her sleep and I kick her back, hard.

The anger that resides within us, customarily in abeyance, has been roused like uncharmed snakes.

We leave for home on the first flight the next morning, exhausted from packing and the laborious politeness we have adopted as a stand-in for the rage coursing through us like deadly poison.

She brushes against me and apologizes.

"No, *excuse me*," I say.

The more beautiful it is between us, the closer we are to dying alone.

It is a week before we stop being painfully civil. I tell her about the tour guide and she can't help it, she laughs.

She shows me the bill for her lingerie and French perfume and I roar at and kiss her roughly.

She sighs, softly. We are back on.

THE NEXT MORNING, Annabel presents me with a script rolled into a Soft White Bimbo bread bag tied with Chanel ribbon.

Ultraviolence TWO: I open it and see there are just a few notes, some maps, and drawings.

"I didn't know you were making a full-length sequel, " I say anxiously.

Kray will not allow this to happen, regardless of what Vivienne says.

"Legally, are you even allowed to make one?"

She tells me her lawyer has worked it all out and I wonder if she is telling the truth, then realize these forensic issues are the least of my concerns.

She wants to move beyond the flash films, she tells me. The plot is all in her head. In her story, Sid, who is now a timid old shopkeeper, meets a girl, Veronica, who changes him.

"Veronica is a sadist and criminal," says Annabel, "but she loves Sid. He's afraid of her at first and then a romance grows as he becomes more feminine and she, more masculine."

"What do you mean? Does he start carrying a handbag?"

"No, I'm using these gendered terms loosely in order to invoke dangerous ideological inventions that hurt women and deform men."

"Oh."

I am not sure what to say.

"Wait. Isn't that like that the stuff in your book?"

"Yes, but the book is more academic," she says. "The film is an imaginative iteration of its premise."

"What's it called?"

"*Church of Dork*," she says, and shows me a picture of a trashed old tabernacle with the words spray-painted over the altar.

What does she mean by this? I haven't the faintest idea.

Whenever she is frowning over her critical-theory books, painting them with her squeaky pink highlighter, I pretend to be absorbed in the most boring-looking book I can find. Currently, I am on page two of *The Mill on the Floss* and have been for weeks.

I think it's about a candy factory, I'm not sure.

It pleases her, though — "I love Eliot," she says, and kisses me — so I soldier on, reading one word at a time and holding it up to the light to try and see what's inside.

She catches me mouthing a phrase and frowning.

"Don't read it for me," she says, taking the book from me and putting it aside.

"Oh why, why do you love me," I ask, like a stupid oaf.

"No anguish I have had to bear on your account has been too heavy a price to pay for the new life into which I have entered in loving you," she says.

"Did you just make that up?" I say, turning away my ugly face.

"No, but now you will never know where I found it."

"Stupid flossy mill!" I say, retrieving the book and starting again as she covers my face with little kisses.

"My angel, my big man," she whispers until I feel myself inflate and grow young.

I read and let my fingers creep inside her. My mouth attaches to her neck, leaving half-moon marks until she arches her back, mates her own book with mine, and we are pulled into a dark flood that pulls us under and we drown.

SHE HAS RAISED the money for the film through modelling. I never knew she was all over glossy magazines in Europe and Asia, plus several in the U.S. that I managed to miss.

She gives me a *Vogue*: she is on the cover in a rose-colored Giambattista Valli gown and about a hundred crinolines, standing by a murky pond, holding a black swan.

Her hair rises in two white-powdered wings; her eyelashes are long, arched feathers: the swan's hooded face rests on her flushed cheek.

"Do you like it?" she says like a hard slap.

"I love it," I say, stammering. Yet again, I feel the power of her beauty, like a hammer to my ugliness.

"You do?" she says. "Because I think I look disgusting."

I snap my mouth shut, scared.

She tears the magazine apart in a frenzy, crying, "I'm so ugly, I'm so ugly," as she does.

"I don't understand," I say. "The other magazines, your films."

"I control the films. I destroy the other magazines," she says. "I'm all in ruins," she says, and I gather her to my baggy sweats, consoling her, knowing, at that moment, exactly what she means.

The flaw is in the reflection.

What others see.

"To me, you are the loveliest girl," I say after I have coaxed her into the shower, where she sees her perfect self in my eyes.

And mine in hers; amidst the smell of eucalyptus and coconut milk, her damp, ripe body fits into mine like a piece in a puzzle about the mystical muscle of love.

ANNABEL AND I fly to New York.

She is rounding up her film crew and doing a MAC-sponsored tribute to Hedy Lamarr—the inventor, she tells me as she tries on wig after wig, of spread-spectrum technology.

I love her in the shoulder-length congeries of platinum blonde curls and insist she keep it on, with the ropes of pearls and textured, skin-tight black chiffon dress.

By the time our car pulls up to the Plaza, the dress is shredded and covered in mad-dog foam.

I cover her with my jacket and the concierge appears at our suite within moments to take the garment to "someone discreet and fabulous."

"This gentleman repaired *Lindsay Lohan's* apparel," he says, letting the mauled frock dangle from one finger. "Daily and nightly," he adds, retreating, as we fall to the bed, my darling in pearls and new, springy curls and I, still somewhat shy, in a robe she unwraps as she murmurs, "There is no modesty between us."

"And besides," she says later, as I smoke and happily recall the most virile of my many moves, "you look best of all like this."

"In the raw," she says as I rooster around, admiring my thick haunches and big, brawny chest.

"*More,*" she says, snapping her fingers.

She is Hedy Lamarr in *Ecstasy* and the pale-green carpet is the field she runs through naked, exclaiming the onset of a colossal orgasm that I grab a piece of, filling my hands with blades of grass and tender pink flowers.

"I want these pearls," she says as we lie on the floor, watching the sun set in white bars across our still, wet flesh.

"They are yours," I say.

I will blanch at the price tag the next morning when she is away at the shoot, and soothe my worries after securing a flight to Buffalo to meet the boy who called her an animal and cut her face with a lawn ornament.

His name is Rory and he is, to my amusement, a docent at the Albright-Knox.

I find him standing beside a strange sculpture by the artist Jacob Kassay, a white doorway leading nowhere.

A small group of high-school kids listen to his rap about the white chunk's ability to "narrate our own movement through space" and clap when their teacher, who is swallowing saucer-sized antacids, hisses at them.

I wait until they leave, and size Rory up.

He is short and lean, and his scarred face narrates his movement through enough street fights and domestic violence to warrant a government-sponsored rehabilitation through the magic of art.

"You grew up in Toledo, didn't you?" I say, and he nods.

"You like this work of art?" I say, standing close to him.

"Sure," he says, nervously. "But —"

"How about this one?" I say, showing him a picture Annabel has texted me of herself standing beside a horse, draped in white moiré and the pearls, worn as a single, waist-length strand: she calls this image, more painfully beautiful than anything in this gallery, *IOU and Xo.*

"Jesus!" he says.

"Yes," I say, and ask if he remembers her, and what he did.

I ask him many times, punctuating the question with fast, brutal punches to his stomach, kidneys, and face.

"I don't remember," he says, then falls to the ground and starts to cry.

I hear footsteps, bend down, and cut his face, ruining it.

Or improving it, I think, and laugh.

"The docent is unwell," I tell two guards, who thank me and hurry to his side.

In the airport washroom, I discard the jeans, sweatshirt, wig, and glasses I changed into when I landed in Buffalo. I put on a suit and carefully cleanse my hands and shoes.

Order a large Scotch in the lounge and unwind, reluctantly, from the rush.

I managed to take a picture as I strolled away: Rory's inert, pasty hand in an impressive lake of blood; it is a still life with broken teeth, curds of fast-twitch muscle and bone.

At the airport, a little kiosk prints it for me as I bite my cheek to taste what I feel, which is elated and starving.

I place the photograph in *Vindicta,* a file I am assembling for Annabel, who meets me at the airport in faux-sable stoles, a sweeping cloak, and brocade slippers.

"You owe me," I say, and she loosens her coat.

The pearls are luscent against her naked flesh, rolling in her salt and warmth.

"Your hands!" she says as I flag a car.

"I helped a homeless Iroquois man build a tiny yet serviceable one-bedroom colonial by the mouth of Cazenovia Creek," I tell her.

She is skeptical, then my songbird returns as I remove the necklace, fill her with it, and pull out and lavish each pearl with my mouth, my tongue.

"Oh, that is lovely," our driver remarks, and chirps and calls along, opening the windows so that a great hybrid flock joins us, singing and drifting, leaving us, in the end, spackled with feathers and each holding a single pulsing egg.

The next morning, it occurs to me that I am too happy, especially when I read a small item in the *Buffalo News* about a "tragic assault on a local man, who may never walk again."

Scrolling further, I see that an imprudent nurse has informed the reporter, "He's as ugly as that Elephant Man."

My heart flattens in pleasure and then rolls up, gathering starlets of joy.

I check on our eggs in the natural nest I demanded the concierge make, and call the United Way.

I make a donation in honor of my alibi and imaginary Native American friend, matching the price of the pearls and requesting that the funds go to the Iroquois Healthcare Alliance.

One egg has started to hatch!

"Baby, hurry," I call out, and my dark queen rustles to my side; our hands cover our dumbstruck faces as a wet, grizzled head appears from the shell, peeping angrily for food and explanations.

WE START SHOOTING in three days.

When the birds hatch, we check out and transfer them carefully to the driver, who, luckily, lives in an apartment that is more aviary than home.

He promises to send pictures, and we leave him seeds and honey sticks, a massive Victorian cage, small period accessories, and a fair bit of the money Annabel earned.

We marvel over and blow kisses at Francis and Zelda and just make our flight.

On board, I wonder out loud if I should model too, which earns me an explosion of laughter and her a brooding and angry flight companion.

Near California, she calls my name and I turn and she takes my picture and says that I am terribly handsome; everyone in the rows around us agrees.

"It's true," she says. "And I'm sorry, but I want you all to myself."

"Mile-high club much?" I say to the homely steward a half-hour later, and he rolls his eyes.

We are home soon and then Annabel is all business.

SHE HAS SCOUTED and secured the locations, one of which — Sid's bedsit — she builds herself in our living room.

I meet my co-stars: Colette, an attractive woman my age who plays my ex-wife, and Damian, a maddeningly good-looking young man with a cool fade and a lean, cut body.

He plays Sid in flashbacks and I hate him on sight.

We have a read-through in our kitchen with a few other minor characters.

Annabel has used proper software to turn this into a screenplay. I read my first line:

INT: SEAMY APARTMENT—NIGHT.

SID DELACROIX, a broken-down old man, sits
in his boxer shorts, drinking a bottle of beer at
his rickety kitchen table. HE STANDS.

SID

I am so washed up. I look, what did John Ford
say, not like the ruins of my youth, but like the
ruins of those ruins.

A HUNDRED CHICKENS fill the room.

"Wait a minute," I say, throwing down the script. "Is this about the film or is it about me?"

Damian stands up and stretches, baring his rib cage and shredded abs. "This is tense," he says. "Relax, Sid," he says, unfastening a memory I cannot—

Colette and, God help me, Annabel are watching him with undisguised admiration.

Breathe, I tell myself: there is cement in my throat.

I pick up the script and resume.

SID

I wish a mythically beautiful girl would kiss this
frog and save my soul.

A HUNDRED FROGS FILL THE ROOM.

I put the script down and look at Annabel, who is looking back expectantly.

"This is it? Cheap effects to make you look edgy? Let's not forget the *La traviata*–flavored house music and a wholesale fairy-tale exploitation of my life."

"You haven't read it all," says Annabel, distressed.

"And I won't," I say, kicking my chair aside and slamming every door I pass through on my way to the car.

I drive to Las Vegas in three hours flat.

When I am blind drunk at the blackjack table, I call Jerry.

"How's Kray?" I say.

"Better," he says. "Much better. You start production on Monday, so rest up."

I hang up and tap out a text, attaching a picture of myself surrounded by glittering showgirls and stacks of chips.

It is a message to Annabel:

Starting ACTUAL sequel next week.

She doesn't write back. I check every few seconds, then drop the phone into my glass and cash out.

I WAKE UP in bed at the Excalibur with three outrageously beautiful drag queens and gently shake them awake as I look out the window, mildly amazed at all of the colorful turrets.

"Did anything happen?" I ask as I button my pants.

"You gave us all money for college," says the youngest one, a teenaged boy in a tall beehive and daisy-shaped enamel earrings.

The others rub their eyes and one of them says, "Get back in here, honeybunch," but I can't. I leave them the room and everything in the mini-bar and tell them to keep in touch.

I settle the astronomical bill with one of my many new cards, buy a burner phone from the gift shop, and have the valet bring my car around.

I call home and a stranger answers. "I'm the cleaner," he explains.

"Let me speak to her," I say.

"She left a half-hour ago," he says.

"Where did she go?" I ask, lighting a cigarette and doing a messy bump of coke off my fingertip.

"She just said she was taking off. Sorry, guy, she's a fine piece of ass."

"The finest," I say, disconnecting and hitting the gas.

I play George Jones songs and sing along like an old, howling dog.

I RETURN TO a spotless home, with nothing missing except a few of Annabel's personal items: a quarter-rack of clothes, a bag of shoes, her makeup and hair-care stuff.

But the place feels empty, as if all the life has been drained from it and replaced with embalming fluid.

I lie on the bed and play with the new phone I sent Charles out for, adding her as a contact, as my only favorite.

I use a picture of her I find online, one she calls *Mise en abyme*: she is curling her lashes in the mirror, and inside the mirror she appears again and again to infinity, speck- then atom-sized, the lavish lashes that sweep my cheek when she sleeps.

Her Twitter page says, "Movie shut down indefinitely, thanks LK and PW," and her anger makes my belly flop.

Her note is brief:

> I'm staying at my place for a little while, until you stop acting like a lunatic. I will miss you, regardless, and see you soon. Xo.

I SLEEP FOR twelve hours and wake up refreshed.

I decide to sort my life out and begin with a short meditation.

Sitting like a lotus as some fruity pan flute plays, I ask myself why I punished her so badly.

She humiliated me, I think, and unfold my legs, ignoring the red curve of the devil's lips as, gratefully, he pushes the word *pride* into my mouth.

I take a long, punishing run.

Several ladies with first-class facelifts chat me up as I pass their gates.

I thought that Annabel would take my new looks with her, and she did. But she left something she can't take away: my cruelty, which makes me less good-looking, and far more intriguing.

I don't need to get in shape, I realize. I need to nurture what is sick in me and let it flourish into a hard shell.

I begin by calling a randomly chosen name from my contacts list.

It's Cotton and I'm glad: he is a shaky fuck and I want to get high.

I ask him to come over and play cards and he sounds thrilled. Our little horror movie has gone on to become a much-watched "FCKN MASTERPIECE" — this according to user GoreLVR666.

Cotton arrives and immediately starts chopping lines of coke. He pulls out his phone and begins filming me, and I slap it out of his hand.

He picks it up and says, "You are completely different," with admiration and distress in his voice.

I am thin and dressed in black, the color my hair has darkened to, from its vee to the raven's quills I have scraped back.

"I know," I say indifferently.

I let him hang around and we drink and do lines until we are confidants. He tells me about his doting, concerned parents, that he left Cat — "her and her mind games" — and a quite disgusting story about a friend he hit with his car.

I tell him about Gary, the old beagle that wandered up Lola's and my steps one day with no collar. He was at least ten years old, the girl at the pound said, and would not be adopted.

I kept him for one afternoon: I fed and washed him, ran with him at the park, and brushed him until he shone, hoping Lola would fall for him too.

"We can't afford an old animal," she said when she returned from class, and walked away.

I drove him to the pound and brought him inside. He just stared at me, trapped in that long, dear, silvery-brown body.

He cried, and I ruffled his fur and said, "See you soon."

I sat in the parked car and slumped forward, thinking of the dog's confusion, of his high, frightened barks following me outside.

"That's brutal," Cotton says. "But it sounds like you did the right thing."

"No," I say. "I never should have left him."

We just keep working on the coke as the night winds rail, bringing with them the sound of old, ruined creatures, bawling that we love them.

That we stay.

THE WEEKEND IS a vacuum, removing all of my feelings of love and kindness.

And desire, more or less. The coke has opened up deep old wounds: I can feel it. And it makes me talk too much, which I cannot allow.

I will stick to drinking out of the tulip-shaped crystal glasses the bartender at Cindy Club used to talk about, wistfully, as he poured the house gasoline into red Solo cups.

Annabel writes me a note on Sunday night: "Normal yet?"

I smile, but I think of how she used me, and her obvious hot pants for Damian.

I will write to her when I feel better. At the moment, I am still in the odious thrall of her awful screenplay.

I remember that I have a copy and decide to read it that night.

I do, and am chagrined to see there is a lot of good in it. It might only be the makings of a small art-house film, but some of the moments, like the writer herself —

"Make me draw in my breath," I write her.

She sends me a GIF of a tiny pageant queen dancing lewdly.

The next morning, I show up for Kray and a proper read-through in a street-sized office at MGM.

This will be the first time Kray has filmed in America. He is fragile, but still powerful.

So am I.

I meet his gaze and nod; his eyebrows rise.

The script, which I read over the weekend, is slick and seamless. Loaded with chic violence, brute sex, and terse, fiendish dialogue, it resurrects the original while breaking new, majestically evil ground.

I will be acting with huge stars, who all greet me as one of their own—greetings I return coolly, and with a suggestion of disdain.

Where were they when I needed them?

THE TRADES CARRY news of the film's pre-production, and I am interviewed more, photographed more, and gossiped about more as spring collapses into broiling summer, and I am now three weeks away from Annabel.

She is modelling in Paris and teaching a section of *Cinéma & audiovisuel* at the Sorbonne, and while we exchange feverish letters, we have not seen each other since my blow-up.

It's mainly a scheduling problem, but, although I don't like to admit this, she was getting too close to me for comfort.

I wake, gasping, from dreams of her soft, aromatic skin against mine, of being gripped by the heat and muscles between her legs, of bottomless, carbonated kisses and fast, piercing bites.

Then I shake my head and lose all this sugar.

I start escorting Gala to events. A high-class call girl, she charges me a fortune, especially when I decline to sleep with her.

Often, I retreat to the various foyers, sink into a chair, and open up Annabel's web site.

One night, I see there is a new video called *Past Perfect*. In it, shards of Tchaikovsky play as Damian puts a glass platform shoe on her foot and she turns into a dragon.

I call Rabi, distraught. He says, "Damian is gay, stupid."

I hang up and dictate my misery and relief into a text to Annabel that reads, "Blub blub."

And, "Hurry home."

At this point she can live *inside me* if she wants.

Too impatient to wait for a text back, I call her.

"You're my honey-damp Queen Bee," I sing to my sleepy, tousle-headed, brilliant, cherry-flavored baby doll.

"I'm beautiful to everyone I see," she says, as my mind fills with a slick, mustache-wearing Frenchman lying beside her—"*Caaaam to bed, chérie!*"

"But I filled my cunt with concrete before flying here, *mon amour.*"

I am so happy I cannot speak.

She tells me about her class, about the photo shoots and her room at the Plaza Athénée.

I listen, hearing only music.

"Wait for me?" she says. This I manage to decode and I say yes like a newborn beaver.

They mate for life, I remember. If I had a tail I'd slap it on every flat rock in town.

We phone-kiss until she is late for her shoot with Virginie Despentes.

They are going to dress in flowered hats and cocktail dresses, carry nail-studded bats into Porte de la Chapelle, and beat rapists to death, she says.

Wistfully.

"Good luck, honey."

When she hangs up, I look up some of the words and phrases I picked out: *semiotic shock, cavilling administrators, pluperfect inconstancy, collective postwar shame, armscye, rose madder, Ladurée,* and *fin'amor.*

I consider some; others I wander away from, into the field of poppies with Darkling, who is always curled up in the corner of my mind, legs twitching and ready to spring up, like me, at the perfume of a soft tail and crushingly big, fluttering eyes.

I HATE BEING alone now.

No matter how much luxury I heap on myself, I cannot shake the bad years.

I will drink a champagne cocktail in my huge claw-foot tub, inhaling one of Annabel's hand-blended soaking potions, drifting, only to hear, "Wake up, you useless has-been!" being shouted into my ear.

Drop the glass, run soaking outside, and hide under a tree, shaking until I feel safe enough to dart to bed and bury myself below the Porthault sheets and hand-embroidered comforter, a reproduction of details from Louise Dahl-Wolfe's fashion photographs of flowers, of farouche nudes, of the sea.

Someone did this to me, someone I owed money to, I can't stand to remember. If I do, the whole rotten stinking mess tumbles down, smothering me until I am sick.

Rabi is in Calcutta, on business. What business, I have no idea.

And so the call girl is pressed into service again. Annabel would likely kill me if she knew, but how to explain?

She never asks questions, and she does what I say. Except wear the mask I have made with a paper plate and string— of Annabel's face.

AFTER A FEW meetings, Kray decides to start shooting.

He finds locations and orders sets as he goes, hires new cast members along the way, and rewrites the script from scene to scene.

I am tricked out in a bespoke striped velvet suit and a white shirt by Anna Matuozzo, with a pink Hermès tie and heavy black boots from a thrift shop. The makeup team defines my cheekbones and fits me with heavy sable lashes as I go over the first scene.

Kray wants to have Suicide's "Frankie Teardrop" play as I walk in slow motion into Belle Reve, Sid's old haunt. Kray did the same in *Ultraviolence*, a technique that not one critic failed to remark on, usually calling the scene "chilling" or "hotly predatory."

Kray puts a new spin on the shot by speeding up everything else so it looks like I am moving in a different dimension.

As I walk through the bar, everyone stops speaking and stares.

Suicide's Alan Vega starts wailing and I stare at the bartender, walk toward him, and grab his collar, pulling him close.

"Otis, you old cunt, how are you?" I say, and the music drops, stops, and rises as "Cold, Cold Heart," performed by Tony Bennett.

The room explodes with relief and happiness: glasses strike one another, couples stand and dance as confetti falls like heavy snow and then speeds into a dizzying whirl.

Otis and Sid dance too, in a clumsy box step, and laugh. Otis is still laughing when Sid pulls out his gun and shoots him in the heart.

He crosses a name off a list and walks back, briskly now, through dead silence and a loaded mass stillness.

The word REVENGE drifts by as Sid pulls Star—Lana Del Rey—to her feet and marches her to the door.

"Why?" she says, and he cocks his head. "One down," he says, pushing her through the door and into an idling black Cadillac.

The Violent Femmes sing about rat finks and the heart of hell as they speed away, and so begins the modern Senecan tragedy—or "black comedy," as Kray calls it—that is *Deadly Nightshade*.

"It's good," I say.

Yum-Yum, one of the makeup artists, is powdering my flesh silvery pink and jewel-smooth.

"It's *brilliant*," he says.

WE SHOOT THE scene in five takes, a record for Kray.

He asks me to have a drink with him to talk about the rape scene we are shooting the next day in "Star's apartment stairwell."

I don't want to talk to him alone: he is repellent.

But everyone has left and he is already uncorking a bottle of Gran Patrón.

He pours us shots that taste like scorching bliss: I drink and I drink.

"I want you to hurt her," he says. "Fuck her so hard."

I am unsteady by now, but tell him that I know how to act and not to worry.

"I'm worried you don't know how *not to act*."

He laughs.

"I want her pussy to bleed," he says.

I thank Christ when Kray's assistant walks in and takes the bottle away, scolding him that he is not to drink after his near-fatal stroke.

Kray allows himself to be led away mutely and I realize I am not afraid of him anymore.

I walk in Sid's measured pace to the door, recalling another revenge tragedy as I contemplate my own *Duchess*.

"Cover her face," I recite to a few hangers-on by the studio door. They are holding old-fashioned pastel-paged autograph pads that they extend to me breathlessly.

"She died young," I say, homing in on the saddest girl, a dump truck in a John Mayer T-shirt, and kissing her livid cheek.

She swoons, splitting her head when she falls, and I drift through the fans, murmuring, "You're all too kind."

LANA DEL REY walks off the set and is replaced with a Keane-eyed ingenue named Kitty Candelabra, a small girl from Lubbock, Texas, with glasses and the mudflap girl's body.

Del Rey tells the media she could not tolerate the violence against her and that there's "something wrong with him."

She means Kray, I think.

We shoot the rape scene in Crenshaw. I hurt this girl as she recites the Angelic Salutation in a meager voice. When her nose starts to bleed, Kray is so pleased he wraps the scene.

She cries behind her script and asks if she can quit. Kray threatens her with a lawsuit and she flees.

I watch her run off, her heels kicking the torn seat of her dress.

"I'm sorry," I say, but I am talking to myself.

THE NEXT DAY, Kray announces that he is revising more of the script.

"Sid will lose all his money at the track. Then I think he should lose everything and fall apart. So you can better understand him."

I sigh; say nothing.

We shoot all day. It is a two-minute scene in which I savagely beat a cashier for not taking my last bet.

The cashier is an actor who once mildly criticized Kray in an interview. I am told to "make it real," and do.

He leaves on a stretcher and we are on hiatus until the new pages are ready.

I take the call girl out for popiah and sticky peanuts and a bottle of 2014 Domaine de la Pépière Muscadet at Button Mash. I am cleverly disguised in a beige wig, an adhesive goatee, and a clownishly large suit I have stuffed with padding.

"It's for a new role," I explain.

She nods, eats with one hand on mine, and laughs warmly at everything I say.

A tiny part of me, I am embarrassed to admit, longs for a submissive armpiece like her as she walks, calling all eyes, to the washroom.

No. I want my girlfriend back. So much so that I am instantly disgusted with myself for spending time with a hooker because I'm too chickenshit to be alone.

I signal for the bill.

What if someone sees me and tells Annabel? What was I thinking?

My date is nonplussed. A stack of bills makes her smile return, even when I decline to drive her home.

Let the terrors invade.

And invade they do: at 3 a.m., I am standing behind my bedroom door with a tennis racquet, shaking.

"I'm not afraid of you!" I call out, meaning everything and lying also. The days pass so slowly I think I will die of heartbreak, and then Annabel calls.

"I'm coming home," she says, and I fall down, pawing at the floor in long, crazed strokes.

"Parnell?"

"Yes, that's such nice news," I say. "I was asleep. Call me when you've arrived?"

She says that she will and I move through the house like a prizefighter, arms raised, and weak from my brutal victory.

Annabel calls back.

"I'm already here. Come get me?"

I dress instantly, open the door, and there she is, creamy from the magnolias in her hair to her fluent dress and high, buckled heels.

"Boo," she says.

"You scared me," I say.

She takes my hand, is silent, and I glow.

Annabel always knows what to say, and when to say nothing at all.

WE STAND THERE forever, turn into dust.

"Why was Damian in Paris?" I ask her.

"His boyfriend lives there," she says.

"I don't want to see him again, ever," I say, my grip tightening.

She tells me she has thanked him for his kindness to her long ago, thanked him enough.

"But you, what will I do with you, jealous monkey?"

She has melted a vein of silver from the hard ore of my heart.

"Let's start here," she says, pushing me toward our bed and elbowing my ribs hard enough to make me fall.

"And here," she says, jabbing my chest with her fists and burying her knee between my legs.

"And here," I say, rolling to my side, kicking backwards, and knocking her to the floor.

She gets up, drops her georgette dress — she is naked underneath — and takes off my clothes with a folding carbon-steel knife.

"You are killing me," she says after pulling me vertical and roughly pushing herself into me.

"I was almost dead," I say quietly, and stay still as she fucks me hard, cums, and slides me out of her.

"But," I say, looking at my still-hard cock.

"Oh, fuck," she says, sighs, and gets me off with her mouth quickly, spitting noisily when she is done.

"Now leave," she says, although her fingers are still inside her pussy, feeling the last of the seismic vibrations.

"Where will I go?"

"To the kitchen. I want a glass of milk," she says, pulling her dress back on and finger-combing her hair.

I turn and hurry downstairs, slowly filling with feelings that I thought I had cauterized to death.

I DRINK MORE and more, worrying about the movie.

The day after Annabel returns, she posts a new video.

I watch it while she is out shopping for dinner.

Called *I Was Cured, All Right*, and set to Dre's "Let Me Ride," it shows her wearing a bloody sheet as a toga and doing a *movimiento lento* Mashed Potato with a penguin, an actual penguin.

Is he supposed to be me in a tuxedo? I wonder of the stiff, waddling thing.

She is so alive, I think, as I very often do, and feel a muffled happiness struggle to exhume itself inside of me.

"You are sublimation," I type, as penguinman1, and then I get up and dance: naked, ridiculous, and blistered with pain and pleasure, each leaving its own mark.

ON THE MORNING of my last day off, I grab Tubby and briskly sew him a cheery yellow sports coat, turtleneck, and slacks, and wrap his head in a bauble-covered turban.

I hand him to Annabel.

"I took a class, on Berkeley," I say, and she throws her head back, laughs, and hugs the bear.

In the middle of the afternoon, as I drink boilermakers on the lanai, I get a text directing me to a page on NewHive called "Sweet Tubby Bitch."

Devoted just to him, the site shows him on horseback, at a masquerade ball, and sleeping, oh blessed Virgin, with Annabel.

Her eyes, closed, are angelfish hiding in the gleaming fronds of her tensile candy hair; her mouth, agape, is the rouge entrance to heaven —

Who took the fucking picture.

There are only a few living particles left in me. Now, another is gone.

Beneath all of the love emojis and messages of adulation, I write "Murderer," which could mean anything.

"It's a selfie," she says to my drunken ass much later, and clucks.

"You scare me sometimes," she says, and I growl. She exits, pursued by me.

PUDGE FINDS MY spare key under a planter, lets herself in.

We hear her, go downstairs.

Annabel hugs her and goes back to sleep.

I make tea with a single Tetley bag and warm water, and she tells me that she is failing school and she doesn't know what to do, for chrissakes.

Bored, I leave a message for Kray, who calls back instantly: Pudge can play the coatroom girl in the nightclub scene he has just written.

I tell my daughter, who hugs me for the first time since she was a child and asks if she can stay with me for a while, having been thrown out of her dorm for the sleep violence I am pretty sure is cruelly conscious.

"Yes," I say, pointing to the guest room in the back. "But if you sleep-bash *me*, I'll hit you back so fucking hard you won't need accommodations anymore."

"Fuck," she says, stunned but unmistakably impressed. "I'll make coffee tomorrow, Daddy," she says, and excuses herself.

"Don't call me that," I say, my flesh crawling.

"Sorry," she says. "Sorry, Dad."

I climb the stairs and try to remember the day Allegra put her, newborn and oddly silent, into my arms.

Her fingers like ghostly florets latching on to mine, how deeply I felt her as a good, gentle part of me.

I want to try.

I will say this into the night as the sound of her snoring, part power drill, part hog, fills the house until I knock myself out with a mouthful of Xanax.

As I submit to the pills, I hear "Daughter" and see my kid and myself walking into the waves in Cape Cod; I see her holding my hand, shivering and smiling.

That's my daughter in the water

I am still singing when I wake up and my eyes are wet as if I have been crying.

THE CAR COMES for us at five, and we are given our pages. Pudge is given more gestures than words, but does get to call me a "despicable mongrel."

I look at my new pages and see that Sid's downward spiral is beginning: he will lose the gangsters' money at the track, and they will find him at a nightclub with their boss's wife.

He won't have a left hand or much of a face after this scene.

We shoot the racetrack scene at Santa Anita, then travel to a warehouse Kray has decorated with bright ribbed condoms hanging like bunting and waitress stations made up like the windows of Amsterdam's red-light district.

Pudge is dressed in a black shmatte, white dirndl, and cap. I approach her booth and she slaps me, reciting her line.

Like a ventriloquist's doll.

But Kray is pleased: he likes the implication of an indecent relationship between me and my daughter.

I take him aside and ask that she be let go.

"No," he says. "The elephant stays in the picture!"

Then the gangsters appear and start working me over: many of the wounds to my face are real but Kray uses a prosthetic hand for the axe sequence.

Through a megaphone, Kray says, "Now rape him," and everyone stands still. "Rape the little slut," he says to the youngest gangster, who doesn't move.

Pudge looks at me and I start to run.

Off the set and two buildings down, where I huddle and call a car.

When it arrives, I lie flush across the back seat, in case they are looking for me, and ask the driver to take me home.

He turns on the monitor in the back and I watch a cartoon about baby lions lost in the savannah.

They are frightened and hungry but they will hear their mother roar for them soon. I can feel it.

I STAND BY her front door, shaking.

I am still wearing the light-blue seersucker suit, pink shirt and socks, and orange Chucks from wardrobe, along with a dirty, floral-banded panama hat.

Annabel, severe in black jeans and a small SECURITY T-shirt, leads me to the living room, sits on my lap, and pours small sips of her sweet tea into my mouth until I can speak.

"Please talk to me," she says. "Whenever one of us has something meaningful to say, the other is asleep."

I nod, knowing this to be true. I want to tell her everything: to confess, I suppose. I will try.

"I was *sixteen* when we did *Ultraviolence*," I say. "Now I'm fifty-eight—no, fifty-seven, actually. My birthday's in the winter."

It's been so long, I forget my real age most days.

"Kray picked me up when I was hustling. I was doing some queer stuff, the minimum, I hated all the sex work, but it was that or more squatting and more of this—"

I show her the keloid scars under my forearm from cigarette burns and she kisses each one.

He told me he had seen me around and who he was; he rented me a room, lent me money to live.

I started to trust him. I was fourteen, and feral.

He was stricter than a drill sergeant. He whipped me into shape.

Where everyone else saw a worthless street kid, he saw a star.

It was *Kray* who saw something in me, who handed me fame on a platter.

He didn't even mind when I went off with Lola.

"Mind?" Annabel says, confused.

"I mean that he let me be. Kray saved my life: his movie—it made my reputation. And—"

"And what?" she says, and I choke, feel parts of my body light up like the prostrate fat man in *Operation*.

"It's hard to explain," I say feebly, because it is, and it isn't. "He abused—and abuses me. But just verbally. It was bad today. But he's old, he doesn't really mean anything by it."

"It doesn't matter whether he does or not, he shouldn't talk to you that way," Annabel says. "Verbal abuse can do more harm, sometimes."

"More harm?" I think, feinting at images that stick me back.

I stare at my lap and she says, "I'll never hurt you," and we run water in her little nun's tub and squish into it together, shivering, blue, and safe.

AFTER THE STRAIGHTEST sex we have ever had, my girl and I talk, smoke, and drink a bottle of beer.

"Tell me his number," she says.

"You're not going to say anything," I say, dazzled by the sight of her raw, naked skin and lambent eyes.

"All right," she says reluctantly.

I assume I am finished, but Kray calls shortly and apologizes, stiffly. "Sid doesn't need to be broken any more than he is," he says. "Besides, he'll always be my bitch."

He is laughing. I hang up and let his words turn into harmless fingerling potatoes that I lower into boiling water.

I REPORT TO the warehouse set in the morning and Kray is furious when he sees the bite marks on my neck; he snaps his fingers for a makeup girl.

"Fix her," he says, and she and I both sigh: it's going to be a long, hard day.

It is.

I am beaten once more and again. My daughter is fired. "Thanks a lot, *Dad!*" is her parting salvo.

My heart takes a stab at going out to her, before Kray orders me to walk on glass and hot coals.

At lunch, we make a beeline to the taco truck.

The old man silently hands out silver packets while a young girl with long, dark hair and a bubble butt, wearing a tight pink Taco Machine uniform and cap, flirts with Kray.

"Gordita for you, *gran hombre?*" she says, and he becomes kittenish.

"I'll need an *extra-grande, novia,*" he says, and the girl smiles, turns her head, and spits.

After lunch we are reshooting the hand scene: this time, Kray asks me to let the axe glance my skin.

I have never seen the actor before, the big bald one with dead eyes who is holding the shining tool.

Kray is leaning forward with anticipation as the other actors hold me down.

The bald guy raises the axe and I hear Kray say, "Fuck, no!"

Then he falls to the ground.

Everyone swarms him.

"Call an ambulance," the lead showgirl says, and, after trying to revive him, I say, "Don't bother."

Kray is dead as a doornail.

We all start moving farcically toward the bathrooms, eliminating as we stagger, sick as hell.

After a thorough purge, I stand by his body and tell one of the less-stellar actresses, who is dressed as a bawd, that Christopher Marlowe, Kray's favorite playwright, also died swearing, in a tavern.

"He did? Oh my God, that's fascinating," she says, and takes my hand. "This is so upsetting, right?"

The medics have arrived and are zipping him into a cozy black bag.

"I'm devastated," I say.

I am. I move to the corner and devise a text to Annabel: two hearts, pink and blue, swooping around our bound initials.

FILMING IS POSTPONED indefinitely. Tributes to Kray fill the world.

I am asked to speak about the one and a half films we made together while I am still violently ill.

The nausea from what the police say is severe food poisoning has turned into a high fever, chills, and delirium.

Annabel takes care of me: I sweat through the blankets as my temperature spikes and carries me to the barren lakes of the moon.

"Kray's genius," I say to an NBC anchor or possibly Dr. Phil, "has a great deal to do with perspective. It lies in his ability to locate what is fearsome in the ordinary, then recast it, as Kubrick does with the notion of the average family in *The Shining*, as recessed or latent horror."

I am reading, badly, off one of the index cards that Annabel has written for me.

"He had," I say, tossing aside the cards, "a wonderfully current sense of style, though he himself was as repulsive as Voldemort."

Green auroras fill my eyes; my skin looks like a wet chicken carcass.

Annabel waves at me to wrap it up, and I do.

"I thought the sadistic bastard would never die," I say, and there is a moment of audible silence before I am disconnected and falling back onto the pillows, envisioning two magpies, Annabel and me, squabbling over a diamond ring sparkling below a candlelit tree.

"Make the branches," I say to her, tearing off my soaked pajamas and lying back down limply.

She understands somehow and, as unappealing as I am, she rolls below me and lets me pound her, slowly, until she calls my name and illustrates my back with the tree: its spindly limbs and flame-red leaves.

She sighs and I fill her with at least three babies. I tell her so and she scowls.

"I was spayed like a cat after an abortion a few years ago," she says, pulling away from me.

I know I should ask her what she is talking about, but I can't. My remark was not at all hopeful.

The fever spikes again, and she and I are pushing a carriage through Marrakesh inside the lush Majorelle Garden.

When the police take her away in handcuffs, I call out, "And where hell is, must we ever be."

SHE CALLS ME from the county jail.

"I have been arrested for killing Kray," she says.

"That's preposterous," I say, reaching for my clothes and steadying myself.

I am still febrile and sweaty: now I am confused.

"Baby," she whispers. "Take out the trash. It's filthy, just throw it away."

Right. This is code for *the weapon is in the garbage*, I surmise.

"I'm waiting to be arraigned. Call my lawyer," she says, and I refuse.

"I will find you someone not working in a strip mall called Apollo," I say, thinking of her former lawyer. I hang up as she starts to whimper.

Drive to her place, toss the trash, and find a McDonald's bag — a clue! — and open it, in spite of her coded request. I see a black wig, a Taco Machine uniform, foam padding, and a vial of something that fumes and bubbles when lifted.

I call Jerry, who calls Robert Bernstein, who, after being forwarded a large sum, promises to visit Annabel tonight.

I toss the evidence into a garbage can right outside of the police station, walk in, and ask to see her.

"Your lawyer called. Nice guy. Gave us all bonuses," says the stout, lantern-jawed cop, whom I recognize from a YouTube video in which he is kicking a homeless woman awake.

"Love your work," I say as he leads me to a sordid little room, then escorts Annabel in: she is grimy and abject; she cannot raise her head. Someone has cut MI PRETY into her hand: I kiss it.

"Can you get me out?" she says.

I tell her about Bernstein, who will get her an early hearing — he had better, given the variety of "incentive bonuses," including bribes, he demanded.

She is contrite.

"I have money," she says.

"I know you do, but please allow me," I say, knowing that she — basically broke as she cannot bear to part with the things she models — hasn't got *Bernstein* money.

Her clothes, half couture and half vintage finds, occupy a room in our home that other couples would have nervously earmarked as a baby's room.

'These *are* my babies," she said to me early on. "The kid can sleep in the dresser drawer in the bedroom, or with us unless you crush it with your fat ass."

"*My* fat ass," I had said, eyeing her distinctly callipygian rear and, of course, flying at it—

I see that even her jail-issue dress has been altered. The collar is cut into a daring vee, its sleeves are missing, and she has managed to sew sequins all over it. How, I cannot begin to imagine.

"My cellmate is in love with me," she says, rubbing her hand. "She's pretty old, but tough. I'm scared."

My eyes fill with blackness, issuing, I am certain, stygian ejaculate.

I whistle for the cop and have a short, urgent talk with him. He smacks his fist into his open palm as I fill his pockets with balled-up bills.

"Hey, you. Yeah. *You*," we hear in the distance as I coax Annabel onto my lap and whisper to her about the islands we will visit, about her body under a skin of warm, green water, about her face, which is all I ever see.

She falls hungrily to sleep and I carry her to her now-empty cell and place her on her cot. I whistle for a mop and take care of the blood.

She doesn't need to see that.

I don't care. That part of me, my empathic connection to the world, is almost completely severed.

It is only Annabel I care about, plus a few other supporting characters in this play, a decidedly Caroline story of vengeance and depraved love.

"I'll have you out in a day," I say, and her eyes pop open.

"*Buzz*," she says. How rarely she calls me that now. "I wish we had a baby."

What a horrendous thought. I try to keep my gaze steady, composed.

"I see him," she says, grabbing my arm urgently. "He is chubby and perfect, with your eyes and my —"

She is nearly asleep. I turn away.

"Buzz," she says, and I turn back to her. "That is what I'll call him," she says, and smiles so brightly the room is lit with Holy Mother blue with Holy Mother gold.

"Blessed are —"

"*We*," Annabel murmurs, her arms cradling the little beastie, a crown cast in shadow above her serene mother's face.

THE JUDGE IS beguiled by Annabel, who is dressed in an acre of white organdy and holding a pink silk parasol.

Bernstein irritates him, but His Honor is persuaded, after demanding a significant amount of bail, to let my jailbird fly — which she does, right into my arms, *oof*, I squeeze her and once more carry her, still frail and shaken, to the car, telling her over and over, "Never again," as she promised me the day she rescued me.

"DID YOU MEAN to poison him?" I say when we are at my, at *our* home and she has showered until she is raw.

"This is all a big misunderstanding," she says, lying at the foot of the bed submissively. "The police say that a woman *of my description* was flirting with him just before, well —"

"But the day after I told you about how Kray treated me, he died. "

"Do you think that I killed him?" Annabel says. We are sitting out the end of my poisoning in her bed, watching yet another tribute program that features a number of pictures of young, sexy me.

"Turn it off," I say, self-conscious, and she says, "Why? You're still beautiful."

I rest in her lap and she pets me some more.

My head hurts: I want her to be innocent again; I want to do the wet work in the family.

I get up and pick up my car keys.

I want her gone.

Sensing this, she runs after me.

"What are you afraid of?" she says, and I let the question pass by me like the feathery moth she was once—

Not heavy with need and screaming unborn babies.

I SPEND THE night at the Chateau Marmont and sleep dreamlessly, and well.

Awaken and have a very late breakfast with young starlets who ask me if their mimosas taste "like spunk" and laugh and tell me how cute I am.

Cute.

My eyes tell them something else and they disperse quickly, as if I am a soap bubble and they are flakes of pepper.

I call Annabel's lawyer, who tells me that he is close to having the charges dropped.

"It's a travesty of hearsay and guesswork," he says. "A civil-rights violation! Besides," he says. "I have it on good authority that Kray wasn't poisoned."

"He wasn't? My stomach is still advertising for a spacious vomitorium."

"Nope. You didn't hear it from me, though."

"What did it cost me, this chat?"

Robert laughs. "More than you can afford."

I almost go home to tell Annabel the news, but I remember that *Exterior* is playing at the Egyptian.

I kill some time shopping, softening enough to buy her an antique key that I attach to a bayadère necklace so she may escape any further prisons.

I sit outside the theater watching the Hollywood hustlers and shudder, remembering the night I cleaned the empty star.

And I contemplate the meaning of violence, as I have been asked to by too many interlocutors to count.

Kray and I had decided to stick to a straight line: that the film was "darkly comic" and that I was surprised by the reaction, the fashion craze I started, the copycat rapes and murders.

But I was not surprised.

Having the strength, the power, and the nerve to *take arms in a sea of troubles* and *end them* is the correct answer, I think, as Hamlet, and know of myself.

What would it be, to be noble?

I would have to die, I think — and shake the thought loose.

It is an early show. I manage to buy some pot from a kid outside. "This is the chronic," he says. "Watch out."

He hands me a joint, having assumed, incorrectly, I would not know how to roll it myself.

I smoke it in deep bursts, hacking and shouting, and halfway through, realize I have made an error.

When you are young and stoned, you can go home and look at your face, your beautiful face; walk around your crummy flat and console yourself with the future, that glitterball—how it will light up the foyer of your joyous life.

When you are old, my God.

It is not only my bony, spotted hands that horrify me, but the realization I now have more in common with the evil chimp than the kindly horse he tortures.

"I cannot breathe," I say to Annabel. I am in the lobby, scarfing popcorn and weeping.

"Come home," she says. *Home*, she says, at last.

I am so moved, I ask the concession-stand girl for more popcorn to take home, certain my girlfriend will understand what "These are the pearls that are your eyes" will mean. I get a box of Dots too.

Ohmmmmygod they are so good.

THAT NIGHT, AS we wait to hear from Bernstein, I am distracted by a call from Crispin Morricone, a famous haute-pulp director. He's a fan of my films, especially those made during my fallow period: *The Evil King of the Evil Empire* is his favorite.

He asks if he can come over and talk about his taking over *Deadly Nightshade*, and arrives with a bottle of Armagnac and a board game based on a short-lived TV show I appeared in called *Murder, He Committed*.

Annabel meets him, dazzles him, and discreetly retires upstairs. She thinks he is here to discuss another project.

We drink and talk, then play the game. I use my own figurine — me wearing a tan leisure suit, holding a scythe — and beat him two games out of three.

He outlines his ideas: he is perfect for the job.

"I heard that Kray was an asshole to you," he says as we are winding up.

I shake my head and don't answer.

"Well, that's all over," he says, and I feel bubbles of happiness levitate from deep inside my belly.

I know I am betraying Annabel, but I can't stop myself.

Still. I just want to be warm beside her, watching Netflix and eating the little pupusas she makes for me and serves with ice-cold beer.

On the very good nights, she wears a scalloped apron and heels, rubs my back with her hands and elbows, and scratches BABY into my scalp.

I want to be decent and true.

Fear me, demons. I mean it: decent and true.

I AM DEEPLY relieved when Bernstein calls the next morning.

"It's official," he tells me, exultant. "All charges against Annabel have been dropped. He had a stroke!"

"But she —"

"Tried to poison him? I don't think that's true. Do you? And anyways, the cops obtained the information illegally, by threatening an extra. His testimony is sitting somewhere with, I'm guessing, a wig and a taco-truck dress."

I say nothing, but I understand. The win is everything to him.

"Stroke?" I say.

He laughs. "Can you believe it? I just read the report."

I thank him and frown. *Mendacity*, I think.

Annabel is sleeping: I will wake her soon and tell her.

Right now I want to remember what it was like.

As I performed perfunctory CPR on Kray, I'd slid a barely visible obsidian scalpel into his pterion, the soft spot behind the temple, causing an epidural bleed—not unlike the ravages of a stroke.

Bernstein has learned that "stroke" is what the creaky old coroner scrawled on his report. And when his young assistant queried the small cut, he said it occurred "in the fall" and, angry at her impertinence, added an exclamation point to the original Cause of Death box.

"The son of a bitch has half a liver and an eight ball of cocaine crammed up his nose!" he said. "Food poisoning would barely have registered. And that little cut. He was probably shaving with a dull razor. Anyways, it's all good."

Kray had opened his eyes and seen me. "And kiss his lips to death," I said as I roughly faked mouth-to-mouth.

I place the cold necklace on her shoulders and she wakes and holds me: such innocence. "You are free," I tell her, and she smiles, stands, and admires her new piece of jewelry.

She looks so good. I will stay on this bed forever somehow, watching her, *my privy gerle wythouten spotte*, fastening the ornate clasp and turning back toward me for a kiss. This leads somewhere, time passes, and I am content she is in my arms. But still, we are moving forward with the dumb velocity of a discharged shell, and when it stops, what iniquitous damage will be done.

"WHAT ARE *YOU* afraid of?" I often want to ask Annabel. She, the girl who was completely sexually impaired when we met; who still shivers when I take charge, and routinely starts rifling through the end-table drawer for handcuffs and ligatures.

We never speak of the poisoning. I'm scared, I think, that she is becoming too much like me.

"Like you're so bad," she would say to me. But I am, I am.

I speak at Kray's funeral after I am let off the hook for having been interviewed while violently ill, and tell the solemn gathering stories about his intractable nature, the force of his genius, and the magnitude of his legacy.

Later, I embrace Vivienne, who discreetly hands me Annabel's screenplay.

JUNK, Kray has written across the title page and several others. Vivienne apologizes.

"He was not himself near the end," she says as tears run a train on her pancake makeup.

But he was. And he wasn't entirely wrong.

My own ex-wife, Allegra, appears in a mourning veil, crying as though Kray were *her* husband.

"I loved him, I always will," she says, as I step as far away from her as I can: he fucked her, I know it.

We each leave a rose in the newly made grave. When it is my turn, I drop the red bloom and make the sign of the cross.

My thoughts assemble with daisies in their hands as other thoughts approach like the National Guard, with rifles pumped.

I GET A call on our way home.

It is Kray's lawyer: I have been named in his will and he wants to meet with me.

I tell him I'll come by shortly.

"Did Vivienne mention the screenplay?" Annabel says, demure in her black pillbox hat and Chanel suit.

"At her husband's funeral?" I say.

"Sorry," she says, lighting one of my cigarettes. "I'm sure he thought it was junk anyways."

AT HOME, I watch a short documentary about Kray as I change out of my rumpled John Phillips suit.

No one is sure where he grew up, or who his family is. He is believed to have been the expatriate son of a Brooklyn widower who worked in a smelting factory and parlously neglected his small, quiet son.

Kray left home and became a painter, working in a slaughterhouse during the day.

He never spoke of the work, except to say it was "just another job, but louder, with more mess."

His paintings are large acrylics that depict crime-scene pictures of dead girls and boys: always street kids, and always savage.

Private collectors ate the work up and he parlayed his fortune into short films: dark stories he wrote himself, billets-doux to crime.

Ultraviolence is his sixth and most successful major motion picture. Written and produced by him alone, it bit off the first half of *A Clockwork Orange* and spat out the rest.

"Entirely too moral," was his terse review of Kubrick's film.

Annabel's book, which I am still struggling through in page proofs, says that "*A Clockwork Orange* uses *Paradise Lost* for a model: Alex-Hero, like the grandiose Lucifer, is slowly taken apart and, ultimately, reduced to a broken captive of the Pandemonium of his own devising."

Kray's work, on the other hand, "enlarges Satan, and adores him as the BBQ apron–wearing killer of the paschal lamb."

I think that I understand what she means, but I have never read the Milton book she pressed on me along with so many others.

Or I have, depending on who it is I am talking to, and why.

As I give my shoes a fast shine, I learn that Kray never had children, that he was a chess grandmaster and a fine horseman, and that he asked to be buried in a T-shirt that says "I'D RATHER BE GOLFING," the fucking maniac.

KRAY'S LAWYER IS located on South Hope Street, in a hundred-storey green-glass building carpeted with plush dollar signs.

I wait for Mr. Lamprey in his Olympian reception area and watch, with more than a little bit of lust, his two secretaries, who are conjoined canary-blonde twins with pocket-Venus figures and lovely chiselled faces.

"Mr. Wilde," says the skeletal black man in a spotless white suit. "Please," he says, gesturing to his impossibly big office, to the aircraft carrier–sized oak desk where his throne and my toadstool await.

Lamprey begins by staring me down. He loses, blinks, and busies himself with a sealed envelope.

"Mr. Kray was suffering from Alzheimer's for the last few years," he says. "He wished to keep his condition secret and I hope that you will respect this wish."

"Doubt it," I say, striking a match and lifting it to the unlit Lucky Strike I have jammed between my lips.

The lawyer sighs. There is so obviously no smoking permitted that he cannot bring himself to mention it.

I call loudly to the girls for an ice-cold glass of vodka, admire their ample bottoms as they walk away, and wait.

"Well, my client said you would be difficult. And he retained me for two reasons. He asked me to apologize for hurting you. He does not say what he did to warrant the apology."

"And?" I say, expressionless.

"He has left you the rights to *Ultraviolence* and the sequel. It is up to you now who directs and stars in the new one, and all past and future revenues shall be paid to you from this day forth."

"Why?" I say at last, having turned all of my attention to an amazing pigeon fight on the windowsill.

"He states, and I quote," says Lamprey, reading from the document: " 'Parnell is like a son to me. A prodigal son, who will either safeguard or ruin my legacy. I am curious, dead or alive, to see what he shall do. He will likely crash and burn, which is unfortunate, but *darkly comic.*' "

He has the decency to blanch as he reads this to me.

As I advance, with flames in my eyes, he throws up his hands.

"He could be wrong," I say, grabbing the papers and what is, essentially, the key to the kingdom: more money and power than I can imagine.

"He could be right," I say, as I see myself roasting thousand-dollar bills on weenie sticks, surrounded by thieves and avarice.

"Good luck," Lamprey says, and I know, suddenly, that Kray has told him everything.

I want to crawl out of the office, but then I shake my head.

Why am I intimidated—and by who? Kray's mouthpiece?

My lit cigarette glances his face: he yelps and the freaks rush in as I walk away in slow motion as a private tribute to Kray, my very own, disgusting, Magwitch.

Great Expectations: there's one book that Annabel pressed on me that I tore through, to her inordinate delight.

I read it because I once harbored such feelings; because she rewarded me at the end of each chapter with a happy ending.

I AM LIVING like a prize pig in our new and still costlier home, but never have I been more miserable.

The nightmares resume, are more lurid; insufferable, even.

I dream one night that Annabel hands me all of her teeth. They sit in a little pool of blood in my palm as she starts strangling chickens.

I wake up, gasping. Annabel is out somewhere. She left a note with alphabet fridge magnets that said C U LTR ALLIGTR, and has not called or texted me since.

I am afraid to fall asleep again. The next dream will be about Kray, it always is.

Of him dead and kissing me or rotting in the bed beside me; of him, a man I once thought of as my father, flaying my skin in long, spiralling strips.

I GREW UP without a father, something my drunken mother never tired of mentioning, so great were her hardships.

I never told anyone, not even Annabel, about the nightly attacks: about her stripping and scalding me with the hot iron, the TV antenna, and worse.

Occasionally, she was in love with me.

She would bring me into her bed and brush my hair, kiss me flush on the lips and call me her dearest boy. At twelve, with my face often mashed into her large, naked breasts, this was confusing and loathsome.

Annabel told me that her mother, though cold, was "as good to me as she could be: I think she had a broken heart."

This was enviably normal to me. I didn't want to admit another nauseating aspect of my past.

It was Allegra who knew, and Allegra who said, "Some kids are targets because there's something not right about them and it shows."

I am a convicted felon, by the way. That was the night I caved in her face, then sat by the front door, waiting for the cops I called myself.

"I'LL TELL YOU what I'm afraid of," Annabel says.

I have her on speaker as I drink from my tumbler of Glenfiddich and cycle through the channels on my jumbotron.

I can barely hear her.

"I'm at a Kraut show," she says, and hangs up.

I heard Alexander's band was playing at the Palladium, but I have no idea what she's doing there.

Looking for a younger me? No, impossible. Alexander is grotesque.

I don't know when she got tickets; I didn't know she liked his band. Although she has been uncommunicative and moody lately, we fooled around earlier today. I hold the pillow I slipped under her ass to my face reverently.

Drop it. I am angry she took off—and to Alexander's show, of all places.

I understand her less and less these days.

I resume looking at the TV and drop the remote when I see *Ultraviolence* is on. I am so drunk, I wish to watch it for the first time since its release.

It begins with Cézanne apples filling a bowl.

A young man and woman walk through snow, their hair dense and white, their long black coats dappled with it.

They turn a corner and their footprints slowly disappear, and the street and horizon join like interlocking crystals, intricate and smooth as clockwork.

I cry, the scene is so beautiful.

Cry, as the anguish starts up around the dead corner and the film cuts to the man that is me, slashing the woman to pieces with a dagger and spraying the snow, the screen itself, with her dark, wanton blood.

"IT'S RIGHT DOWN the hall," says a satisfied yellow canary of a girl as my Sid walks out of her bedroom to a wall-mounted telephone, wearing only his jeans and a rattlesnake belt.

"Bring Baby and Bint," he says, naming two of his gang members. "And more rounds too," he adds, inspecting the gun he removes from the small of his back.

Kray used dark makeup to make me look older. He added hollows under my eyes and liner to make them pop.

"*I'm so young, I'm so young,*" I say involuntarily as I look at myself noticing a slender black girl powdering herself with a big white puff.

"Hello, sweet thing," Sid says, moving, terribly, closer.

"Leave her alone!" I yell, and when I throw the remote at the TV, it disgorges its batteries and the channel switches to one with a live feed of a fish tank.

I am tailing a shy jewel fish hiding at the base of a pirate's chest when Annabel calls.

She is crying and I stand and do a few quick wind sprints to sober up.

"I need to see you," she says.

She tells me she is a few blocks from the Palladium, underneath a bright green Ferrari.

I call the car company and ask that someone fetch her.

I push her out of my mind and go back inside to inspect my face.

Not bad: my last round of injectables has left my face smooth and embonpoint.

I comb my hair back and change into the white chambray shirt and black jeans she likes, Harford's boots.

I want her home safe, but I am afraid of hurting her.

"*Leave her alone!*" I hear myself saying, and see Annabel being led to me in a torn dress and a black eye.

"WHEN I WON the essay contest," says Annabel, "they flew me to New York. I pretended my parents were chaperoning, but I went alone."

She is cross-legged in a suspended ball chair, a brancher in a nest of black chenille.

"I wore my medal and walked all over the city. I walked until it was night: I wasn't hungry or tired, I felt high.

These boys stopped me in Central Park."

She has told me this story. I understand that she must tell me again, while I am wide awake to be certain I understand everything.

And to take over.

"This is *my* story. My life," she says, her voice rising.

She lights a cigarette, accepts a glass of beer, and continues.

"The good-looking boy was dressed like you were in *Ultraviolence*, and I thought he was an angel.

But he wasn't an angel. He raped me and he kicked me in the stomach when he heard someone coming.

Two women.

They walked right by me, like it was nothing to someone like me."

She starts to cry, and I hand her a stack of linen handkerchiefs; carefully hide what I am feeling.

"I put my ripped clothes on and ran like a deer all the way to my hotel, and cleaned myself with a metal brush. But not the boot print. Look," she says, and I understand what *ne obliviscaris* has meant all along.

"I'm sorry," I say, ashen.

"I'm sorry too," she says. "For tracking you down. I *did* like you. But when I came looking, it was to find him."

I remember her tossing my apartment and flinch.

"But I ended up falling for you," she says. "You know that."

And when I look into her eyes and see us being led out of Eden, still hand in hand, her defiant words strafe the accursed fruit trees.

All places thou.

She sees me understanding, and resumes.

"I went to see Kraut tonight with a model I know. She's dating the bass player, and we went backstage. The lead singer is your son."

And then, "He is the guy who raped me."

I am walking in tight circles, like a wretched lion I once beheld in a Paris zoo, living in a prison barely larger than him.

"Je vous connais, vous êtes moi," I said and the old lion wept, what will I do for blood—

"I attacked him and he fought back," she says. "But he won. Again."

She bursts into fresh tears.

"I thought I would avenge myself one day, but look at me."

I look at her.

She is so small, and frangible.

I think of my son.

About the trips he took to New York, to visit colleges, he said.

About finding my film costume and makeup in his room, and his easy response, that he was writing an essay about me for class.

About telling him he was too young to watch that movie, and how he laughed, then checked himself.

"I closed my eyes during the sex and violence parts," he said.

I close my eyes and calculate the distance to the Palladium.

"No," she says. *"Please."*

Walk out and leave Annabel suspended, rocking as she sleeps and cries.

I see her understanding, and resume.

I BASH ON the backstage door, and just as security is about to slam it shut, I see Alexander and raise my second finger, whirling it in the hurry-up sign I taught him when he was a child.

"Oh shit," says Alexander. "I know this guy. Come in!"

The guards open their ranks and let me through the door into *Satyricon*. Alexander is undressed to his torn jeans and black Converse sneakers; three girls crawl over him and a dozen more stand in an orderly line beside him. His bandmates are being serviced along with the roadies. One naked young girl is demanding the entire band fuck her and then set her on fire.

He pushes the girls off and stands up.

Hugs me and says, "So you caved, after all."

I say nothing, and he starts to twitch.

"Did you like the show?" he says, still keeping one track-marked arm around me.

He obviously likes me better as a success. The memo line of his last check, sent to Elsinore, guilelessly read, "Enjoy the twenty bucks, you scabrous failure."

I cashed it.

"Yes," I say. "I like the show you put on at twenty-one about visiting prospective colleges."

Not to mention all the other lies, and the depraved behaviour I ignored because I wanted to love you, because —

"I was afraid of you," I say, surprising myself.

I unpeel his arm from mine and face him. Sad, but not afraid anymore. Of him, or anyone.

He looks at me intently: he is sizing me up.

When his crew advances, he signals them away.

"What do you want?" he says like ice.

I say, "I want you not to have raped my girlfriend when she was a kid." And push him.

The room freezes.

"Which one is your girlfriend? Not the cunt who attacked me tonight?" he says, pointing to three deep scratch marks on his face.

"That would be her," I say pleasantly, and punch him so hard he spits blood and falls down.

The gun keeps everyone else where they are. It is a contraband TEC-9, and I look like I want to use it, badly.

I knock my son down, kick him, and hear a snap.

"I hate your band, by the way," I say.

But I am kneeling on the ground, cradling his neck and holding him. He cannot support his head (his peach fuzz–soft head in its blue bunting

Daddy's gone a-hunting I sing I swear he smiles and)

"And I hate you."

I cannot remember the tears, the bubble of blood and saliva like a snow globe we are inside of, and I am carrying my child on my shoulders.

"But I love you," he says. I do not hear him: I let him go.

Holding the weapon with two hands, I maneuver my way backwards, through the door and down the hall.

It is snowing outside: I walk down the street and into an alley.

My driver, Larry, is waiting, waiting by the building that is sending out feelers of smoke. It is on fire, and the snow is ash, descending from the top floor as the inferno musters its strength.

As we drive away, an armada of fire trucks appears, black-suited madmen listing from its sides.

ANNABEL REMAINS IN the round chair, a constituent of Melvin Sokolsky's creation *Bulle*: a photo series of models in haute couture locked in Plexiglas balls and suspended above the streets of Paris.

She will write in her diary:

Love is clockwork, with its cold steel.

RAPE is surgery performed with a rusty saw and staple sutures; what is removed is vermin, plucked with dull pliers and flicked into a bin of amputations and red gauze.

The wings are dissevered and cooked in smashed Corn Flakes and lard: she will never fly again, *tant pis*.

Her mechanical wings exist only for exhibition purposes, for the filthy men, the lechers and scum.

Not long ago I found a bird—*mi alma*—mauled and chittering beneath our persimmon tree, and I lay beside her as her heart slowed to a stop.

My friend, I said, and her tiny eyes found mine and blinked in assent, blood leaving her in filigree, the blood that beat in me when he fucked me slow enough to make me feel it.

Do you feel me, feel how hard I am? he said as I became uglier, until I became putrid.

I worked hard on my false beauty after he changed me, avoiding the mirrors that revealed the chirality. My rape lives in glass and shows me, my face opened up like a shotgun wound, leaking venom.

Parnell sees my mutilation and loves it, loves me. Does he share it?

He loves the devil inside me, who is a fallen angel. Rebarbative, beautiful.

I tell my story to the ugly ones with every photograph; many send back pictures of their gorgeousness cut from stem to stern and brewing poison.

Yes, I tell them, I too am a bird.

Sí, mis hermanos y hermanas, los veo.

WHEN I GET home, I scoop Annabel from the hanging chair, deposit her into a hot bath, and join her.

"He will never bother you again," I say, and she sighs, that's all, just sighs and holds me tighter.

"We are sleeping beauties," she says, and smiles. "And princes."

Annabel lies against my chest as the bath bombs detonate and color the water pink, then blue.

"What happened?" she says.

This scares me. I am losing the memory. My mind has discovered a tremendous way to contend with trauma: selective amnesia.

But I love you

"I saw him, and saw red," I say, tightening my hold on her.

"Red advances, blue recedes," she says dreamily. "In one of my *Clockwork Orange* chapters, I talk about the title cards, about how Kubrick uses them like Rothko."

"Kray copied that outright. But he got the order wrong, didn't you tell me?"

"He did," she says happily. I so rarely mention her work. "But that was calculated. He —"

She turns and notices my hair is a shock-white shampoo bubble.

Pissed off, she dunks my head underwater. I emerge sputtering, which makes her laugh, and vainly I straighten my plastered hair with my fingers.

It is a beautiful night. We see Andromeda through the skylight, see its milky white haze, and I feel like Perseus, having saved the most beautiful of all creatures from the monster who lives deep below the surface.

"He's dead, isn't he?"

I don't answer.

The bath simmers like a cauldron. I squeeze her harder, and she laughs like Poppin' Fresh.

"I love you," she says, and I nod, get up, and dry off.

"I know."

"What kind of an answer is that?" she says, standing up and shaking off the colored sludge. "I just told you that I *love you*."

Breakfast at Tiffany's is on in the bedroom: we are both distracted by the lost cat and swelling score.

"You know what your problem is, lassie?" George Peppard says woodenly to an indifferent Audrey Hepburn.

"You're chicken!"

On and on he goes. He is incomprehensible.

I look at Annabel, who is repeating the words soundlessly, tears falling down her pretty cheeks.

"I hope you're crying for that cat," I say. "It's soaked to the bone."

"Baby, you're already eating suet," she whispers as Hepburn steps onto a golden perch and sings of love; as Annabel shows me, in faint scratches and joyous chirps, what I mean to her.

"All night long," I boast later to an appalled Rabi.

"She can't live without her heart much longer," he says, and spits, as that very organ leaks through the lace handkerchief she has wrapped it in, spraying my pocket like a frightened little skunk.

LATER, AS SHE sleeps, the buttery moon alights on her back, which has been freshly inked.

The words are from Zora Neale Hurston—the end of her strange tautology about women's memory.

The dream is the truth, reads Annabel's cinnamon-script. It is barely distinguishable from her flesh, so I trace it, and remember how I forgot about killing Kray, and forget that I remembered.

The dream is the girl who tried to take him out for me; the woman who keeps giving me her strength until she is wasted, each vertebra on her lustrous back visible, her neck limp against her stem-thin arm.

I give her something so small in return, I think as I roughly finger her, rolling her over so she can face and lacerate me, crying, "It hurts so much."

Shining with blood that pours from new gashes and old scars, I tell her, "Yes," and, "Never stop."

"WHEN I FIRST met you, I acted pretty cool, didn't I?" says Annabel.

It is almost dawn, and we are airing ourselves on top of the stained, glutinous covers.

"But when I was thirteen, I had a big crush on you. I *laminated* those shots of you with the daisy. I carried them everywhere, like Tubby — hey, where is he?"

"You have him," I say nervously.

"I do," she says, reaching for her bag and pulling him out. He is dressed like a fire marshal, damn it.

I click on the TV and we watch the chaos on CNN.

"At least one dead," the crawl says. "Dozens injured."

The Palladium is pictured, blackened but still standing: dazed, hairless people wander around a tier of ambulances.

"You?" she says, covering her face.

"What? No, my God."

She is staring at a covered stretcher, at girls howling as the name Alexander Wild — he dropped the *e* years ago — fills the screen.

The phone rings and rings.

My son is dead, I think, as I turn the ringer off, plump the pillows, and emit a *what have I done* into the almost viscous air before falling into a long, vacant sleep.

ANNABEL WAKES ME and hands me my phone.

"It's your wife," she mouths anxiously.

All I hear is rattling snot and wet huffs.

"I'm at the police station," she says. "They want to talk to you."

ALLEGRA HAD GRABBED the telephone from the detective's hand as he dialed me, it turns out.

I sit with him in a glass-walled room as Allegra talks to an officer at his desk.

"I was there," I say.

"We know, several witnesses saw you."

"Several?" I say, arching an eyebrow.

"All right, they're almost all dead. But someone saw you."

"Was it the roadie I saw raping a groupie?" I ask. "Or the insentient junkie?"

"Where's the gun?"

"At home in a strongbox with its carry permit. Why?"

"Why did you bring it to a concert?" asks Detective Alberto. He is a handsome young Dominican man with huge, barbellate forearms.

"To show Alexander. He loves—he loved—guns," I say, and cough.

"Did he like getting beat up?"

I tell the detective about Annabel, about what I learned, and he nods grimly.

He has my son's record spread out before him.

"I have to arrest you," he says.

"For what?"

He's a fan. Bernstein has already been dispatched.

I am led to a relatively nice cell, where I nap until my lawyer springs me.

"They have nothing," says Bernstein, leading me out.

The cop who booked me says, "Call me if you remember seeing anyone running away or anything about that fire," and hands me his card.

I do remember. I remember a girl begging to be burned alive—

"And, ah, would you mind—"

I sign the *Ultraviolence* poster he has run to his office to tear from the wall: "To Joey. *Make the bad bleed.*" It is a line from the movie and he repeats it, slowly tracing my signature with huge, reverent fingers.

Annabel laughs when I call and tell her where I have been.

"I thought it was another woman," she says.

"No, we are both habitués of the same jail, that's all, taking togetherness to new and daring heights."

"Get back here, sweet Daddy," she says. Which is all she ever needs to say, and I'm gone.

"FUNNY, ISN'T IT?"

"What?" says Allegra creamily.

She has invited me to dinner at Musso & Frank the following night: she wishes to celebrate my release from jail and to commiserate about Alexander.

I arrive late and she is perched stiffly at the bar, primping her obvious wig and assaulting her compact with a filthy sponge.

We are escorted to one of the snugs by a black giantess with natural and pure orange tiger's eyes.

She orders an onion tartlet and rare steak, which sickens me.

I order a large salad and a baked potato, and marvel at my vegetarian girlfriend-slash-sorceress.

I go on about how while Alexander looked something like me, Pudge bears no resemblance whatsoever.

"She kind of has my eyes," I say. "And that's it."

Allegra tries to change the subject by admiring the many flans on the menu.

I say, "Pudge has a prominent nose. And Kray, Kray had quite the beak, didn't he?"

Allegra starts yelling. "Stop torturing me! All right, all right, the kids are *probably* his. He seduced me, the devil, and then he wouldn't leave his wife."

She buries her face in a napkin.

"Why?" I say, standing to my full height and towering over her. People are staring. I squeeze her shoulder, and she quiets down immediately.

"You never loved me!" she says as I return to my seat. "He made me feel attractive again. You hadn't touched me in a year."

I look at her, and she could be anyone. I have no love for her, which is what, I realize, I felt throughout our marriage.

"Okay," I say. "Enough crying."

She stares at me, tears pooling in the reptilian folds around her eyes.

"What is she like?" she asks quietly.

"She's exceptionally smart."

Then, more sharply, "What is she like in bed?"

I prevaricate, then fold under her death stare. "Like a perverse archangel," I say, and my ex-wife holds herself up stiffly, stands, and walks away.

She smooths her heart-littered red dress over her stout rear and large paunch and exits the restaurant, leaving me to feel a nauseous combination of distaste and pity.

When we first met, she embroidered my name on a set of vintage handkerchiefs.

"I'll never need these," I said as I lifted her in my arms. She was so small I called her my bag of feathers.

I never did need them. I lost them all, though I do have a vague memory of cleaning a shoe with the last one, soiling it irreparably.

Oh, you rotten prick, I think as I salt my salad with my remorse and her steak rebukes me from its estuary of blood.

ANNABEL HAS BEEN sleeping on and off since the night of the show.

When I get home, I stand in the bedroom doorway and watch her.

She is naked, angelic.

"I have questions," she murmurs, and I tell her to go back to sleep.

"Look at the list," she says, and I do.

DID YOU KILL WILL?
DID YOU KILL YOUR SON?
DID YOU SLEEP WITH THAT WOMAN?

"There's more," she says, "but I forget."

"I have questions too," I say, lying beside her and pulling her close.

"Why are you so pretty?" I say, and she frowns. "And, have you ever cheated on me?"

She shakes her head. "There is no one like you," she says.

"All right," I say, preening. "Here are your answers. No. Almost. Who?"

"The hooker," she says. "I have eyes everywhere."

"All right," I say, flustered. "No. Never."

Among Kray's papers, also bequeathed to me, is a scribbled note with Harford's flight number crossed out and the comment "Does he think I'll shoot the fucking plane out of the sky?" followed by a row of happy-face emojis with tears of mirth in their eyes.

It was just good timing, it turns out.

Alexander was Kray's son, I'm certain of it. So was he, and he left both kids some money, which I am supposed to disperse, and Allegra a few hundred dollars and a valentine heart that says "Slippery When Wet."

I have already forwarded the money to Pudge, who spent it instantly on a handsome fancy man and an interest in his art-therapy business, which is located in Folsom State Prison.

Alex's share goes to the fan who sends the most sincere card: "When he sang," Rachel writes, "I put down the razor for good and let his voice pull my pain away."

A cutter.

She is, or was, another trail of blood that leads right to me.

Of my odiousness and anemic dreams of truth, I sing: *My soule, poore soule thou talkes of things. Thou knowest not what, my soule hath sliver wings.*

"My poor baby," Annabel murmurs, and we sleep on the flight feathers of argent pinions that speak of moments, dazzling moments, of release.

I TEAR UP Allegra's card and cringe on her behalf: hand the money to the first indigent person I see, a topless old woman pushing a stuffed monkey in a stroller on Mulholland.

"Did he leave me anything?" my ex-wife calls and asks me at dawn, sounding like a whipped dog.

"Yes," I say. "There is money in an envelope that reads, 'Forgive me.'"

"Thank you," she whispers, and I make a note to get this fabrication to her quickly.

I thought I had more questions, but I forget them because so aromatic is my girl asleep beside me, emanating Mitsouko, vanilla soap, and amber shampoo—and, better, her raw, velvety gash: part seaweed, part honey.

My mouth catches on "I love you" and swallows the phrase whole.

"I know," she says in her dream, the one where I am decent and valiant and we live forever.

THE FOLLOWING NIGHT, at Annabel's apartment, I dream of Alexander.

He is five, pulling feathers off an injured bird he has found on the street.

"Stop it," I say, and toss the bird into a hedge.

"That was *mine*," he says, and kicks me in the shin as hard as he can.

"I'll tear off that foot," I say, and hop after him.

Annabel shakes me awake. "I want to talk," she says.

"No," I plead. "It's four in the morning, I want to sleep."

She gets up and boils water for tea. Reluctantly, I lift myself and join her, splashing cold water on my creased, burning face.

The summer is now full-blown. Her useless ceiling fan churns the hot air around; she and I sleep in underwear that she has kept in the freezer all day.

"Look," she says. "I know that the screenplay is no good. I find those old forms inhibiting and boring. That's why my book has no bibliography or notes, just a disclaimer that says, 'My memory will have to do.' But I could do something with Kray's screenplay, which is very good, but backwards. All of the intimations of the epicene, the context of female radicalism, are gone. Which is why my short films, the ones about you, are so much better."

"They *are*," I say, remembering one devoted to a particularly faded area of my jeans.

"So you'll think about it," she says as I kiss a beeline down her belly and into the damp recesses of her bird-covered bikini briefs.

"Yes," I say, though to what I am not sure. "Yes, yes," as she snaps my shorts off and fists my slick cock.

An idea begins to take shape as she pushes me back and presses herself against me, fucking me gently to the mechanical prayer of "O Superman."

What if I gave Crispin her screenplay, the parts I highlighted, and asked him to mash them into his?

If I show him her films, the story of love and danger that they tell—the lit and *sauvage* visual poems, as Rabi calls them—he will agree.

She is poignantly sincere, I think, making another note to buy her the cardinal-red metallic vinyl poms I saw on Melrose: two for her, and the Columbia blues for me.

"I can't wait anymore," she says, her face screwed up and doe's eyes shining. I let go like a bottle of shaken pop, knocking her, amazed and delighted, off me and onto the bed, where she keeps coming in waves filled with coarse salt and deliriously happy little fish.

SHE IS OFTEN sad after our trysts, and then she is irritated by my need to cackle and fuss like an old pullet.

"No, I don't want *tea*," she says, as though I have just offered her a bottle of baby formula.

She is breathtaking when she is cross.

Tonight, she stands in a black half-slip and structured vintage bra that makes wired torpedoes of her breasts, drinking gin from a jam jar, a cigarette affixed to her full, ruby lip.

"We are bad people," she says, and my memory jams, stutter-starts, and stops.

"No, we're not," I say, although I know, without knowing, that I am.

"You're not half the devil I am," she says, flattering herself while expertly blowing Cheerio-sized smoke rings.

She brightens and pulls on a sheer pink robe that I have snatched from Wardrobe after many fantasies about her wearing it.

"Why don't we write down our sins and eat them?" she says.

I go along with her and write about ten things on the scraps of paper she provides. Chew and swallow them with difficulty.

"I feel better," I say, and she says that she does too.

We have tombstones for eyes; we are gaunt and twitchy.

Too much has been left unsaid, that's all me, and she has said too much.

Something has got to give, and I pray it isn't us.

"WHAT'S THIS?" ANNABEL says, holding up a shirt cardboard. "Give me that!"

She reads it, one of the many poems I have written about her since she first appeared in my apartment.

"It's terrible," I say. "I wanted to give you something back then and I couldn't afford a bunch of carnations from the liquor store."

She reads it with one eyebrow raised:

> Your eyes are combustible fluids, suspended
> colloids, an amber formula where two zeroes
> lie between brackets and "lesser than" and
> "greater than" equal your smile —

"Oh, that's so sweet," she says, and kisses me with big smacks.

"Tell me what he did to you," I say.

Her face falls.

"I already told you. Does it turn you on?" she says miserably.

I feel struck.

"No," I say. "I'm trying to understand why I have no compassion for my only son lying in a morgue drawer."

The police were still investigating, holding up the funeral service and cremation being referred to, on Twitter, as #burningman2 and #creepella.

The jumbo-sized mortician, wearing more makeup than Allegra, met with us. "Your son is being kept as cool as a cuke," he said. "Please don't worry yourselves with thoughts of decomposition."

Until then, I hadn't.

Annabel says, "The only romance I had ever had before your son raped me was with Curtis Jones, another five-year-old, who told me he loved me and kissed me once on the roundabout. When I came home from New York, I kept to myself. I was too scared to tell anyone what happened, scared even that they'd laugh. Because he's so good-looking and—"

My rage actually leaves my body and becomes a ghost, wild for revenge. "Soon," I murmur to the ghastly apparition. "Soon."

"I realized I was pregnant and had to tell my mother," Annabel says. "She sent me to our family doctor, who told me, privately, to learn to keep my legs shut. He went after that fetus like a burdock root. I bled for weeks."

"Say, what is that doctor's name?" I ask, planning to chisel out some hollow points later on.

"No, I won't tell you. No more of this," she says, and clams up.

I console myself for the time being with the thought of sneaking into the mortuary and cutting the cool air.

Of his dick browning like an old banana and falling off.

I will remember to find Annabel's doctor's name on the way to the funeral home.

And forget about the baby, the shrimp-sized one encoded with pale-blue eyes, with monstrous intelligence and some kind of love.

THE COPS ARRANGE a lineup of a few vagrants who live near the Palladium, one a known arsonist, another a police officer.

They pull in a hundred eyewitnesses, all of whom pick the officer.

"That's him, man. Lookit those crazy eyes."

The arsonist's attorney smiles and takes his client home to the trailer park in the hills, where several scorched husks sit on blocks.

The vagrants' court-appointed counsel sets them loose at Circus Liquor, where they make a small fortune telling their story to Kraut fans.

Unofficially, the police have given up.

Cat Pause, Alexander's manager, is infuriated. "He *knew* the guy!" he says. "They hugged, and talked."

"Yeah, then he knocked him down," says one of the cops. "Look, we've investigated, this is a big case. Your client was, all due respect, a real piece of shit. We found disgraceful juvie records, also battery and sexual-assault complaints, DUIs, larceny, destruction of property—I'm sure Mr. Wilde had his reasons."

"He was a rock star," Pause says, frustrated and angry. "All of that, it comes with the job."

The cops exchange looks.

"Nice work if you can get it," says an officer who is more mountain than man, and whose scowl lifts Pause's bony old ass off the folding chair.

"Fine, fine. So let one of the greatest voices of the millennium die without justice. Be interviewed for the rest of your lives by lugubrious fans and intrepid makers of conspiracy documentaries!"

The cops watch Pause walk away, emitting tiny bursts of gas in his fear and unquenched animus.

"'Tell us how you killed your son's ass," Mountain says, and laughs.

I DON'T HAVE to tell Mountain anything, it turns out, because the groupie whose body started the fire has been located at the L.A. County General Hospital Burn Unit.

Her name is Nancy Maddox: her face is the only part of her left partially untouched.

She tells the police I had a quarrel with my son, and that's all. That he was fine when I left.

I visit her with a thick envelope of cash and the medical video game *SnowWorld*.

"Why did you lie for me?" I say, touching her sad, sweet face as I rest gingerly beside her among the cold gel packs and worn plush animals.

"He helped make me this way," she says, and winces. We throw virtual snowballs until her body relaxes.

"He had sex with me when I was twelve. It was my fault. I went backstage dressed like a little harlot," she says. "But he hurt me, he hurt me so much."

I capture her tears and I rage inside, tell her that no, it is entirely his fault.

"You sort of look like him," she says, and smiles shyly.

"I'm sorry," I say, and curve my hand around her skull.

"No one will ever kiss me again," Nancy says, so I kiss her and we kiss until I am shooed away and *the nerve* flies like a bullet through the corridor. But she was smiling when they unlatched me.

ON THE DAY of the funeral, Annabel puts on a long beige dress and matching loafers, braids her hair into a circle on her crown and wears no makeup other than brown eyeshadow.

I wear a good black suit and a white camellia in my lapel.

We sit at the front of the Bel Air Presbyterian, listening to interminable acoustic tributes and unintelligible eulogies.

My wife and daughter decline to speak. They are too distraught.

I stand at the podium after kissing my son's cold, waxen lips.

"Alexander was a rock star," I say.

One mourner says, "Fuckin' A," and is silenced.

"A rebel, an outsider, and more of a Sid than I ever was. I will not miss him, nor did I love him. But I am here to tender my admiration for the ruthless way in which he lived his short life, and to be certain he is cremated. I intend to sprinkle some of his ashes on the steps of the Downtown Women's Center, then spread the remainder over a urinal puck."

I feign discomfort.

"I beg your pardon," I say. "By *urinal puck*, I mean the cheap stinking blue cakes found in men's toilets. Thank you."

I step down to shocked silence and a few loud, excited claps.

"Have you thought of a career in writing disgusting eulogies?" Annabel asks when I sit down, and I laugh.

"The cops are here," she says nervously.

"So what? Sweetheart," I say, "could you please run home and change before the reception? You look really bad."

She runs out of the church and I wave after her as if she is getting something from the car.

Annabel will tell me what I said later and I won't believe her. My anger appears out of nowhere, like a murderous twister, then scarpers off, leaving my mind in shambles.

I suppose that being near Alexander again was traumatic. I did, after all, beat him to death.

Wait. That can't be true.

He died in a fire, the poor bastard.

At the reception, I dance with a small, curvy brunette who says she liked my speech and rubs up against me so much I toy with the idea of walking her to the coatroom when Annabel returns in a short black dress and heels, her hair loose.

"Was that so hard?" I say.

"Why are *you* so hard?" she says, glaring at the brunette and pulling me into a tango that very quickly dominates the floor.

"PLEASE HELP ME, help me, God."

Annabel wakes me. Adrift in moonlight, she asks what is wrong so gently that I finally feel the brittle shell crack.

"I don't want to feel anything, it hurts too much," I say.

"It hurts to keep it all inside," she says, and I blow up.

I run through the house, wailing and falling. She chases and finally catches me by the kitchen sink, where she gathers my body against hers and pats and rubs my back until all of the black toads and deep-blue bats and small white snakes have crawled out of my mouth; until I can cry clear liquid and not murky, sulphurous waste.

"What will I do?" I say. The moon is high in the sky, sheer and curved.

"Ask to be forgiven," she says.

I rest my head on her lap and tell Jesus, who is raising a barn for the waning moon, that I have not been myself, that I have behaved very badly. He stares at me with His gelid eyes for a long time and says, "Really?" in a sarcastic voice I am surprised to hear the Lord use.

I fall asleep inches away from paradise. When we wake, several hours later, I have chewed through her pajama bottoms and she is basking in the good vibrations.

I AM OUT of control, in danger once more.

Time to get on that wagon, shape up.

I fill three boxes with liquor, Class A narcotics, tranqs, some mescaline, and a brick of hash, and leave them on the curb. They are gone before I reach my door. I have the dogs groomed and quarrel with Rabi about the pets he insisted on sitting. Now he wants to keep them.

He tells me that Pepita, Odorosa, and the Bandit, the skunks, are fully grown and deeply attached to him.

"And all of the wild birds flew away," he says, and I am not surprised. I never understood how Annabel coaxed them inside to perch on her and make nests in her stocking drawers in the first place.

We compromise and he brings over a box containing a baby possum, a Komodo dragon's egg, and a tiny achondroplasic kitten with seven toes on each paw.

I call my trainer and agree to work like a fighter every day. I quit smoking and fill the refrigerator with organic leafy and fruity items, with soy milk and almond butter, quinoa loaf and flax pita shells.

And write contrite letters on monogrammed cards.

Annabel has moved back in completely, bringing with her the color and light that vanished when she left, when I dressed all the windows with black blinds.

The dogs act like she has never left, while baring their teeth at me constantly and snarling when I touch her.

Jerks.

She cries over the missing pets, but the new ones attach themselves to her. The egg cracks instantaneously when she holds it.

"We are getting a rescue hippo," she says, and I agree, weak as the kitten she calls Peewee.

I write to Pudge at Annabel's insistence, telling her that even though she is not biologically mine, she is my daughter and I love her.

I put my pen down.

"But I don't love her," I say. "Not really."

"You told me you were close when she was little," says Annabel, worried. There are twenty cards to go.

I sigh, and recommence.

"Please remember to be a good girl," I conclude, signing my name with a flourish.

"She's just going to throw it out," I say, thinking of her mouth tightening like a sphincter as she rips the thick card stock in half.

"Keep going," Annabel says. She is proud of my resolve and has promised me a "dirty swim" after the letters are done: I can't refuse.

I write my ex-wife that I'm sorry she's a whore, and am told to correct it.

"I'm sorry I called you a whore," I write, adding that I wish her well.

I write a bunch of people I was mean to or neglectful of, including Cotton, whom I so seldom call, then beg for a break.

Annabel puts the envelopes in her purse and strips to her polka-dot bikini. I discard everything.

"If I don't fuck you to death, I'll write the rest," I say, chasing her, stark naked, into the water, and mauling her like Jaws.

Later, in a hot bath, I say, "I still feel good. Cleansed. But something is missing."

"This?" asks my beloved, easing a finger into my ass, then two, a completely repulsive gesture that confuses and excites me.

We stay in the tub until the water is dark and dirty and we are asleep, facing each other, and the sun drops past the window and into its charred, moon-battered hole.

THE NIGHT ANNABEL formalizes her return, she has a miserable cold and can speak only in whispers.

She is determined to make the place feel more homey, and places pictures of us on the ornate tables. In my favorite, taken by a passerby, we are standing on the Champs-Élysées, our arms filled with leafy vegetables, flowers, and bread.

We had planned to make faces, but this stranger—was it Brassaï?—captured us just as we spontaneously dropped the bags and clung to each other.

My hands are tilting her face to mine and our eyes commit indecencies that our bodies have already begun.

We drag some pillows below the pictures and drink ice-cold dirty martinis.

A flood upstairs that I thought I had staunched knocks the paint off the ceiling and Oriental blossoms drift down — I am reminded of cherry blossoms — and latch on to my skin, my face, my eyes.

This must be what falling in love is like, I think, and she says, hoarsely, that she fell long ago.

"From heaven," I say suavely, blowing it.

"Sure," she says.

Annabel is a nice girl above all, and patient with my defect.

I wait until she falls asleep and announce to her curved ear that this really does feel like love, as a whirl of air lifts the last of the rich, pink paint.

She snores quietly, and a small part of me urges me to wake her and *tell her*, she is so beautiful and good, and I have never —

"I think," I say, and she opens her eyes, expectantly. "I think that we had better get to bed."

She sighs and we stand, brushing off specks of dust and flakes of paint, yawning and downcast.

Goddamn my faint heart.

I MEET WITH Jerry at the Palm and tell him I am going to attach some of Annabel's work to the sequel.

Jerry says I'm thinking with my dick, or he is starting to say so when some of the old illness returns, like a determined criminal.

He can eat shit.

I look at the Hollywood mural, the vaulted wood ceiling, and think of bringing Annabel here.

I get up and throw my napkin down.

"Lunch is on you," I say. "Now find me a few small parts to revitalize this fucking project."

Jerry nods and lowers his head.

I'm getting better, I think, as I slap the valet with my ticket.

I must be in love.

WHEN I GET home, Annabel is standing in front of the window in the bedroom, stroking her suddenly-big belly.

I cough and, startled, she pulls the pillow out from under her dress.

"What are you doing?" I ask nervously.

"Practising," she says. "What if I *can* have children?"

"But I thought you —"

"Is something the matter?" she asks, walking over to me and grabbing a box of condoms out of the drawer on the way.

"No," I say in an unusually high voice.

"Wouldn't you like to throw these out?" she says, biting my ear and squeezing me passionately.

I think of her enormous in a sitz bath, her body marred by fat, wormy lines.

Gross. No.

"Of course," I say, stalling. "But is now a good time?"

"We don't have to have a baby," she says, and my relief is palpable.

I lift and toss her onto the bed and fuck her from behind, pulling out to bust on her back.

I get up and go to the bathroom.

Sing as I clean myself and comb my long, prolific hair.

When I return she is still lying on her belly, her back cradling a basin of fishy goo.

"Get up and clean yourself," I say sharply, and she does.

When she returns, I hold her face, which is puffy and red.

"Are you crying?" I ask, and she says no, but I am lost in a reverie of how her back cracked when I chopped it, of being deep inside her, thinking, *You're my baby, you're all that I need.*

I FEEL TRACTOR-BEAMED into Tiffany's, where I buy a ring—a four-row band of blue diamonds pavé-set in platinum.

I'm too frightened to look at the price. Also, I am too absorbed with planning a romantic proposal.

Cocktails at the Tropicana, then dinner at Mélisse, where I will get on one knee in front of the room, open the robin's egg–blue bag and the black velvet box, and offer her its blazing contents.

She will cry, the room will applaud—

I put the bag on the dash of the Jag and speed home.

Annabel is asleep on the sofa in boxers and one of my T-shirts.

She is bleeding.

I shake her awake: "You have your period," I say.

She looks down and starts to cry.

"Charles will clean the sofa," I call after her magnanimously as she runs upstairs.

But my plans dissipate: I make no calls as I trundle after her, just put the ring in the vault.

I lie down, close my eyes, and hear his voice.

"Who loves me?" he says.

This is how it always begins. I swallow puke and fright.

Annabel walks in and says, "I was bleeding because —"

"I know basic biology," I say, and turn my head.

Hear her run off again, maybe sad, maybe angry.

I'm doing well. Things are good.

MAYBELLINE OFFERS ANNABEL a TV commercial.

The money is insane, she can't say no. But what she does do is insist that they use one of her videos in their TV and digital campaign: she sends a sample short of her swimming naked in a lake of celadon to the tune of "Black Pearl" and they are thrilled.

Annabel is too.

"This will be my mainstream breakthrough," she tells me in bed. Then, sadly, "You seem a little uncomfortable with me lately, anyways. Maybe a bit of time apart will help us? It usually does."

Even hurt, she is all grace: why can't I throw myself at her and babble at her goodness?

I am dumbstruck.

"Maybe it's time," she says, "for me to stand squarely in New York, look that fucking city in the eye, and start over."

"I will miss you terribly," I say. I have fallen asleep listening to her, and she is gone.

I kiss and kiss the *L'Heure Bleue*–soused rupture in her pillow, and wonder what has happened and why it hurts so much.

I AM LOOKING at one of the PETA emails she has signed me up for.

I see a list and wonder: does she know?

Hesitantly, I text her the index of cruelty-free cosmetics and an unhappy face. Maybelline is not mentioned.

"I miss you already," I write. I want to go on and on, but I am still stinging about what she said.

I don't feel uncomfortable with her.

All I can remember are the thrilling things—carrying her up the staircase like Rhett Butler, her resisting faintly in red velvet and crisp white lace, the two of us kidnapping the weeping mastodon from La Brea and releasing it by the Hollywood Reservoir, so many formal dinners, on Turkish beds and tiny, ornate chairs, speeding around the hairpin turn at the end of the Snake, dancing at the Mayan—

I am standing in our bedroom, holding myself, swaying, lightly swaying as all her birds break in and fill the room, diving and coursing, the outrageous show-offs.

"Oh" is the text I get back and I think, *someone's in trouble.*

I MISS HER SO much I can't breathe.

We talk every day, but when she tells me things like, "You said I looked like a pregnant Kardashian that day at the beach," I am mystified.

I tell her I may have a brain tumor and how delicious is an expecting Kim or Kourtney, for that matter?

She warms up, but urges me to make a doctor's appointment.

I do, but it is with a therapist: Dr. Lisa Jain, whose card I find on a bulletin board at the hippie food co-op that Annabel urges me to visit regularly for spelt, amaranth, and freekeh; repulsive-looking vegetables still caked in dirt and covered in scars and blemishes.

There has been a cancellation: I can see Dr. Jain the next day.

Fragments of memory begin to assail me: "Don't you have any friends?" I am shouting at her as she joins me on the sofa to watch a movie.

I don't think it happened? It couldn't have.

The day is shot.

I go back to bed and run my hand along the memory of Annabel, now feeling the mattress, long and slender, C-curved toward me.

"Kiss me," I say to her absence, and my eyes water, I am such a baby.

A baby! I cry, and turn away from the circle we make every night to watch the bright-pink hibiscus on our Juliet balcony crawl toward the sun that looks like a mentally ill person has drawn it — it is a fat, spiked yolk in the center of the pale-blue sky.

"You're such a baby," a cruel voice spits, a girl cries, oh Christ, I said this, I think, my stomach blasting acid, as sleep quickly and safely contains me.

MY FIRST EMAIL from Annabel in New York is a film.

She is leaning against a wall in Spanish Harlem, dressed in a pink body stocking, Docs, and a crown.

A light-blue radio perched on a high windowsill mews the Supremes: *I hear a symphony.*

She starts to move and ten little girls dressed like her appear and dance behind her in a vee.

At the end of the song, she says, "I miss you, boy," and slaps the camera out of her way.

I watch it three times in a row.

"This is good, honey," I write, and delete COME HOME NOW.

Everyone always leaves, I think.

I am watching my mother, tarted up in a clingy dress and pumps, walk down the street.

I am hungry and scared.

I eat noodles I pour into a bowl of hot water and fall asleep holding a kitchen knife.

This time, she is only gone two days.

She is gone five when they find her body in a bedsit in Lewisham, cut up and pulverized, bloated to twice its size.

I GO TO see Dr. Jain, who is slight and almost plain until her big smile pops, showing off deep, fetching dimples.

My hands start to shake. What will she say? That I have murder in my eyes?

She plays something strange she tells me is called *The Drift*. The singer sounds like an old crooner on his deathbed.

I like it.

"Should I start with my childhood?" I ask, reluctantly.

"Start wherever you like," she says, lighting a cigarette and grasping a squeaky plush toy.

"There was a field of poppies," I say, then talk for fifty minutes straight.

Her frown tells me we are out of time.

"I never even got to meeting Lamont Kray," I tell her at the end of it all. "Or my girlfriend's recent departure."

"Let's meet again," she says, and hands me a large blossom she has made by picking at the plies in a tissue.

I slip into the adjacent washroom and am about to toss it when, remembering the pleasure of her quiet company, I fasten it behind my ear with the bobby pin holding it together.

"I miss you," I text Annabel as I hit the street.

"Me too," she writes back. "Talk soon." She adds bee emojis one by one, making a swarm.

I think about her as my iPod shuffles and wails, *anger is an energy*.

When I start my car, my eyes are half-closed and leaky; my flower is askew.

OCCASIONALLY, ANNABEL USED my computer to update her sites.

I open up my photo folder, linger over a bunch of us that she uploaded for me, and watch the racy home movies, mouth ajar.

I see a new file called ham.doc and open it.

It is a video, but unlike any of her other work: it is some kind of puppet show and it is so creepy.

The background music is whatever city noise is seeping through an unseen window: ambulances, blasts of music, brief outbursts, an unpleasant sonic haze.

Dominating the screen are two unfocused figures: a female character—a decapitated rubber chicken on a fork wearing a pink-dotted head wrap—and a male, who is an old, navy-blue Tonka truck.

She jabs at him with one loose tine and he reverses, then flattens her.

The truck trails tin cans, each bearing a name and skull. It dumps a melted plastic baby on the ground that the hen spears, then carries, weeping, to a bowl of water.

"I'm sorry," I write her, and she calls me in the middle of my night.

"I know you don't mean it," she says, and I am not sure that I understand.

Asphodel, bluebell, carnation, daffodil, everlasting daisy—

"Sing to me," I say, and she does.

She sings a murder ballad and I fall asleep before the madman is felled by Wild Elderberry's axe.

When I wake up, she says hello.

She waited for me: my heart almost explodes.

SUMMER IS COMING to an end.

Annabel's Maybelline campaign and her antagonism toward it are a smash hit: she is trailed by little mental patients and elderly captains of industry all day long, fawned over and offered the world by admirers, publishers, filmmakers, and more.

She doesn't care: I have never understood this part of her.

She spends an hour every morning answering lonely, barely literate comments on her social media, but blows off a meeting with Graydon Carter because "his hair makes me nervous" and lunch with Anna Wintour: "What if she's wearing fur?"

Her date request from Drake has me playing Othello, but he is also dismissed with a perfumed note: "I'm afraid I am otherwise engaged," she writes in her fluid script.

I have flown to New York to visit, to watch her at her pink ivory wood desk in a red rippled moiré peignoir, dashing off stories and letters and RSVPs.

I arrive at her hotel late at night, carrying bags of Chinese food and calla lilies.

She takes away the bags and my carryall, places them neatly on the bed, and fucks me in the doorway, murmuring hellos at passing guests.

"Tell me again what you see in me?" I write later on an insane fortune-cookie slip declaring, "Your tight ass will take you far."

I hand it to her as she steps out of the shower, wrapping her wet hair in one of my old T-shirts, one of her model tricks. She laughs and agrees.

I point to the other side of the slim paper, dying of embarrassment.

"I'm not exactly sure," she says, and I feel myself coming apart.

"All I know is that we work together," she says. "And that you are one hot *specimen*."

I scoop her up as she protests, *but we just, my hair my eyelashes I'm late*, and burrow inside of her like a common warthog, snuffling and gratified.

She reclines as if bored but there is no missing the walls of her pussy slamming shut, then open, like a magical iron maiden.

WHEN I RETURN home, I rehire Charles, whom I fired in a rage when Annabel decamped. He has the gardens tended to, the windows washed, dead rats scooped from the pool, and so on.

He takes Fang and Lupe, the dogs, on long walks every day, and Annabel keeps in touch with him and sends things. I overhear him one day saying, "Your mama is sending you both the nice donuts today," and smile, thinking of her taking care of us.

Time drags: Crispin is tweaking the screenplay, and the work that Jerry cherry-picks for me invariably involves me walking into a scene and slapping, choking, or killing one of the principals.

My allure heightens because of this. Rabi visits and shows me hundreds of fan pages, some by adolescent girls, many of which are outright filthy: "I want his boner in my vagina so bad!"

I look like a soft forty-five, at the most: my hair has grown and I wear it in a loosely gathered ponytail; I have a girl at Bloomingdale's teach me how to contour and make my eyes look "like a panther's," she says, batting long, jew-elled lashes.

She is beautiful, but I feel nothing.

I only want Annabel, in the long grass, feeding poppy seeds to ants; arch-Annabel, powdered, parading around in tap pants and red sequined heels; and Annabel Victrix, quickly writing the last line of her book and murmuring it to me: "Having carved my way out of their thrall, I spit at Sid and Alex: *The boys are behind me one hundred percent.*"

When she is away from me, I am left with my muddled memories and calling for Darkling until I lose my voice.

And when she is with me, I turn on her. Not often, but once is often enough. When she was working during my visit, I repented to every priest in·Manhattan and three other boroughs.

When I return, I stand inside the painted golden vault of St. Vincent de Paul and, at last, the queen of heaven fills my arms with poppies.

As I breathe in their smell, Annabel appears with my joyous dog and we chase the sun's poky passage over the sky.

MY MOTHER BECOMES more vivid each day, each night, occupying my dreams with her spatulas and cheese grater, her wooden stick and the rest of the arsenal.

My teachers think I'm an idiot and ignore my bruises and cuts.

"With no father around," one big, boxy old woman says, "it's good your ma is keeping you in line."

The dirty little slapper," she then mock-whispers to another of the teachers. They laugh until I sink my teeth into her fat, furry leg and have to be pried off.

"WHO'S MY BIG man?" my mother says, letting her smoky hair fall into my face.

I had been sound asleep under my bed, having heard footsteps in the hall and pounding at the door earlier.

I tell her and she laughs. "Oh, that was Bernie, he's so madly possessive. He's gone, my lamb."

"Tell me about your night," she says, pulling me onto the bed with her and kicking off her shoes.

"I watched a movie called *White Heat*. It was good."

She doesn't care. She rubs my back, then asks me to rub hers.

I don't want to.

"Why don't you love me?" she says, and is suddenly a whirling dervish, slapping me, stepping on my toys, ripping my drawings from the wall.

"No one loves me!"

"I do," I say. "Please."

"Please, *what*?" she says, knocking everything off my dresser with one swipe.

Please wake up is what I say, and I do.

Then, I tiptoe, *in my own house*, unlock a drawer, and withdraw a bottle of the single-malt Scotch I definitively prefer.

I am drunk in moments, and feeling fantastic.

I select a package of Silk Cuts and light up, feeling my lungs perforate.

I almost call Annabel but ring Charles instead, demanding that he join me for a nightcap.

It is 4 a.m.

He comes to my room and stands in the doorway warily, dressed in his white sateen robe with black velvet piping.

I toss him the bottle and he takes a little sip.

We drink for a while, and I sing for him and get up and do a little soft-shoe number.

"Really impressive, sir," he says, pecking at the bottle.

I slap him on the back and roar, tears zooming from my eyes I am so happy, happy on my hands and knees emptying my stomach, happy braying about demons and desertion and death to no one, for Charles tiptoed away a long time ago.

There is only the lunatic's moon, and me.

GOOD, YES, THINGS are going splendidly.

Crispin is blocked, he says, and is headed to Nepal to "wrap my head around this thing."

Charles, frightened I have fallen in love with him, sets me up with his mother, "for companionship, sir."

She is a bald fossil who speaks in a growl and weaves tapestries of the celestial birth and heraldic death of Princess Diana.

I sit with her every night while she works at her loom and drunkenly adore the work that emerges, the jets of cerulean blue and hammered gold.

Because she is deaf and speaks little English, I never do learn much about her. I tell her how lonely I am, and she rewards me with damp hand-clasps and gentle, commiserating sounds.

She loves *Entertainment Tonight* and one night we watch an episode I PVR'd for her as she puts the finishing touches on a heroic portrait of me dressed as Lawrence of Arabia, riding a camel into a salmon sky.

She shakes out the tapestry, hands it over, and walks away regally, her brittle bones snapping with each step.

I hang it on the rail of the canopy, replacing a nude of Annabel on all fours in a lake of cum. "Milk, it's supposed to be milk," she said.

Okay, I wrap myself in her portrait and pretend it *is* her, crying out, "Oh, my darling!" and "I'm so happy you came back!" until Charles's mother yells at him and he scurries over, tucks me into bed, and pats my face with a cool cloth as I fall asleep, all windmill arms and spazzy legs.

I SLEEP FOR two days, waking to drink the power smoothies that Donna — this is Charles's mother's name — makes for me, eliminating into zip-lock bags that she removes, frowning, yet not angry.

I call her "Mama" one day, and it sticks.

"Go to that doctor," she tells me, and I do. I go to her waiting room and pay her next client to hit the road.

I feel a bit guilty, because the woman had cross-hatched scars on her wrist and a dead animal in her purse, but I'm not feeling very well.

DR. JAIN GREETS me and sits in an enormous beanbag, watching a projection of stars lace the ceiling.

I tell her Annabel has not contacted me in a while. That I read she is making a Maybelline video called *Bunny*, but she has not told me.

"Isn't love strange?" Dr. Jain says, and smiles.

I release all the breath I have been holding — forever, it seems — and throw myself onto the other beanbag.

"It is a miracle," I say, and together we point out the formations and make up names for the ones we don't know.

Twink Majoris. Ursa Andress.

"She's coming home," I say, drifting on my spacecraft.

"How wonderful," she says, and, with some difficulty, we both stand and wave goodbye for now.

"WATCH ME," HER text says.

Tonight is the TV and digital debut of her first Maybelline ad. Teasers of her in a vintage Playboy Bunny outfit are everywhere.

I watch the ad alone, in my bedroom.

It begins with her in the outfit, pink ears alert, being made up with the new "Bunny" palette. Suddenly, her own video starts: an actual rabbit, sick and shaved, is being jabbed with mascara wands and force-fed stalks of lipstick.

Annabel appears in a pink lab coat and cradles the dying creature, closes its blood-red eyes.

The commercial stops and an old one kicks in.

I open my laptop and watch Twitter explode, then jump around, trying to find her.

Which I do.

At LaGuardia, informing a reporter to "tell my baby I'm coming home."

I hurry out to meet the breeder Charles located.

Rush home with flowers and two striped baby rabbits, one black, one white.

When she comes in, they are capering on the bed, eating dwarf carrots and rolling in hay.

"I'm in a bit of trouble," she says, scooping up the white one.

I adjust my eyes to her beauty and tell her how proud I am.

We are careful to avoid our new friends as we tear up the bed and she cries after.

"I wish you loved me," she says.

I blot her tears with one of Jain's tissue flowers and hold her, my darling, twitching bunny.

"You know how my heart beats," I tell her, rocking her to sleep. "We will both be fine," I say, sorry to lie, yet grateful to her for holding on anyway, and anyway.

It is true enough, this cottontailed night.

ANNABEL SLEEPS AND sleeps.

I unpack her things, pausing to watch and fuss over her.

After several hours, I pull out her arts-and-crafts satchel — she likes to make me dioramas, bell jars containing pipe-cleaner lovers and killers running amok under suspended salt-crystal snowflakes, and diminutive chiming tin mobiles, among other delightfully inept pieces that I keep in a box under the bed.

Finding a large piece of bright-red construction paper, I fold it, then cut out a half-heart.

On it, with a gold gel pen, I write:

> Between your legs is
> Alabaster, apricot
> Bee's feet
> Champagne fizz
> Duckling fuzz
> Ebony slit
> Flowers dripping pollen
> Girl goo
> Haute hotness
> Indian milk
> Jams and jellies
> Kisses that enter sighing
> Liquid nirvana
> Monster's milk
> Nest for tiny birds
> Orgasm O's
> Pussy galore
> Queenly dew
> Rills of cyprine

Sluicing salty spume
Two lips, rosy pink
Underwater divers, breathless
Vagina divina
Wet joy
Xtra slick slide
Yarrow — the devil's nettle
Zillions of plays, "Your Sweetness Is My Weakness"

I leave this folded into one of her shoes and am exhilarated. My mind is whole enough for now, I think, as I lie cautiously beside her and then I am reading at the Agora in ancient Greece.

Medu Neter, the gathering whispers, then shouts.

MAYBELLINE TRIES TO sue Annabel, whose contract, composed by her, is bulletproof.

They launch instead a series of infomercials of their laboratories in China, where animal testing is mandatory.

In it, the creatures apply their own contour and rouge, gradations of hot-pink shadow, while hopping around a cage lit up with strobes and glitter balls.

"Zhège hěn yǒuqù!" they say. This is fun.

WE TALK FOR days, calling in for food and clean clothes.

She tells me about walking through Central Park and how she jumped when a boy handed her the handkerchief she dropped by the little castle.

I tell her about my new therapist, whom I want her to meet, and about feeling like a post-surgery Chang or Eng without her.

"Either one," I say, as she shakes her head.

She finds my poem and slips it inside of her bra. I tell her about the alphabet game, and never even having reached F before.

"Fear," she says, handing me a Virginia Woolf book about a painter and the same letters that I swear I'll read later.

Because now she is back and just the same, but more powerful—and more gaspingly beautiful. *Look at your hair, look at your eyes, look, look,* is all I can think to say.

She is happy to spread out on a bed of pillows like my *maja* and let me drink her in to the last heart-shaped (naturally) freckle, located on the lips of her—

I have been indiscreet before.

Better to say that I kissed her in all the tender places I had longed for: firm, yielding places that seem to kiss back.

That at last I fed her truffles, chocolate and rich, fruiting fungus.

WHEN FINALLY WE leave the bedroom, it is to shop at the farmer's market for pinwheel-sized sunflowers and loaves of soft, grain-pocked bread.

A vendor tells her she has a nice ass, and when she ignores him, starts to follow her and calls her a cunt.

I am in the middle of a joyously brutal beating in the parking lot, where I have frogmarched him, when she finds us and pulls me off.

"You're lucky," I say, spitting on his prostrate, fetal-shaped body and shaking some canines loose from my hand.

An elderly man sees me as we re-enter, whistles, and says, admiringly, "Aren't you the pretty boy from *Ultraviolence*?"

"Fuck off, you old fruit," Annabel says as I try to hide my trembling with a fast stride.

We stand holding hands in front of a bin of walnuts.

She pries one open, shakes out the center, and swallows the meat of our terrors.

We decide to see Jain sooner rather than later.

Then I get on my knees, take her hand, and sing Little Dragon's "Don't Cry."

I heard it at the doctor's office. We made felt puppets and everything.

"THE PSYCHOSIS OF Sir John Everett Millais, the crew of the *Red Dragon*, Movie of the Week template, takes an axe to Act Two's inability."

I am reading—discovered under our mattress— Annabel's abstruse diary, berserk in its feminine detritus. It has a pink-and-white candy-striped velvet cover featuring Winnie Harlow as a centauress, a pinking-sheared white silk bookmark, and a lock shaped like a heart that I pick with a metal shaving.

The diary is about writing and nothing more.

Occasionally she scribbles our initials in hearts, sometimes filling an entire page, but I am otherwise absent.

It is, in fact, so devoid of intimacy, I wonder if she knows what diaries are.

I buy one that closes with a lock and toss the key. On the first page I write, "Well, this is daunting!"

Dear Diary,

Having a nice day with my girlfriend, Annabel, who is very pretty and smart.

We may go to the beach tonight and have a bonfire, or stay in and watch movies.

Whatever we do—

I end it like that, as if she has just come into the room, and hide it under one of the bed pillows.

I am nervous for the rest of the day. Will she read it, and amend hers? What *does* she really think of me?

After dinner, she yawns and says, "How about that bonfire?" and I run upstairs, calling back something about a bag of kindling.

I grab her diary and skim the latest entry, dated today.

It reads,

I have been asked to do an ICA talk in London, based on the book. I think I will talk more about the optics in *A Clockwork Orange* and *Ultraviolence*, about the ways in which they—and this is more *Alice* stuff, to be sure—force us to consider <u>perspective</u> in such an unsettling, active (i.e., assaulting the passivity inherent in viewing cinema) way.

I feel like a dick. Even her half-assed line drawing of her lips with my initials on them, floating on a blank page, does nothing to assuage me.

Annabel texts me from downstairs:

How much kindling do we need ffs?

"Coming," I text back, and call Rabi.

I ask him to meet me tomorrow and he sulks for a bit—it has been a while—then says, "Okay, Planet Hollywood at noon."

He hangs up as I wonder: is that really still a thing? I smash one of the guest-room chairs, ball up some pages from one of Mama's Nora Roberts novels, and set back downstairs, confused but still puppyish, love's young nightmare–like.

I HAVE NEVER told anyone I loved them.

Not my mother, not Lola, Allegra, Pudge, Alexander, even Annabel.

It was hard with the kids. They sensed I was holding back and tried wheedling, extortion, and outrageous tantrums to get me to respond to their hopeful, mostly outraged admissions of love.

I deployed verbal trickery. "You too," I would say, or, "Hey, that's so nice to hear."

Allegra said I was gutless.

In the middle of a formal dinner party, her eyes cloud and she says, "I love you, my darling." As the silence grows and grows like a swarm of locusts gathering strength in the distance, I answer, "And I love this papaya-based sauce," swirling my finger around my empty plate as the guests scatter.

"What are you afraid of?" she says, slapping and scratching me as I work very hard to restrain myself. "Of love, of being loved, of being rejected? Which is it?"

"Nothing," I say.

"So what is it then," she says. She sits down, hair unkempt, eyes swollen and running.

Few things are sadder than the truly monstrous, I think, and tell her: "I don't love you or anyone, for that matter, and that's all there is to it."

I show her my steady hands. "Look," I say. "No fear. Not much of anything," and leave her to her manky crying self, walking past my sleeping kids' rooms and thinking, It's not like I *hate* them, then walking out.

One of our guests, a well-built redhead whose husband is home ill, is waiting on the porch.

"I knew you'd come," she says, and we climb into the back seat of her car, where I lift her spangled dress and fuck her ass and molest her tits until I do.

She, more dreary tears, more talk of love, does not.

"DO I LOVE Annabel?" I ask Rabi at the Backyard, my choice, my treat, where we are pinned by the sun, miserably fighting off striped throw pillows on a blindingly blue sofa.

The dazzling blonde waitress doesn't ask him for ID, even though he has chosen to wear a terry-cloth shirt, baggy jean shorts, and suede booties.

He smokes and speaks with such authority, he is never challenged. He even gets the girl's number.

"You're nine years old, what do you want with that?" I say, irritably. The girl doesn't appear to know I exist.

"Don't worry about me," he says.

We sip horchatas and I tell him about Annabel's diary, and how I don't love anyone.

He stares at me like I'm stupid.

"Not her diary," he says. "That's a decoy."

Goddamn.

"You love everybody, suckhole."

"I do not," I say, and he is all over me, tickling and jabbing me, demanding I say it, *say it!*

"All right, I like you!" I say, out of breath and cross.

"I know you're lying, yaar, but to say love is hard for you. I get it," he says, and, as I protest, slaps down cash over the check. "Love means pain, no matter how good it is."

He's right, as always. "If I *could* feel that way," I say, "you'd be in the top five."

"Get outta here," he says, and laughs as the blonde returns in her street clothes and pulls him to his feet.

"I could just eat you up," she says.

"That's the plan," he says, and leaves me alone with my thoughts and what will become a disfiguring sunburn that Annabel laughs at and covers with zinc, while I brood about her real diary and its whereabouts.

MEANWHILE, ANNABEL AND I have started to see Jain often, and I once more get my drinking under control.

At Annabel's insistence, I hire a team to manage my finances. On the same day, I bring home a tiger cub I have named Sandy and take him for a walk on a jewelled leash in tight leatherette shorts and a diamond sun visor.

Everything is returned, by me, as my girlfriend pinches my ear—except Sandy, who is taken directly to Tippi Hedren's Shambala Preserve and donated to the animal sanctuary with both a hefty maintenance check and the name of the Craigslist lunatic who sold him to me out of the back of his pickup truck.

I am lectured about conflict-free diamonds versus blood diamonds, animal trafficking, gluttony, and invidiousness.

Told to mend my relationship with my daughter and there'll be no more sex for me until the harridan I call my girlfriend says so!

I rebel, naturally. Once more, I drive to Vegas and, just as I spot a glimmering roulette wheel, a stupefying showgirl, and a tray of chilly martinis, she calls.

"Baby, please come home," she says.

Home. The word hits me like a silver striker on a still triangle.

"I'm lonely for you," says Annabel. She says it again and by then I have already grabbed my keys from the valet. I am slamming my foot down on the gas and heading toward the voice that begins in the base of her throat—

It is a lustrous black bird with long, curved flight feathers in mid-ascent.

I am flying to this voice, which starts as deep, desiring tympani, and bumps its pitch higher and higher into her own string-crossed cries; cries I match with the blood in my heart, the blood pouring back and forth into the smaller chamber,

a white jug, painted with pink roses, bearing her name

ANNABEL, IN A batiste shift and chiming ankle bracelets, greets me at the door and wraps her legs around my waist.

"I came home," I say, carrying her up the stairs.

"I'm so glad," she says, and when I lay her on the bed she is all girl — open and warm and candy-sweet in her readiness for me.

I CALL PUDGE.

She is living in Sacramento and burning through her money on cosmetic procedures and the Petrossian Royal Ossetra caviar and Dom Pérignon her fancy man likes with each meal.

Allegra has called me to tell me this, worried about her daughter and, for once, wanting me to intercede.

"The prison job lasted a week," she says. "Christine looks like an enormous Joan Rivers. And that man! My God, he's a lard-ass too, a gigolo and a cokehead."

"I've never seen a fat cokehead," I say, genuinely intrigued.

"Would you *please* just talk to her?" she says, and I promise that I will.

"Pudge!" I say when she answers the phone sleepily at 3 p.m. "If you do not stop spending money like a drunken sailor on shore leave, and if you let that eurysome villain stay with you a minute longer, I will have you taken care of by professionals."

"You've been in too many B movies, Dad," she says, adding a sarcastic spin to this sparse term of endearment.

But her voice is shaking.

"All right, kid. You were warned."

I hang up and make a few more calls, humming.

Annabel comes into the kitchen and smiles.

"Did you tell her you loved her?" she asks.

"No, that's not going to happen. But I helped her. And I'm about to help a lot more."

She squeezes me and we change and go to La Scala. She wears a vintage black faille Balmain gown with a melon-pink peekaboo lining and jewelled Miu Miu heels; I wear a black Brioni suit with a flowered chiffon shirt and striped Balenciaga tie.

The waiter is obsequious: we are impressive. People take covert photographs and rehearse their approach to our table.

"*Vorremmo che l'insalata verde, e alcuni spaghetti al pomodoro e basilico,*" I say. "*Per secondi, la melanzane alla parmigiana, e mousse al cioccolato per dessert. Sì, e una bottiglia di 2010 Brunello di Montalcino, grazie.*"

"Was that your way of ordering lamb chops?" she says as my phone vibrates, and I excuse myself.

I slip into the cloakroom to listen to this voice mail:

"Dad! I'm in the hospital with a broken arm and my boyfriend, Atlas, is gone! My money is gone too, what am I supposed to do?"

I text:

Inch by inch, life's a cinch. Yard by yard, life is hard.

Then I return to the table, feeling mellow, and swirl the wine in my mouth, feeling it address each of my taste buds by name and in turn.

"Two thousand and ten," I say to the sommelier, "a good year."

He agrees in a near-frenzy and I think, For *wine*. I sip

from my glass, hold my girlfriend's hand. I feel I am through with the past.

"We have arrived at last," I say, as the cameras start clicking and Annabel reluctantly poses, flashing the smile that keeps the Colgate dividends arriving, and clinging to me possessively.

I shoot my cuffs over my scars and beam also.

Life is beautiful.

PUDGE SELLS HER story to TMZ. When I am asked to comment, I say, "I don't give a fuck," and advance on their mobile team, a clip that is played and replayed online.

Which serves to make me seem more dangerous, and more cool, and my fan base drops in age and rises in number.

None of this pleases Annabel, or "Parnell's ladyfriend."

"You were supposed to make things better," she says.

"I did," I protest. "She was ruining her life." I grab her. "Can't we be a family, just us? I want to start over."

She chews on her ragged lips. There are dark circles under her eyes; she is thinner than usual.

"Pudge called you a gold-digging cum-dumpster," I say, and she makes a flicking gesture.

Says, "Fine. It's just us, now."

That night, I find the real diary in a laundry hamper.

It is a plain Mead notebook filled with shopping lists and the occasional reference to events and dates.

I call Rabi, triumphant.

"*Chutiya*," he says. "That's decoy number two."

I add TRUTH to one of the lists, then feel stupid and cross it out.

What is she hiding?

"ARE YOU ANGRY at Annabel for poisoning Mr. Kray?" Dr. Jain asks, smiling as if pleased by my girlfriend's ingenuity.

"No," I say, taking Annabel's hand. "She was trying to protect me."

"And Annabel, are you angry about Parnell's actions?"

"It excites me," she admits. "No one has ever loved me, not like he does."

After a weighted pause, Jain remarks that we seem very comfortable with violence.

She has no idea.

"Do you hurt each other?" she says, and we chew on that for a while.

"He gets a bit rough in bed," says Annabel finally. "But I'm rougher."

Annabel lifts up my Death Row T-shirt to reveal a kaleidoscope of bruises and lash marks.

Jain stands and traces the damage with her cool fingertips.

"It is not my place to judge," she says, "but—"

Taking out an old Polaroid camera, she shoots a picture and writes MAP on the tab below.

Over my wounds, she draws fluffy, leporine arrows, pointing up and out.

"Refer to this as the way out of hell, if you like," she says.

Annabel holds out her wrists, which are also scarred, but deeper and more efficiently.

"From missing you," she says, and I go to her as our doctor says, "Cheese," and makes one last map.

WE GO HOME and she wears her holster, black thigh-high boots, and nothing else.

She whips me and cleans the raised lines later in the tub, and when she goes to her dressing room, I follow.

I arrive in time to see her adjusting the large framed photograph of Ondine, in *Chelsea Girls*, over her dresser.

Later, when she is watching some tedious Agnès Varda film, I slip upstairs, move the picture, and find the safe.

I don't have the combination, but the real diary must be in here.

I text Rabi: "BINGO."

"Third decoy?" he texts back, and I am deflated, then taken aback by a shot of him and the blonde waitress, whom he is riding around his living room, on a saddle strapped to her back.

"Is that even legal?" I text, and he responds, "Stop jellying. Find the book."

"Daddy?" says Annabel, and I whirl around, pantless and scared.

"I was just ordering you something sparkly," I say, and she is pleased.

"Look what I got you," she says, unclasping a bulky platinum chain from her waist.

"I look dope," I say, and her eyes widen. "I mean," I start maundering before she closes my mouth with an amused kiss.

WHEN WE WAKE up, it is 1 a.m. and we can't sleep.

We look at our phones, and she shows me a shot of Pudge, baggy and blonde, her nose bobbed to the size of a thimble.

"My father is an evil and dangerous man" is the caption, and I shake my head.

"What is she talking about?" Annabel says.

"Some horror of a Barbie I neglected to buy her, in all likelihood," I say.

I would have bought her anything back then, but the way Pudge asked! It was like being swarmed by those awful little bugs that live for one day and never stop advancing.

"I had the best Barbie collection when I was eight," says Annabel. "My mom's co-worker's kid died and I got all of her stuff. There was even a canopy bed."

I almost ask how the little girl died, but she is so happy.

"That was my second-favorite year," she says.

"What was your first?" I ask, knowing she will say this one, and that I have the code for her safe.

THE THIRD DIARY is frightening.

It is a black notebook bound in elastic bands and covered in silver imprecations and dire warnings.

I open it trepidatiously, and it is empty.

Except for this:

STOP LOOKING FOR MY DIARIES OR ELSE.

I almost laugh, it is so childish, but a part of me has always been afraid of her and her strange magic.

I will stop.

For now.

The TV, always set on an entertainment channel, announces, "Comeback Star Parnell Wilde's Daughter's Explosive Revelations!"

Not again.

After a number of sickening commercials for candied pig snouts, comical rectal thermometers, and kale-flavoured condoms, the revelations unfold.

"I have been to a therapist," a much-altered Pudge announces. She is finally thin. Loose-skinned but thin, in a ruffled brown bodysuit and, inexplicably, an eyepatch.

"She put me under. And told me, she told me."

She stops, covers her face with her hands, resumes.

"That he molested me. He's not my biological dad, but still. I can barely look at myself," she says.

The female host puts her arm around her shoulder, and Pudge looks bravely forward.

"I'm not afraid of you anymore, Dad!" she says while tousling her frizzy yellow hair.

"Just disgusting," the male host says in closing, and I leave the room to find Annabel watching the same show in the bath.

"Pervert," she says, and I gasp.

Then she blows me a bubble kiss and says, "As if."

I climb in with her, fully clothed and shaking. She strokes my face and sings broken old country songs about black-hearted ladies and male tramps bearing raccoon-skin coats and frogs in black velvet boxes.

I CANNOT DEAL with this.

Annabel can.

She wards off Allegra and finds Pudge.

"Tell me what his cock looks like," she demands.

"Like . . . a small pencil!" she says, picking up her hotel-room phone to call security.

"A small pencil," Annabel repeats so scornfully that Pudge puts the phone down. "What else can you tell me?"

"He touched me, he made me touch him!"

"Bitch, he did not," Annabel says. "Why are you making up this *shit*?"

"Because he never pays attention to me, because he ruined my life, all right?"

It is better than all right: Annabel has recorded the outburst.

It's harder to undo damage than create it, but she is a hot sell, and several of the big outlets invite her to play her recording and talk.

She does, and she looks straight in the camera when she says, "It's like a club. Or a mutant cucumber — with a cute little birthmark, but I'm not saying what *that* looks like, just in case."

The hosts are uncomfortable but Annabel is so charming, such an ingenue in her checked pink dress and white Mary Janes, that they smile.

I smile at home, watching her.

The mark, it's a star.

I want it between her legs so badly I can't stand it.

On TV, her lips part and I know she is thinking the same thing.

"Isn't Mr. Wilde twice your age?" someone asks.

She replies, "More than that!"

And then, "He is so much more than that," in this breathy voice that leads the host to shift in his seat and end the segment.

She walks away and he watches, along with millions of viewers. Knowing this, she flips up her skirt, shows her bare bottom, and causes a Twitter spike, #wildeass, that persists for hours.

"I'm sorry you are such a miserable person," I write to Pudge, and have Charles bring a box of new Barbies to her hotel.

His mother has died. After learning her story, I sent her to visit her lover in Barcelona, and after a long, happy reunion, she never woke up.

Charles is devastated. Pudge, sensing this, kisses him and yes—

My daughter, long story short, is now happily married to my butler.

PUDGE MOVES IN and shares the cottage with Charles.

Love suits her.

She lets her hair grow back to its natural chestnut color, gains a bit of weight, which Charles loves, and starts making nervous and sincere visits to me and Annabel, whom she comes to see as a sister.

They talk about clothes and men and Regency romance novels, and I lose most of my *froideur*.

The day my daughter bakes me a cake shaped like an S and says it means she is sorry, I am happy enough.

I cut into the curve and eat a big lemon-gooey chunk.

"It's all right," I say, hugging her as I pat and pat all of the tears and shudders away.

For this little while, it is all right. Better than that.

Then I start filming *Deadly Nightshade* and find the final diary.

And we see Jain for the last time together as Annabel, caked in makeup, is coaxed to reveal the bruise covering her eye and cheekbone.

She says, "Don't you understand? He loves me."

I cast around, trying to match the cuts on my knuckles to the atrocious purple starfish on her face.

She hits me, when did I start? She cut me and I knocked her off of me, and kept hitting—

I see my hand as a fractal; I see the larger shape of my illness—

Amnesiac, batterer, cunt, dumb fuck—the letters are falling away.

Dr. Jain—Lisa—stops smiling, and says she cannot see us again.

"I see how this all ends," she says. "It cannot be otherwise, and it is too sad for me."

She hands us knitted facecloths at the door and says that ideally, love is kindness, sweeping like a clock's hand across fear and pain.

I attend to a worried, distressed Annabel with one of the cloths, soaked in witch hazel, and say that I never meant to hurt her, that all will end well, as she watches enormous seabirds through the window and sits in their sovereign shadows.

But hell rapidly breaks loose, and I disappear.

You will see me soon enough: sitting at Hollywood and Vine in a torn, crappy Michael Jackson costume, with a Styrofoam cup in front of me and enough liquor inside of me that I slosh when I moonwalk.

FOUR

PARNELL, SKID ROW, 2018
(THE WORLD) WILL BEAT YOU TO YOUR
KNEES AND KEEP YOU THERE

I AM SLEEPING on a big white painted polka dot in Leimert Park, with a newspaper blanket and inflated-plastic-bag pillow, dreaming that I have rented an empty apartment in Paris, with big covered windows, a mattress, a ladder.

Annabel leans against the wall, shirtless, in tight jeans. Her hat, black with red roses, lies on the bed with her fleecy white coat.

I am kicked awake by a cop. "You want to get killed?" he says. "Move along."

I get up and start walking.

Make it to Melrose as the sun rises, and dodder along, my head filled with Annabel, a deck of images I squeeze in the middle and speed-shuffle: her kind, limpid eyes; her lush vegetable hair; the tiny freckle below her left eye she sometimes embellishes with a pink pencil.

I am staring into a shop called SLTS, at three mannequins dressed in leather masks hitting each other with whips.

"Parnell?"

No, *no*, not this.

It is an admirer, some jackass dressed like Sid aiming a camera at me.

"Looking good," he says cheerfully, even though I am grimy and dressed in a child's ski jacket, wide-wale, flared yellow cords, and one gaping shoe.

I have to make him stop.

"I read that you broke up with your lady," he says. "I'm sorry, she is *bad*."

I do the worst thing I can think of to stop him.

I shit in my hand.

A tour group of elderly women start crying.

I say, "Okay, ladies, let's get *information*." Then I laugh, beat up the Sid guy, break his camera, and run.

What happened?

Listen to many, speak to a few.

Listen to me, just listen to me.

ENTR'ACTE

PARNELL AND ANNABEL,
THE PACIFIC PALISADES, 2018
THERE CRACKS A NOBLE HEART

IT IS ANNABEL'S birthday in two days.

"A pony, a dragon ring, my name tattooed over your heart, a first edition of *Dubliners*—"

She is sleepily listing the things she wants. I tell her she is getting a coupon for a perm in the Valley and a set of golf clubs if she doesn't stop.

"You talk then," she says.

I hold her and graze her hair.

I say, "When I was in elementary school, I made a picture for art class: the world, with NO ONE HERE GETS OUT ALIVE lettered over it. My teacher told the principal, who asked if everything was all right at home. It wasn't, but I told him that my picture was not about my life."

"What was it about?" she says, laying a hand on my belly.

"The fact that we all die, but don't believe it will happen."

"You don't think?"

"No. And we don't seem to realize that there are worse things than dying. We can live so poorly, so swinishly, that a long nap in a satin-lined coffin is, relatively, not so bad."

"Tell me that when you're dead," she says, and laughs.

"Promise to sing 'Baby Got Back' at my funeral?"

"You're joking," she says, and bursts into tears.

Annabel: my arms filled, always with flowers—

"Don't die," she says, and practically breaks my neck, holding me as she falls asleep.

She would walk down the street and sick, miserable old men would brighten, open their rusted-out throats and sing "She's a Rainbow."

Annabel, walking in colors with the juice of peonies between her legs, behind her ears.

At the end of her rainbow is me, is nothing. At the end of my rainbow—

"Don't *you* die," I say as I try to make her small, so small that I can hold her, my wild little wren, in my hand.

She breathes and tiny painted eggs spill from her mouth, she breathes her birdsong and spins the *Saliera*, a vitreous enamel vessel where we, *terra e mare*, repose in gold, in ivory, and brood over our baluts.

ANNABEL IS BUSY with the party planner, so I go driving around aimlessly and then see a fortune teller in Tarzana.

I listen to the woman ramble on about curses and my flair for numbers, smack her *gypsy fortune teller*'s hand off its crystal ball and grab it—she is as much Roma as I am.

Tell her that I think I am in love and keep talking, staring into her frightened eyes, until I mention that my son raped my girlfriend—well, my fiancée, I guess.

I am thinking of how I plan to propose during dessert tomorrow night.

The dumpy lady in veils pulls her hand away.

"Why was your son dressed like you?" she asks, her eyes suddenly shrewd.

I look back, warily.

"He wasn't. He was dressed as a character I played."

"A character she thinks is sexy. Who made her climax during the rape," she says.

"How could you possibly know that?" I say angrily.

"How do you think?" she says, and laughs at me.

Enough is enough.

I reach for her as she smiles lazily and leans back in her chair.

My hands fall to my sides, defeated, and I turn to leave.

"Don't go away angry," she says.

I run off and stand by her door, breathing hard.

It's all coming undone, I think, as my heart rumbles dangerously.

At home, Annabel kisses me hello.

"Did my son make you hot?" I ask.

She slaps me so hard my head hits the door.

"Well, did he?" I call after her as she runs up the stairs.

I do not follow.

Instead I stand in a scalding shower swatting at images of my girlfriend conjoined with my son, of her jerking off later, her head filled with him.

When I have dried off and am smoking, wrapped in a towel, in the kitchen, Annabel comes in and hands me a book.

"It's a journal," she says, named *Signs*. "I wrote about this," she says, pointing to the table of contents and to her article, "Reverse Cowgirl."

"It's about rape and anatomical politics," she says, nervously twisting the hideous puce cover until it tears. "And about—"

"I can read," I say mildly.

"The pleasure is involuntary," she says, so quietly I can barely hear her.

I pretend I can't, and say everything is fine; shoo her away so I can change.

She leaves and I flick *Signs* away. It was different when it was rape. I could only imagine tears and pain. Not pleasure.

She makes me sick.

It is the beginning of the end.

O heart, lose not thy nature, let me be cruel.

I USED TO think that I was afraid everyone would laugh at me. Then everyone did, and it was bad, but not unbearable.

Annabel, I know what I am afraid of.

CRISPIN WRITES TO me: he is back at work, and I will "dig" what he is doing.

"Sid meets a woman, this martial artist–slash–neurosurgeon, drop-dead gorgeous," he says when we talk. "He falls in love for the first time. *But the chick dies.*"

"Why?" I say.

"Because it's a revenge tragedy. No happy endings."

I see myself holding Annabel's dead body, racked with remorse, breaking open the sky with my grief.

Then I remember that I can change the script—or can I?

"Keep writing," I say, and get out of the car.

I am the new face of Fendi, and have some ads to shoot.

"WHY DON'T YOU model anymore?"

"I didn't like it. Neither did you. You told me it made you sick to think of all these guys jerking off to me in their wives' magazines."

"You were so pretty," I say.

"Were?"

She still is, but I miss seeing her in priceless dresses, laced in jewels and posing in magical gardens, held aloft by Green Berets at the center of a bloody riot.

And I *was* jealous.

I wanted her to make *me* beautiful.

Sensing this, she tells me how good I look in my pale-pink shirt and red jeans, how rich and shiny my hair is.

Then, how deep I am inside of her, that it hurts, but don't stop, she pleads.

Did she feel like this with Alex?

When I left the fortune teller's apartment, I went to the call girl's place and fucked her for the first time. Hard, over a table, and she said the same stuff about my cock, and moaned the same, and came just as hard as Annabel does.

"Why can't she be you?" I say to Annabel that night, Annabel whose face I have buried in a pillow.

She can't hear me.

I shudder to a stop and feel sick. All I can think about is my son as Sid, making her pussy wet for the first time—

Taking her first.

I'M A MONSTER.

I can't look at Annabel anymore, or talk to her.

I hate her cowlike confusion and sadness.

Late that night, blistering drunk, I call a distress center while she sleeps and tell a volunteer named Miss Pringle the whole story.

"The body is a dumb slab of meat," she says. "Pound it, and it feels pain. Tweak it, and it feels pleasure."

"She has a brain," I say.

"Do you?" says Miss Pringle, and I am stumped.

"Your girlfriend's reactions *just happened*, pantywaist."

"Pantywaist?" I am lying on the floor, numb.

"Your virility is threatened by the violence your bastard son committed."

"I'm in distress!"

At least I thought I was. I stand up, slowly.

"*She's* in distress."

I let the phone fall out of my hand and go lie down beside Annabel. She sits up and her face is a mask of fury.

"I heard you," she says, flicking my face steadily and sharply.

"I'm sorry," I say, and start to panic.

"No, don't be. It's a legitimate concern. Your son was gorgeous."

I stand and start to back away.

"And you know how it is, right? Didn't you feel good when Kray fucked you?"

"What are you talking about?" I say. Looking down, I see I am gray.

"You know what I'm talking about, you old twink."

She is magnificent, really. Kneeling on the bed nude, pointing at me with her long red talons.

"Not true," I bleat, reaching wildly for something to hold on to.

There is nothing. I fall down, and the ambulance ride is the same as the last one except she declines to join me, or to visit throughout the many lonely nights in my empty room.

I BREAK DOWN and call Rabi. I ask him to bring me a contraband wet bar and he does, along with a bouquet of daisies.

He and I watch Oz, Dr. Phil, then Ellen. Three days in a row.

"Ellen is so happy. It's infectious," he says, and I cannot agree more.

"I hope that glass addict moves out of her mother's house," he says. "What did Phil say?"

"He said that we make our own happiness in life."

"Yes, that's it. Phil!"

My machines beep and hum. We are careful not to mention Annabel.

I concentrate on forgetting what she said, the crazy bitch.

SHE TAKES EVERYTHING: her clothes and cosmetics, her books, music, pictures, pillows, kitchen stuff, sheets, drapes, chair, desk, and all of the animals.

Except the psycho Komodo dragon, who is clearly desperate to kill me. I have a comfortable muzzle designed and sleep with the beast, I am that lonely.

All that she leaves is the real diary, next to a bottle of good Scotch and a carton of American Spirits.

"Enjoy your suicide," a notecard says.

It is taped to one of those awful Moleskine notebooks.

It is full. I don't open it.

I pour a drink and start screaming.

WHEN I WAS still on the streets, Kray talked to the admissions board at RADA and to Welthorpe, the director of my first film, as well.

At that time, he was in a closeted relationship with Simon, his very pretty thirteen-year-old boyfriend, a jealous little queen who forbade him from so much as looking at anyone else.

And Kray never did. He was in love with Simon, and tortured by his heroin overdose. Simon died on Kray's property, and two of his men dumped the body on the street corner where they met. This was shortly before Lola left me, and Kray invited me to stay with him while we shot *Ultraviolence*.

At the back of Kray's palatial property, I have my own little cottage — still filled with Simon's S/M accessories, perfume bottles, and movie magazines. I feel cautiously hopeful about a new life.

I start looking for my own place, and dating, occasionally.

And then Kray has his first small stroke. It changes him: his cruelty, usually seen only in glimmers, has mushroomed.

The night he returns from the hospital he wakes me with a slap.

"Who loves me?" he says, and rapes me, with extreme force.

It doesn't occur to me to fight. I close my eyes tight until all I can see is a hazy white zero floating in black space.

My cock gets hard and my prostate twitches. My body disgusts me.

He rapes me again, and when I protest, feebly, he uses a metal bar while pounding my face.

When I won't wake up, he drags me to his car and to a clinic known to him.

I fall in and out of consciousness.

In the car, he says, "I thought you were tough. Stop crying." He asks for a particular doctor, who is on call, and curses when Dr. Kalita emerges.

Kray decides to bluff: "The faggot is hemorrhaging on my good bedding," he says. "I don't care what he and his little friends do, but now he's gone too far."

Dr. Kalita must see the misery in my eyes. He brings me into one of the curtained rooms—"*Alone*, sir"—and conducts a lengthy, very careful examination.

"This must stop," he says, and sends me out, after kindly pressing my shoulder.

I don't know what he says to Kray. I hear shouting, and he emerges, wide-eyed with: what? Is he afraid?

I am transferred to a hospital to heal. I have deep fissures and broken bones, and my teeth are gone—these are replaced with expensive, pearlier ones.

Kray never touches me again. He *says* things, but even then—having developed a tic—he looks around for the surveillance equipment he tells the crew is everywhere.

"You're on in five, princess," Kray says, and we shoot the last scene of *Ultraviolence*, which J. Hoberman will say is "like discovering Jacobean theater for the first time: vile, lofty, harrowing, exultantly London-based, as 'No clime breeds better matter for your whore.'"

In this scene, Sid avenges himself. He shoots all of his enemies in Whitechapel after lining them up in an alley and firing a machine gun into the night sky.

They fall slowly as he slide-steps back into the street, dropping his gun.

He crouches, then leaps for joy.

The cast and crew burst into applause: a heavy rain had blown in out of the blue, and I acted through it. The scene is perfect.

Kray makes me do it sixteen more times, using the first take in the end.

At the wrap party, he puts his arm around me and says, "Why do you think your little friend didn't call the cops?"

I don't answer. Shrug him off.

"Because he has eyes on me!" he says. "He's in deep with the filth, that bastard."

He smells cops, and wants me out. I am a serious liability. In my haste to get away, I don't even pack a bag.

I know the doctor has scared the mercifully paranoid Kray, and I thank him and I thank him still.

I find a room downtown and entertain in it like Caligula, and you know the rest: Kray's renewed interest in working with me, my move to California, his role in my ruin.

My retrograde amnesia, cured all right, by Annabel's departure

And whenever I speak of Kray, I say, "The man saved my life."

It is what I told Annabel, early on.

"Cut the shit," she said, and tenderly kissed me, moving me to cry out, hurting, happy, maybe.

I STAY IN bed, not moving, eating, or drinking.

I remember everything: every sound, texture, and smell.

I fish a receipt from my pocket and read the writing on the back of it: "Rape is retardation, the cessation of growth that posits violence as a membranous sac of seeds, tiny lashings."

The receipt lists

1. Two whiskey sours, neat, with Bing cherries
2. Three bottles of Tsingtao
3. Plain white side dish. Customer has decorated it, and insists the plate is his (no charge)
4. Shot: Jägermeister
5. Shot: B-52
6. Irish Car Bomb
7. Large curly fries
8. Four (bald) hamburger buns
9. Dry martini
10. Potato: customer is moved by its "dear face" (no charge)
11. Three pepper shakers: customer has named them "Dear Friend," "My Sweetheart," and "Annabel" (no charge)
12. Glass of champagne
13. Jar of customer's tears, labelled by customer: "Love's Marinade"

$70.00
Thanks!
Heather ☺

Having misplaced my wallet, I hitchhiked to the bar with a teenage girl, who cried the whole way and kept asking me if she was fat until I said, "You are so thin I cannot see you. Are you a ghost?"

"Thin," she said, and cried harder.

Through her grateful tears, I heard her say "the first time" and when she dropped me off and drove away, I thought, "Where have I heard that before?"

Oh yes, Annabel's sexy triumph. It is so painful even to recall the caption of this memory.

I concentrate on the jacaranda blossoms framing the doorway, then I see an entire street in Santa Ana, where she and I once spent a weekend, filled with masses of the bluish-purple blooms. There were so many the sky appeared limp from elbowing its way through.

And the sweetness of the smell! We filled our hands and lay in them later, a little unwisely: they are a sticky collision of honey and egesta.

When their seeds let loose they floated upward; they looked like what a plaintive Annabel called—I don't want to remember. In miniature—

Dead babies.

Annabel in the middle of the night, carrying a tiny, ornate box; the sound of a shovel ringing against stone, dirt on her hands—

Singing of young hearts; standing still before the night bird's song.

Resting my cheek on the stucco wall by the entrance, I call Jerry for some money.

"You sound strange. Are you all right?"

I pull the pocket watch Annabel gave me from my vest; it is inscribed Sweet Daddy, after the Hank Williams song I like to yodel in the shower.

Lord I love to hear her when she calls me sweet—

I tell him I am fine, just late, very late, and return to the hotel bar, where I keep drinking steadily.

Jerry arrives with one of his sturdy colleagues and they settle the bill as I jump into his car and peel out.

They try to stop me but I am like a frantic greased pig in search of a tiny corner of the world where I might rest unmolested.

PUDGE AND CHARLES are in Spain on a bus tour. She has left me casseroles, clean towels and sheets, and a number where they can always be reached.

I ignore everything, push the furniture against the locked door, and manage to have belated birthday flowers delivered to Annabel's apartment.

She will rip the heads off the roses and throw them out the window, giving passersby tender premonitions and vivid new Ascot hats.

I DIAL HER number and hang up, every few minutes.

Finally she answers and I say, "How did you know what Kray did?"

"First tell me you liked it," she says, and I find a clean razor and cut words into my wrists in her beautiful Spanish.

I write DIRTY and WHORE and PLEASE until the blood pours out like a tide and drowns these sorrows.

As I cut, I ask, "How can you be so cruel?"

"You started it," she says, the fucking infant, and I drop the phone into the forest of burning trees, into the bloody maw of a Bengal tiger—

When I awake, feverish from my floor nap, I use an old hotel sewing kit to stitch myself together, splashing rubbing alcohol on the cuts.

I am sorry to wrap my skillfully iterated truth in bandages, but the thread keeps coming loose, and beneath my request—please know that I attacked you because I could not face myself—is a chilling glitter of bone.

Later, she writes to say she is sorry, and that she knew because we are the same person. "The same, but post-mitosis now. Good luck," and this is goodbye.

The dragon stares at me, furious, and drops dead.

I bury him in the backyard in a matte-black shoebox his mistress left behind and recite from *'Tis Pity She's a Whore*.

> Soranzo: *Did you but see my heart, then would you swear—*
> Annabella: *That you were dead.*
> Giovanni: *That's true, or somewhat near it.*

My eyes moisten. He was a brave little man, who never got over Annabel. He has my complete sympathy. I scatter the sun roses he liked to chew on and spike the ground with a cross I have painted with cool red flames over his name, *Tommy*.

Her idea, as with all the small, lovely things.

AFTER THREE DAYS of blinding pain, with no medicine or food, just handfuls of warm tap water, I change my bandages, put on my jeans and boots, layer a sweatshirt over a flannel and T-shirt, and head out after wrestling with the furniture jammed against the door.

I bring nothing but a plastic 7-Eleven bag containing my envelope of treasures, which now includes tiny nail clippings and a flower from the dragon's grave.

As I leave, I take a look around.

Annabel has left a few little things: tortoiseshell hairpins that I smell and reverently slide into the envelope, a hot-pink thong and white camisole I stuff in my pocket, and an almost empty bottle of Mitsouko whose contents I pour into the hollow of my throat.

And Tubby. We play with him less lately, but he is still smartly dressed in a red slicker and matching rain boots, an outfit I picked out after a two-day storm — the weather was so dangerous we holed up and made squiggly pasta and watched old movies and —

The little bear is in the trash.

My heart twangs ominously. I move to pick it up but all I see is her, dripping wet and burnt caramel–colored, her strong, concave thighs open, exposing the pouched, purple lips of the slipper orchid between her legs.

I leave the toy in the garbage and go.

THE CARRIER BAG contains paper towels, glass cleaner, oil soap, a sponge, and a bucket of hot water.

I go to her apartment and spend a couple of hours cleaning her door, doormat, and peephole, remembering the time she cleaned my place. I have to rest for a while: I am weak and sick.

Finally, I struggle to get up, and I am hanging a PLEASE DISTURB sign on her door with my number scratched on it when a slip of paper shoots out from beneath it.

"Get lost," it says in her ornate script.

I do, leaving the bucket in the elevator.

I hear someone say, "Bucket taking a ride," as I hurry to the heavy doors and let them whoosh me outside.

AND SO I roam the streets, starving and burning for something to drink.

I write FAMOUS ACTOR on a piece of cardboard and sit on Sunset, declaiming speeches from *Hamlet* but also selections from *The Love Boat*, a show I appeared on in my decline.

I played a car salesman henpecked by his boorish wife who meets an actual mermaid in the moonlight.

"I want to be with you, Sally," I recite, as people hurry past. "I will jump in the water and grow glorious gills!"

After several hours, I have enough money for a pizza slice and a few shots of Wild Turkey at some dump on Fairfax.

An old barfly latches on to me, eventually recognizing me.

"You're a famous guy," she says, puffing her chest out. In her dingy white angora sweater, she looks like a barnyard hen. "What are you doing here?"

"I am scourging myself," I say, letting my fingers walk on her thin, divoted thighs.

"I have a place near here," she says, tracing her stubble-fronted lips with her short, coral-colored nails.

She reminds me of Siobhan, only worse, so much worse.

I say, "That sounds like a suitable punishment."

She doesn't seem to hear me: "Let's do this," she says brightly.

I get into her dirty, oily bed, flinging aside a few slices of luncheon meat and a cigarette end.

I watch her strip to her beige support pants and tan bra and attend to her when she joins me, eating her cheesy pussy, squeezing her deflated breasts until she cums, pissing in my face.

"Sorry," she says, lighting a cigarette. "I got carried away."

I mop my face with the burgundy sheet and smile. "Don't apologize," I say.

I go to her bathroom and turn the mirror to face the wall. Get dressed and head for the door.

"My name is Anna," she says sourly, and I want to punch her so much.

Sensing this, she throws up her hands. "You're a wonderful lover," she says.

"You're not wrong," I say.

I sleep a block from her house with an old man who may or may not be dead, inside of his cardboard home.

What he is, unquestionably, is a blanket hog.

"Don't you share?" I say, yanking at the scrap of plaid wool as I fall, instantly, into a deep, torrid sleep.

I SEE ANNABEL one day.

A few of the other indigent men and I steal a car and drive to Pasadena to try to sell some of our finds at the Rose Bowl.

We make a booth out of scraps and cover it with broken appliances, used needles, empty bottles, and single shoes. People are disgusted, and avoid us.

She is walking a black pug with a white circle over his right eye.

Wearing a short flowered dress, flowered stockings, and flamingo-pink platforms.

Her hair sways as she walks.

"*Annabel*," I cry involuntarily.

She turns around.

It's not her — or it is, and she doesn't know me.

"Every time you left, I was certain you were fucking someone else," I call after her, and hear several *tsk tsks* of sympathy. For her.

Because I hate myself, *I hate myself* is what crawls silently through my throat like a stoma.

I take off on the other guys and drive back. Sit on a sidewalk in Silver Lake and use a stone to write on the road: MADE SOME MISTAKES.

Maybe it is the vision of Annabel not-Annabel, in all of her lilies and violets and cowslips and marigolds: I am showered in money.

One fashionable young man even kneels beside me and pats my back.

"I made mistakes too, man," he says, and I burp noisily.

"That's it, that's it," he says soothingly, and I squall beside my handsome young mother as the sky fills with blue wildflowers and Queen Anne's lace.

SHE IS SMART and beautiful, but she is funny too.

Some nights, though I don't want to, I remember her making me laugh.

By brushing her teeth and running into the bedroom, foaming at the mouth and snarling, "Rabies!"

By enticing telemarketers as a baby-voiced patsy, or scaring them as a lovesick sex criminal.

By dancing, full on, if "Turn Me Loose" came on in a supermarket or coffee shop, and hitting every high, horrible note.

By subjecting me to "Tick Tack," a tickle assault that always left me begging her to stop, and leaving notes on the fridge like "My chopped-up body is in the crisper" or "Joe and Frank Hardy called re: the Aztec Warrior. Urgent."

And by telling long stories about kids she went to school with, imaginary ones like the Boy with Bug Legs, Gina the Ghost, and Murda.

There's so much more: and the things we made up together, like our decomposed Sonny and sad Cher impression, and an entire private language, but it hurts to think of any of this.

It hurts because it's dead, all of it: the people she invented, the words we used. She knew this when she chucked Tubby into the trash.

I try to think of things I don't like about her but I can't, and that's the way it is with someone you're crazy about.

The bad things become the same as the good things, different-shaped precious and semi-precious stones on a necklace, a one-of-a-kind piece your beautiful girl finds in a junk store, polishes, and wears to bed with nothing else, so you supplicate on each gem; you say, *What joy has filled my heart*.

I sleep with my mouth open, hoping that heaven will lower a golden rope ladder, with blessings descending.

HEAVEN DISREGARDS ME.

Days and weeks pass.

I am quite ghastly. I have not taken my meds, I live on street food or snacks plucked from Dumpsters and cheap alcohol. Ale, bourbon, corn likker—this is my brain on crazy.

My clothes are fantastically filthy, as am I, and my wrists are electric with infection.

At night, some of my new Skid Row associates and I make fires in steel drums, and I tell them about Annabel.

They listen, because I have a naked photograph of her taken with the Instax Mini I gave her with obvious ulterior motives.

She kindly obliged, leaving shot after shot under my pillow until she tired of it.

In this one, oh Lamb of God, she is reclining spread-eagled on our bed, wearing a sheer pink scarf and matching pink knee-highs.

A cigarette dangles from her purpled lips, her free hand holds her hair up, and she has written BIG MAN below a bruise I pulled from her neck.

I flash it at them and tuck it away: "Listen, you guys," I say. "We had it, it was *right there*."

I know they won't ask what, so I say, "Joy, joy was sitting in front of us and all we had to do was take it. But we were too scared, too careless, too dedicated to pain—"

I trail off and roll a cigarette.

Pretty soon we are all plastered, and when one of the guys asks to see my nudie again, I refuse.

"I'm sorry I betrayed you, baby," I cry as they jump and roll me, taking my girl with them, leaving her *big man* blubbering in the dirt.

OVER THE NEXT week, I have a few bum fights, over territory mostly, and learn how to make money doing the same.

I use my anger over losing Annabel to win, and I accept my winnings—moonshine, cash, a roll of grimy Percocet, stolen wallets—with the serenity I have recently acquired.

The serenity is this: I live like a broken-down swine because I am one.

Yet I am, possibly, becoming stronger in my rump, pasterns, and cannon bones. Ernest Hemingway said this about livestock once, I'm quite certain.

In addition to my new-found peace, I think my street-ruggedness and miscellaneous new scars make me look cool.

In the evening, I dream of Annabel as Gustav Klimt's *Hope, II.* Each night, I dream of her in every color, gazing at her beautifully enlarged belly, her eyes closed and doleful because a skull rests there among the pink, blue, and gold fish.

I wake up, sick at what I have given away so thoughtlessly.

My own baby, our baby.

I join the mourners at her feet and cry, and the other bums kick and laugh at me.

My golden queen walks slowly through the nightmares as well, picking them up like little sea monsters on the aqua-lined shore, questions unasked on her deep-red lips.

"He did not make me stronger. What he did dissolved my memory, my decency, and the small part of me still capable of love," is what I answer the glance that asks if Kray made me tough, after all.

The circles on her robe move, stick and unstick: full moons bumping, watery stars.

I gather all of her colors to my heart, and it bangs out another answer: me taking a chisel to my armature and seeing our child, a radiant boy who repairs us.

"He cuts away at our dread, he murders what is past and carries us forward in his small, clefted arms," I say loudly, and she moves gravely away from my sleep.

"No, don't leave me here," I call after her, and there is nothing left but three unbroken threads, saffron, ultramarine, and fuchsia, that I braid as the sun comes up and pisses on the wall of the alley, waking me with its rotten force.

I AM HAPPY, in my way, talking to Annabel and carrying her sometimes, for she is somewhat heavy in her pregnancy.

She is also far more beautiful. Her rosy-fingered face and full breasts, her small, puffy feet like marzipan, candy-darling, I want—

"*What?* What the fuck do you want?"

It seems I have walked up to a compact muscleman in a boar-hair unitard and whispered my delights to his rampant slice of mustache.

"My girl," I say, lightly stroking his long, sunlit hair, which is something like Annabel's, and steam pours out of his ears.

He makes a fist and a young couple yells at him to leave me alone, and then some schoolkids join in and start kicking him sharply, and I am grateful, but anxious to leave, when a man in a good jacket says, "Hey, aren't you—wait, you're *Parnell Wilde!*" and I am busted.

Not quite: I make a labored run for it and manage to elude him, but I know he will get the word out.

My idyll will end soon, that much is clear.

"It has been beautiful," I remark to one of my confrères, who is taking bets for a worm race to begin when the rain stops. "A genuine blessing," I say, fishing around for a dollar to place on a stout, purplish fellow whose segmented body is both stylish and built for speed.

I ROOT AROUND in my Purdy Liquor bag and withdraw Annabel's camisole.

It is stained where the *bouffage* of her nipples left wine-dark tracks on the white muslin.

I fold the cloth into a wafer and place it on my tongue, my eyes closed and effluent.

And commence the epiklesis, *Corpus Maria* —

AS EXPECTED, IT is not long before the media finds me and ruins everything.

It is the day I have traded a bottle of sherry for a zippered red vinyl jacket, a fedora, and short white socks.

"Amma lie becoma truth!" I sing, one rubber-gloved hand on my crotch, the other tilting my hat at a rakish angle.

"MULTI-MILLIONAIRE MOVIE STAR PARNELL WILDE'S CRAZY NEW JOB!" is the headline of the *Enquirer* story that is picked up everywhere.

I know this because a Japanese tourist who gave me a dollar to take a selfie with me shows it to me on her phone.

"I'm sorry," she says. "You are really good!"

"I won't stop dancing," I say, as if anyone has asked me to.

I am deep into "Bad" — "I want you slap my face!" — when the officers arrive and seize me.

"No, no," I cry: my fans are outraged. I dance more, fiercely, dangerously.

"Sorry, MJ," the youngest cop says. "Your daughter wants you home. And your mechanic called. Your Jaguar is tuned and cleaned."

"I am unclean and unworthy," I say, then, summoning Michael again, hold my head up and let the cameras rack and rack their shots of me in my good red lipstick, black eyeliner, and straight shining wig that flips at the bottom like crow feathers.

I hold out my hands and they take me away.

My fans are sorrowful, for I am almost young, and still so graceful.

I AM TAKEN to hospital for examination and to dry out.

After that I am to be transferred back to police custody and charged.

I have the DTs, millipedes in top hats performing for bird carcasses.

My cries of "It's a sin, it's a sin!" die down eventually and dissolve into sobs of joy.

"What's the matter with you?" says a guard, obviously irritated.

"There's this girl," I say, lighting up like bumpers, like poppers and flippers; like the whole backbox she dominates.

"She's the one for me," I whisper.

"So what," the guard says, moving along.

I hold my secret tight, along with my soiled pearl-collar cardigan and pink clutch, and it lights up throughout the night, making metallic snaps and mechanical roars.

I and the other invisible, not visible, devotees of Shinto warm ourselves on this shrine all night, rising only to lay shocks of hyacinth on its cold, gleaming face.

I AM RETURNED to the police and spend a day in a cell, using rudimentary magic to amaze my new friends with the finger-removal scene from *The Changeling*.

Pudge and Charles appear at the station just in time.

A cute little padded wagon is igniting outside and prepared to take me away "for a nice, long rest," according to Sheriff Meaty Balls—this is how I hear his name, and I become agitated that I may have to address him.

Pudge is huge again, but different. How? Charles has plundered my wardrobe, to impress: gold and white-checked Turnbull & Asser shirt, brown gabardine Gucci slacks, gold Rolex, and caramel-colored Ferragamo loafers.

Utterly cluelessly, however, he has tied an Old Navy sweatshirt over his shoulders. This the cops don't notice, even though I wish to slap him with its cheap, saggy sleeves.

They convince Sheriff Meaty Balls—oh, *Mettibals*—to release me into their custody.

"He has to get back on his medication, and he has a film to shoot in three days," Pudge says, with more than a little charm, which is something new for her.

"Just keep him out of trouble," says the sheriff angrily. "He violently *Thriller*-danced into two of my best men."

She promises and we file out, wordlessly, and get into my car.

Charles drives, after cracking a window. I don't mind. I have tremors and stink like hell.

No one says anything until we get stuck in traffic on the 405 and all burst out laughing.

Pudge stammers, "Meaty balls!" and Charles counters with "Zombie-dance attack!" and we laugh, bent over, our stomachs aching, until we ache.

"I'm so glad you're back, Dad," Pudge says, wiping her eyes, and I smile for the first time since Annabel was around.

I am suddenly anxious to get home and shower and read that diary. It's all I have left of her.

I can't go looking for her. I am too humiliated; she sounded so certain.

But Tubby may still be in the trash.

I breathe deeply and close my eyes. Feel something toward my daughter: what is it?

I cannot say, so I reach forward and awkwardly muss her hair.

She laughs; her belly jumps.

Oh! She is so pregnant!

"Four months," she says, and adds wistfully, "It's not Charles's."

"It is," he says, giving her belly a tap. "Fathers are made, not born."

Pudge throws her arms around him. The car swerves as she says, "I know, I know," and cries and laughs.

I look down at my lap. I am neither.

"It's okay, Dad," says Christine, and I wonder at her kindness, her bursting, brand-new joy.

PAGE ONE IS the screamer.

"Is it still rape if you cum? Nothing ever felt so good, and so sickening, before or since," she has written beside the frontispiece, a collage of Sid reclining in a field with several striking, slashed women. *Soiled doves*, she has captioned them. She is one.

She has written these words in pink ink and centered them as if they are the epigraph to her entire life.

I feel different; I have changed.

I am sad and only sad for how my son's illness attached itself to her virtue like a metastatic cancer cultivated on an animal in a cage. On almost every animal is the mark of our gross indecency, signifying its innocence and, occasionally, ours.

Occasionally, prostrate and injured, I called her the Venus in Furs.

As though she, who wears vegan moto jackets and biker suits, would touch a fur; or that her position, as the dominatrix, was anything but a gift given to a girl—truly, yet selfishly—too scared to feel safe inside her own skin.

As if she had actual power over this malignant animal, or its disease.

THE DIARY, ONCE opened, walks me into memory and leaves me there.

We are in Berlin, at the Hotel Adlon Kempinski, drinking glasses of kirschwasser in clementine club chairs and watching elegant couples walk along the Unter den Linden boulevard at nightfall.

Annabel is exhausted: our haphazard tour involves a lot of missed sleep and time changes. She is also the kind of traveller who wants to take everything in, to stare and touch and absorb her surroundings, then photograph and film them.

She begins *Jewel* at the Tussaud Museum after shooting Marilyn Monroe's wax likeness, which is frightening to her.

Edits and shoots more, conscripting local actors and finding costumes, sets. This night she shows me what she has done before our vegetable wursts arrive.

It is horrifying. She has slowed down "Your Body's Callin'" and it blasts over the wax figure that is Monroe, planted over the infernal subway grate, her hands adamantly holding her dress down.

Another image assembles itself: it is Monroe naked, in a dishevelled blonde wig, lying on a shabby, rumpled bed.

Suitors approach, each carrying a single rose.

Her eyes roll up, revealing white shells.

"Rape me," she says as her windup teeth chatter, and they oblige her.

"Wait for Sugar," she says, but she has swallowed her teeth and, anyways, no one is listening.

She sprouts yellow feathers and a slender orange beak.

A man appears beside her, who looks like me, who has my old busted-out tattoo that says BOY ALFRED, which was *my* name for Lola's and my son.

He is wearing a dirty poem that I sent Annabel as a codpiece. As he stands with her, the bed fills with blood that spills to the floor, soaking Jewel, Monroe's small white poodle.

The song catches on the lyric "Here I come baby" as the camera closes in on her mouth, a rictus, on my bare, bloody feet leaving the room, leaving her.

On Jewel's gummy eyes, as an indifferent cop leads the dog to certain death.

Before expiring, Marilyn has managed to write FEAR on the wall with damp rose petals.

WE WATCH THE film and say nothing.

Someone below us is singing, *"Halt dich an deiner lieber fest."*

Annabel rushes to the washroom and returns, pale and naked in a stiff platinum wig, and falls to my feet. "I'm so ugly, I'm so ugly," she cries. "Why won't you help me?"

I don't know what to do. She gets up and starts to run,

out the door and through the halls, and I cannot move, I am so consumed by incomprehensible guilt.

I hear catcalls and murmurs of admiration and drag myself to the hall, where a kind bellman has wrapped her in his coat and is speaking to her as if she were a child.

"You're a good girl," he says, and she smiles beatifically.

"Who did this to you?" I say as I hold her snake-tight in bed.

"What do you mean?" she says, smiling savagely, and then, "Do you love my movie?"

She rips the covers off and ravishes me. All I can manage is "yes" and "but it scared me," when she uses her teeth.

Who whispers, "You're done for," right into my ear later as we lie sleeping?

I hold her closer.

Germany is filled with ghosts and fury. We leave first thing, spreading euro notes like a tarot cross on the bureau for the maid with the yellow eyes and vertical irises.

Soon it will all seem like a bad dream.

To her.

In Amsterdam, we eat kif brownies and we fuck until we both bleed, which thrills her, and sends me to sleep clutching my passport.

She takes pictures: of me asleep, and soaking wet; of the blood Rorschachs on the sheets; of the dirty pigeons she has welcomed as friends, who walk my back all night until I announce I am feverish with homesickness.

We keep travelling, though, through scene after scene of her self-hatred.

"Cut me, cut the putridity away!" she cries, and I retreat, at last, into cruelty, my old friend.

"Pack up, Ugly," I announce one morning in Athens.

She cries so much on two planes that we have to tell people her child died in a car accident.

"My one and only," she says to the flight attendants, who place and replace hot towels on her face and serve her large brandies while squatting beside her with open, caring faces.

"He has never told me he loves me," she says, and we are bumped again, to two seats in the first row, and fed what I am certain is Vicodin-laced cheese and red wine until she falls away.

She never shows anyone our holiday shots and films.

Simply posts them without comment and the fans get in line. "Shock and awe, gorgeous," the responses begin.

I stop reading but I know something: that the power I offered Annabel was a sham.

That I am destroying this girl.

I CONTINUE READING her diary.

It resumes more prosaically. I skim through small worries about my ennui, doubts about her talent, and unknown, untold loneliness:

> My book has been sitting on the coffee table for two weeks. He has no interest in it.
>
> I will probably have to go to my launch alone.
>
> I dedicated it to him.

This is one of the last entries.

I have an hour-long scrub, some broth, and tea, and keep reading. I am medicated but, worried about shocks to my system, avoid most of the disclosures preceding this dolorous entry.

She must have gone to the launch alone. I get the book and return to bed, trace my name with my finger, and kiss hers.

"I'm sorry, honey," I say to the side of the bed I leave untouched, as though she is about to climb in with me.

I bash her pillow so it looks like she has just stepped out to get some warm milk or the crackers she gnashes on, leaving crumbs everywhere.

The bed is clean and crumb-free now. I consider messing it up and must stop myself.

I crack open her book and read—reluctantly at first, but then with genuine interest.

And pride: she is just twenty-two, and so bright.

I fall asleep holding the book and wake up to find myself stroking and caressing it.

I still don't let go.

Miserable, I fall back asleep, and there she is, waiting for me, as a fan dancer this time, angelically spotlit and demure.

I READ THE chapter titled "Optics," which features an altered photograph of Alex DeLarge's eye being slit with a straight razor. I skip the parts about perspective, which I already know, and read

Both Kubrick and Kray are indebted to Milton, the most famously blind writer (surpassing Homer), for if Alex and Sid seem strong in their respective films' ends, they are merely pale shadows of their exuberant selves.

The shootout in the alley in *Ultraviolence* is clearly a feverish hospital dream: as he fires, Sid sees himself in his victims' eyes as small and yellow, then long, white, and masked like a swan. Similar is Alex's Pygmalion vision in *A Clockwork Orange*: note that he is pupating in the final scene, moving toward some kind of transformation, which is germane to his lurid vampirism, his parasitic or insect eyes, and the proboscis referenced early on by his perverse post-correctional advisor. Other texts bitten off here include *Gulliver's Travels*, bound as the in-traction Alex is to his illness and moral deformity, and imprisoned within his (Nadsat-for-brain) "gulliver."

I put the book down after tracing these words on the first page: "This is dedicated to the one I love, Parnell Wilde," an inscription she has embellished with a showy pink kiss, then admire her hybrid author shot: a self-portrait of her dressed like Sid, executing a faceless Alex, who kneels before her as if praying.

In strictest truth, I think of Homer as a bottomless bore and have shredded the Milton, a pâpier maché project from the bad days, and refashioned it as the Holy Spirit, a cyclone of red and black I keep underneath the bed.

Additionally, I understand but do not agree with what she says.

I was there.

I *am* Sid.

I open the book and scratch out the line about the ending of the film being a dream, and write in the margin, "Sid was victorious. He vanquished his enemies and rejoiced in his revenge."

PUDGE AND CHARLES continue to live in the guest house together, and I like to see them. Still, with or without them, I am on my own.

Only Annabel ever stepped inside the orbit of my isolation and changed it.

I think of all the men who have lost their children, and of having been a father, briefly.

I will die alone.

DEAR ANNABEL,

I lied.

I once told my mother I loved her.

PUDGE COMES INSIDE at dusk and makes sure I have eaten the healthy vegetable stew she has made me and that I have taken my medication.

We sit in the darkening kitchen and I say, "Pudge, I don't deserve this. You should go. I will buy you and Charles a home."

"Would you please call me Christine, Dad?" she says. I nod and she moves beside me.

"I was never nice to you either," she says. "I was so sure you didn't love me, I put up walls, never let you in."

"Love," she says, rubbing her belly, "has annihilated my pride."

"And love," she says, taking my hand, "just grows and grows if you let it."

"I love you," she says, and I squeeze her hand and say, "I know" and, "You are such a good girl."

"Do you want me to leave?" she asks, and I shake my head.

"Then let us take care of you," she says.

She makes my bed and I am secretly distraught: Annabel's smell is completely gone, as are her little remnants and the bear.

"Tubby," I say sadly, as she sees that I am tucked in and comfortable.

"That's not nice," she says, and laughs. "I prefer *pleasingly plump*." Then, hearing Charles's call, she leaves me to my cheerless room.

Try to get through this, I think; then of a rainwear-clad bear in the steel mouth of a garbage truck, being chewed up and deposited among all the other remains of what was once regarded with avarice, nonchalantly, with love.

MY MOTHER IS raging drunk.

Pulling me from my sleep, from my bed, and demanding that I leave.

"You wrecked my life, you wrecked me!"

Her robe is gaping open: I see her rufescent Caesarean scar; the argent lines on her deflated breasts.

I stand and tie her robe, tightly. Tell her, firmly, "You are not wrecked."

"No one loves me," she says.

"I love you," I say.

"Well, don't," she says. "Because I hate you."

She slaps me so hard I hit the wall and black out.

I wake up and she is sleeping on the daybed.

I collect a sponge, some Fairy soap, and a bucket of hot water, and clean my blood from the wall. Tidy my cot, then myself, using her concealer on the deep, cardinal gash on my forehead.

Make her a big cup of tea and bring it to her with some ginger biscuits and a fresh ashtray.

"What happened to your face, love?" she says, exhaling a spray of smoke and holding the hot cup in both hands.

"Mum," I say, kneeling beside her. "Don't you remember?"

"I'm sure I don't know what you mean," she says, her eyes narrowing dangerously.

She looks pretty again after some reparations with her compact, lipstick, and kohl. Her hair billows down her back, and she has changed into a black robe with embroidered red frog closures.

"I fell," I say, and she laughs.

"Spastic," she says cheerfully. She waves me away and begins making telephone calls filled with purrs and throaty denials: "O I never!"

I am five years old.

I return to the closet that serves as my room and imagine my insides.

I see the cage bars, my ribs, holding my starved heart, which, beneath my gaze, bursts, revealing a much smaller, chromium-plated, steel organ.

Never say *that* again, I think, and when I open my eyes, I see everything so clearly and sharply, I feel dizzy.

"*Pat!*" my mother calls—my real name, my old name, is Patrick Hurst. "Give us some more tea?"

"Make it yourself," I say, walking toward her, holding a hammer I will not hesitate to use if she touches me.

She does not.

ANNABEL, THIS IS why I don't say it, why I *can't*—

I say this to the silent, pitch-black room, silent but for one strange bird that always stays up very late, chirping in a fractious way—about what, I cannot imagine.

I START TO drink again. Not much, as Christine and her husband watch me closely, but enough to make me drunk-dial Annabel, who promptly changes her number; to have SkyMall gifts sent to her express—a Celtic dragon wall clock, a hand reflexology massager, an Illumicube—all immediately returned; and to send her actual letters, as she appears to have blocked me all over social media and flagged my email address as well.

She does not return my letters.

Charles is kind enough to drive me to LACMA, where I spend all my time in front of Pieter Soutman's *The Raising of Lazarus*.

I buy a hundred postcards of the image: she is the refulgent Christ and I am the dead man, born again in Her.

On the first ten, I write her name in different colors, marvelling at its beauty.

On the next ten, I draw lopsided hearts and fill them with clouds of pink crayon.

Then I start writing short phrases, like "Miss you" and "What can I—?"

Then outright apologies, long, teeny-lettered sorrowings.
Finally, my last poem:

> I found you little bird and kept you
> In a golden box with a jeweled perch
>
> You lay on your side retching
> Seeds and nectar, until the day you flew
>
> Away, your russet wing mended,
> Singing as wild things do,
>
> That to be captive is worse than death;
> That death was everything I knew.

I sign it with a drawing of Annabel, pendent in the sky,
and this one is returned to me with DEAR PARIS REVIEW
scrawled over my crummy poem.

I send her an eight-slice toaster and a windup chip-
munk with genuine emerald eyes, and cry so much that
my daughter comes to sit with me, promising me things
will get better.

Finally, I look at her, directly.

"You are beautiful," I say, and am violently ashamed when
she lights up, then breaks down, my never having praised
or loved her, this innocent child.

ANNABEL APPEARS IN the middle of the night.

How, I do not know.

Grimly, she removes her clothes and I see she is pregnant, but smaller than Christine.

Pulling my bedding aside, she climbs on my naked body and fucks me, hard. I am too anxious to cum. She is not.

She dresses and says, "No matter what, you are the love of my life," before padding out the door and down the stairs.

I follow her but she's not there.

I go back to my room and the bed is crisp and clean.

Could I have dreamed her?

THIS NEVER HAPPENED is scrawled in the mist on the closed window.

I pray that it has, and as I pray my eyes pop open and I am wide awake, painfully alone, and pathetic and dry.

Please, Annabel, I love —

The bed is a raft, the room is a sea of tears, and my adored Annabel is the pole star obscured by the storm that has taken so many lives, another will not matter.

I DO NOT drown, or die.

I shake it off like Tay Tay. I'll never get my girl back like this.

It is time to hit the gym with a vengeance, stick to my diet of kale smoothies and pails of supplements, and make the rounds: hairstylist, aesthetician, cosmetic surgeon, all of the high-end department stores for a brand-new wardrobe.

And some cool shops as well. I like American Rag for sheer, intricately constructed blouses, distressed jeans, and boots. I find a three-quarter-length immaculate white pile coat with a pink satin lining at Lemon Frog, and a black ankle-length military jacket with epaulets and gold buttons.

I will be fifty-eight soon. There is some talk of a birthday party, but all I want is Annabel.

Crispin has finished the first draft, "And it's perfect, *ese*."

I read it in one sitting and am very impressed. It is unmistakably Kray's, but polished, and somehow rougher.

The theme of brutal vengeance is perfectly articulated with gestures to the essential plays and films (from *Death Wish* to *Unforgiven* to *Pretty in Pink*).

Still, something is missing.

I wonder what it is, when it should be obvious.

I look around online and see that Annabel has put up a film, her first since we broke up.

It is silent and uses a title card that says OH NO.

This card appears in every shot, as she, cloaked and hooded, throws herself onto beds and fainting couches and, in the end, off a tall building, holding an antique ceramic doll that shatters as it falls beside her.

I have a revelation, and call Crispin.

"I need to show you some things," I say. "It's important, I'll come to you."

Remember how I wanted to mash Annabel's work into the film? I had this idea, but got distracted — by her all dolled-up, by her thrilling ass, by a song on her lips, what, I do not recall — and forgot.

This can't possibly surprise you!

I drive to Crispin's with my highlighted copy of her screenplay and all of her videos on a USB — placed there, I am unreasonably proud to say, by me.

He balks initially, then flips through her pages and jams the flash drive into his laptop.

He watches, moving closer and closer to the screen.

"She's incredible," he says, and I fall all over myself, assenting.

BACK HOME, STRONGER, with some brandy navigating my system and happy plans, I take Annabel's diary to the pool, sit on one of the cherry chaise longues, and open it at random.

It is only a matter of minutes before I get the picture.

"I missed my period."

"The stick turned pink."

"Not again."

There are long, tangled entries about her feelings, initially optimistic yet frightened, which are awful to read.

I skip to the last entry:

> How can I raise a child with this person? I am so filled with feelings of betrayal, disgust, and pain. I knew he was damaged, but I always felt safe. Not anymore.
>
> Anyways, I would likely miscarry again.
>
> So I am having an abortion.
>
> Am I?
>
> Part of me wants a little part of him, the purest part of him, before he was ruined.
>
> I can barely leave Tubby behind.
>
> What to do, what to do.
>
> Whatever it is, it will not be with him.
>
> My only love.

I thought he was going to change me.

He almost did — it is hard to forget all the crackers he broke.

She signs this with a torn heart; the writing is smudged and running.

Oh no. Another baby, lost.

I race around, pressing hot and cold washcloths to my heart and hyperventilating.

Block my number, disguise my voice, and call her, lying outright: "This is your OB/GYN calling," I say, and she says, "Yes?"

Before she can hang up I say, really fast, "It's my baby too, please don't do it, please —"

"I wondered why my female doctor sounded like an old man," she says. "Parnell, it's done. Now please leave me be."

She hangs up, and I know it's her body and her choice and everything, but I still tear through the house raging, tormented by the image of another of my children being cut away like an ugly, useless polyp and flicked into some medical-waste bin along with bloody gowns and gloves, dull scalpels, and wet paper masks.

I will make the hell out of this movie, I decide.

I summon all of my early training, then forget it. I will act from the inside out, excising memories, ideas, and feelings from the crypt I have sealed for most of my life.

It begins with Darkling, in the field of poppies, rushing uphill.

I show up for work ready and stay longer than anyone, burying myself in the character of a man who is unloved and cannot love, yet betrays his tenderness in every pearl he buttons when he dresses; in his careful combing of his wild, raven hair; in the way he holds his face to the moon sometimes, as if he is receiving a kiss.

THE CRACKERS I broke.

Just one.

Annabel and I are slow dancing to Link Wray's "Run Chicken Run" at the Double Down Saloon in Las Vegas, the only time she ever accompanied me to my favorite retreat.

She tells me she used to love dive bars, and reminds me that the sign above the entrance states it is "The Happiest Place on Earth."

Some drunk, a mystifying obese tatterdemalion with big blond surfer hair, approaches us.

"I paid for this song," he says. "I should get to dance with her."

I flash on my old terrors *I don't feel safe I don't feel safe* and try to escort Annabel off the floor, she a wildflower in a fitted white cocktail dress and heels, her hair scraped back with the tiara I sent her when she was working in New York, after which she sent back a riveting picture, a self-portrait taken with a timer—

It is her, naked and insolent on a divan, a pink hyacinth in her hair; she is offering herself flowers wrapped in flowered paper, the rough string undone.

Now it is framed and carried by me whenever I travel, to place on nightstands, tray tables in first class, various countertops and chair arms.

But the drunk is insistent.

"I'll buy her off you," he says. "What's the going rate for an uppity n—"

He cannot finish the sentence because he is drowning in his own blood. I am raving mad and ready to kill them all when the female bartender, shabby, sympathetic, manages to steer us outside.

Annabel jumps him and chokes him further. *"You fucker!"* she screams. *"You ruined it you ruined it—"*

In the car she apologizes, because she is afraid. It sounds like the ambulance isn't far off, so we floor it. No one saw anything, it turns out.

"LOCAL MAN IN CRITICAL CONDITION," I read online the next day, and feel an itch to kill the local man that I must extinguish. I do, by taking Annabel to Joshua Tree, where we hole up for days, where it is all sex on the half-hour, cactus milk and gin, meals in bed beneath a lovely rectangle of Xiang Xiu embroidery.

We are two wild Xu Beihong horses rearing against a blood-orange sky.

A stray kitten mews at our door late one night, battered, toothless, and missing an eye. "Oh my God, he's been hurt by someone," says Annabel, scooping him up. "What is wrong with people?"

We rush to the twenty-four-hour GroMart to buy cat food and litter, then administer some some basic first aid.

Annabel, who has named the kitten Tad, and I take him to a Washoe vet, who does what she can in surgery. He joins the family easily, curls up on the dash on the way home. When he mews, it is cool: he has a grill, sort of, a row of gold teeth that match his new, aureate glass eye.

Tad never leaves Annabel's side until the day he dies. We never learn why, but he fell away in her arms.

We saw the Virgin Mother reach down and retrieve him. We did.

"Do you like animals better than people?" asks the quiz, a quiz about mental illness that we both fail or pass, depending how you look at things.

The other stories are in *Vindicta*, too many, too grim.

I mean the evil that men, and the occasional woman, do.

WHEN SID FIGHTS for Gloriana, or "Glo," I am fighting for Annabel, and so intently that the actress playing her — Carmen Hayward, a famous blonde known for the ethereal yet callous women she plays — falls desperately in love with me, and eventually has to be talked down by a therapist hired by the production company.

Any time Sid fights, period, I am fighting too for this last chance: to be a meaningful actor, never to be a joke again.

I fill each of his words with my crippling sadness, loneliness, and loss.

Crispin is thrilled, and makes everyone else work harder and harder to keep up.

One scene in which Sid, armed with a hatchet and a flame-thrower, collects money from a colossal gangster is leaked online for a full day. The scrutiny is intense and amazed.

"I forgot Parnell Wilde, the great actor," a prominent critic writes. "Seeing him in *Deadly Nightshade* has brought him, incandescently, back."

Reading these words makes me work even harder: no one will forget me again.

We shoot until October, primarily in Los Angeles, where Sid has emigrated.

Crispin discarded Kray's frenetic opening, and gave the footage to Vivienne.

The scene that now starts the film is all about Sid. It takes place in Las Vegas, and is a long, slightly slowed-down single shot of me walking into the Bellagio, wearing scuffed black Givenchy ankle boots, a black georgette shirt with old Irish lace lapels, and a ravishing black Prada suit our costume designer has expertly cut into a thousand pieces and put back together with loose red blanket stitches and safety pins.

My hair is pulled back with a rubber band; curving tendrils escape and frame my face.

Hands reach out to me, but I ignore them. Women offer their cheeks and — my idea — flowers begin to fall, languidly. There are just a few black roses, then more: flowers of every kind storm my passage to the front desk, where I stand, at last, in a field of fallen blooms, immaculate.

I tweak the single pink rose in my lapel as I smash the bell for service, and all the sound and movement stop and then start again as six men rush to my assistance and the camera resumes its doting track of me striding to the elevator, where I pause and smile lazily at a pretty girl who, dizzy in my presence, falls to her haunches and drops her head between her legs.

The elevator arrives and I step in. The screen turns to the gold of its doors, and the music starts: the guitar riff that drives open the Pistols' "Something Else."

"Fuck, it's all coming through," Crispin says as we watch the rushes, and I nod, spellbound.

I am unrecognizably attractive, as my terrible nature has, once more, cast a stronger spell than Annabel's goodness.

My Gloriana, who is seated beside me, whispers, "I can't wait till our love scene."

"Fuck off," I say. "I'm taken."

I will be. When Annabel sees me like this, she won't be able to resist me, I think, trying to ignore another, more insistent, thought.

She doesn't care.

LATE AT NIGHT, I watch TV in bed, sightlessly.

I so rarely used it before; Annabel and I had so much to do and say.

I watch a Victoria's Secret Angel fluttering around in an aqua teddy, garters, stockings, and tinted-to-match high heels.

And wings, naturally.

I had forgotten she was an Angel.

And that one night I saw her ad in a bar.

As I was admiring her, a young man beside me said, "Damn, I'd like to fuck that one's face and skeet all over her."

I asked him to step outside and boxed his belly, kidneys, and face.

I went home, still angry — angry about what he had said, and because I had done just that to my sweet girl the night before.

THE WINGS ARE something else she left behind, possibly because I asked her to wear them to bed one too many times.

I get up and take them out of her closet, breathing deeply — yes, the padded hangers are still redolent of her — and slip them on.

Charles finds me in the darkened living room, in the wings and my white boxers, drinking a tumbler of whiskey.

"You've got it bad," he says.

"I write her and write her, but it's no good," I say. "It's over."

"Maybe you need to move on, to leave her be," he says, perching beside me, his face pleated with concern.

"Maybe I need to prove to her that I am the most def man alive," I say. I had not realized I was so drunk.

"Check it," I say, spinning the dial on my docked iPod to LL Cool J's "Mama Said Knock You Out" and shadowboxing vigorously.

As the feathers fly and I rap "Don't call it a comeback!" I flash back to the chicken ad and fall down flat.

"Are you all right?" asks Charles, helping me to my feet.

"I'm nervous," I say, and he nods.

"Of course you are," he replies, and, taking my hand, leads me back to bed after gingerly unhooking my wings and brushing away all of the white fluff.

I dream of the day Annabel saved me, how I thought of her as my last chance.

I am out of chances, I think.

"Do you want me?" I ask the vacancy beside me. I occupy the space, her space, while pleading, from my field of red flowers, that she not see me, not see me like this.

I NEVER SEE pictures of her anymore. Her social media has dried up, barring the occasional Instagram video of a pug dog dancing—terrifically—to a wide variety of songs.

She never includes captions beyond the names of the dances: Farruca, Mashed Potato, Watusi. Her web site is under construction, her Facebook and Twitter are dead, and after *OH NO*, her video sites sit unattended and voided of all of her earlier work. She is not modelling; her book is a critical success in an elite niche market, but there is no launch or media.

She might as well be dead.

I, on the other hand, appear everywhere. The advance heat for the film is considerable, and my new agent — fuck Jerry — a young Machiavel named Ash, balances smart puff pieces with impenetrable essays in film journals; exhaustive articles in the *Times*, the *Guardian*, *Harper's*, and *Tiger Beat* — the last a short bit of erudition the elderly woman writer, masquerading as "Chase D. Hunter," manages to slip past her editor by beginning the article as follows: "Parnell Wilde is staring at me with those big green eyes, carving me a new vadge hole."

I am photographed with famous actresses, models, and so on, but always state that I am "involved with a brilliant filmmaker" when asked.

Maybe moved by this, or maybe drunk herself, Annabel calls me on the first of December, my birthday and the day before we wrap.

I answer the phone in the kitchen, where Christine, gigantic now, is decorating my vanilla-fudge cake with white rosettes and bumping into the trailing strings of a galaxy of balloons.

I run upstairs like a kid and throw myself on my bed.

"Hi," I say. "Hi, I'm so happy you called."

"Well, I miss you, I guess. And I know that you are being faithful — why, I'm not sure."

"I am!" I say. "I mean, discounting the call girl, because that was when I was mad at you, and I was so wrong, my

God, and that disgusting woman who gave me the STD, but I'm clean now and—"

She has hung up.

I go crazy, redialing her number until I get a mechanical message that my number has been blocked.

I call throughout the night: with Christine's phone, with Charles's, with Rabi's, Crispin's, Dante's, and Cotton's— my party guests—but no dice.

As we eat dinner, I tell everyone what happened and Crispin says, "Why did you tell her that?"

"I blurted. I was so excited to hear her voice I couldn't think straight. Besides, we didn't like secrets."

"But secrets like you," says Rabi—wisely or not, I don't know.

I am an actor: I feign happiness capably for the rest of the night. More people arrive and we listen to the band Charles has hired, an atrocious Nirvana cover act called Kurdt and the Kobains. The lead singer is a mean little woman with a black mullet wearing a flannel dress and Keds, who inserts cruel lyrics about our appearances into the songs.

Still, we dance, and I blow out candles and make a wish and open my presents.

Rabi's is last.

It is one of his photographs, beautifully framed in cherrywood: a large black and white shot of Annabel and me at the old apartment, eating Korean takeout on the lumpy bed in our pajamas.

I hold it and stare; my heart speeds up.

I am wearing a *myeon*, a glass noodle, as a mustache, and she is laughing, her head thrown back, her neck long and arched.

Her hair is loose and messy, her eyes squinched.

The room becomes ruthlessly quiet and I put down the picture and say, "Thank you. This is so thoughtful," rubbing the heels of my hands into my eyes and concealing my tremors with a frenzied little dance move.

"I fucked up," Rabi says. "I thought it was sweet, but—"

"It *is*," I say. "Sweet, so sweet. Would everyone please go? I'm so sorry, I am going to be ill."

I stay in the room as everyone leaves, moving faster when, holding the picture tightly and speaking to it, I start to retch.

"I was hurting *myself*," I say, as Christine stands somewhere in the shadows. "That woman, those women. There has never been anyone but you, why won't you forgive me?"

I hear my daughter crying and am startled.

"Please leave," I say. "And thank you. I can't remember the last time anyone even mentioned my birthday."

She moves toward and then away from me, trembling.

I look at the picture one last time, break it with my face, and throw it, savagely, into the fireplace.

Walk upstairs quickly, animated with rage.

Yes, there it is, the anger that I have struggled with my whole life, the anger that elbows aside feelings of pain, of weakness.

I feel my face harden below its mask of blood and I hate her, how I hate her.

The heartless bitch, I think. I intend to write this down and, after tossing my desk, find a pink envelope that once housed a card she gave me; it pictured two smooching turtles that say *yum* in weird, fucking adorable voices.

I crumple the card, smooth it, throw it out the window, scramble around in the dark looking for it, and finally lay it gently across my ass, after falling face-first onto the bed.

I dream of long, hunched shadows that glide behind me as I use a tawdry angel for target practice.

"What are you afraid of?" she says, and I laugh.

In Rabi's picture, we are sitting right beside a mirror and, in it, we look just fine.

"Not a goddamned thing," I say, and weep for our stupidity, born of vanity and fear.

WE WRAP THE next day, and the last scene has me throwing myself off a bridge for the love of Gloriana, who is nothing but a gleaming skull I carry in my hands as I fall, grimly, without making a sound.

"I hope it works," I say to Crispin as the wrap party winds down.

"It may, it may not," he says nervously.

We are speaking of Annabel's work. It doesn't matter anymore, but I feel honor-bound to use her strange, splendid footage.

He promises to do his best; he has gestured to her screenplay by throwing all those frogs into a shootout at the Santa Monica Mountains.

I made sure they were unhurt, and given a large terrarium-trailer.

Maybe he's leery of me or maybe he's a decent guy. It's a bit of both, I think, as I clap his back and thank him.

"You salvaged the best of me, and almost obliterated the worst."

"Oh, I think I did a bit better than that," Crispin says with his endearing arrogance.

We go to a titty bar and spend a fortune.

Big things are about to happen, we say, slapping palms, to more than a few lap dancers, and the girls, the lovely, curious girls, cautiously extend their own grubby little pincers for stacks of sweet-smelling, newly minted cash.

And a few specks of love they paste to their nipples and shake for us until the night hits the wall and cries, *Mercy!*

IN JANUARY, *Deadly Nightshade* sweeps the Golden Globes after the fastest release turnaround in cinema history.

Best movie, screenplay, director, actor, and actress. We are going to take the Academy Awards too; the odds in our favor are overwhelming. The reviews are ceaseless raves.

Every time I win, I think of Annabel admiring me, envying me, wanting me.

And brush her off.

She is nowhere to be found, so I have no idea how she is reacting to my silent treatment. I have Ash arrange for an in-depth interview with Barbara Walters. I will tell the kind lady everything, and coax out Annabel in the process.

We talk for an hour about my career—a "fever chart," she calls it—about my troubles, she says delicately, and my love life.

"Is there someone special?" she asks, and I lean back, legs open, my chin on my steepled fingers. I am muscular and fresh from my assemblage of groomers, wearing a rose velvet suit and jade shirt with short, red suede boots and hair bound with a pink ribbon. I look so ripe that Barbara leans in hopefully.

"Someone who—?"

I punch ellipses into the air, pause.

"Left me," I say, strategically dropping my head.

I scratch my shoulder, where an old fentanyl patch is still releasing small fronds of opium, and feel the sympathy and desire I have aroused.

I feel thousands of cunts—maybe tens of thousands—throbbing my name onto silk gussets.

Nervously, I feel Annabel's displeasure as well. I have lied by omission and she is already standing at her cauldron, twisting into it foul roots and using an eyedropper to release smoking drops of revenge.

I'm not afraid, I tell myself. I am almost dead already.

Still, there are things to do and say.

I HAVE USED my anger as an engine throughout, to carry me through the tedious post-production of the film, the award-bait press and interviews, and the hope that has been implanted in me like a microchip by anxious producers, having sunk a fortune into a has-been and an extremely late sequel.

My PR people tell me to keep my sob story to myself.

"The old bags feel sorry for you," they say. "But nobody else. You two were a hot couple, play that up."

Their ruthlessness appeals to me.

I am so tired of being angry.

And I am better by far sequestering myself inside of my memories, where something living, expectant, is still lodged and prepared to burst.

And so when I am named *People* magazine's Sexiest Man Alive, I replenish my patch and offer the magazine several shots of me and Annabel: intimate, happy pictures of us in the pool, riding quilted rafts and splashing each other; smashing milk bottles with hard balls at the arcade; sound asleep and dishevelled in the back seat of a limo that has pulled up to a big industry event.

When asked about our status, I am coy. "Let's just say that we're soulmates," I say, "two broken pieces that, when fitted together, make a perfect whole."

It is possible that I pick this remark out with a knife while befriending a butterfly called Severin.

"She took up the faux fur–trimmed whip and said, *Bleed for me*," I may have said as well, but the interviewer is practised at ignoring drug-induced psychosis and is, she tells me, on my side.

"I hope you get your girl back," she says, timidly holding out her hand for the gift of the butterfly, who will perish before she reaches her car.

As I conduct his funeral — "Severin loved not wisely, but too well," I recite — the magazine locates Annabel, but she declines to comment because she is "hard at work on a new book about Freud, Hitchcock, and Edith Head."

When I appear on Conan, I am basically clean. I cannot locate the pharmacist, whose shop is belted with police tape.

I have a finger of vodka, cross my fingers, and when he mentions Annabel, I say that she and I are "on a brief hiatus," an ambiguous remark I bury quickly by talking about us taking a yoga class once and disrupting it by deciding to share a mat and invent a move we called "downward doggy–style."

I almost get censored but the story gets big, generous laughs and the host's scandalized reaction, combined with a shot of the beautiful Annabel, secures the moment.

Later, I am afraid the press will ambush her and she will deny the story, but she does not.

When TMZ corners her at Ralph's holding armfuls of greens and big, veined melons, she smiles and says, "We did do that, yes. We never could get enough of each other."

I get a note from her later: "I said that to make you look good. I know how important the movie is. But the truth is, we *have* had enough of each other."

This hurts so much I feel winded. I write her back, "I have not," and receive an error message.

So she never receives my weepy sad face :_(or my RIP Tommy.

"Your loss, baby," I say loudly, swallowing tears. *Our loss.*

The anger is now entirely sadness.

I have known the purity of pure despair.

I BRING MY bird poem to an open-mic night at Small World Books on Ocean Front.

I am immediately recognized, which causes a frisson of excitement.

"I am here to listen and to share," I tell the group, who seem to be waiting for an announcement. "I am a lousy poet and broken-hearted bastard, nothing more."

The mostly young writers welcome me, beckoning me to a good seat near the front and elbowing one another fiercely in order to sit beside me.

I listen to poems about the choppiness of the ocean and the ocean chopping onions and crying its salty self sick.

A long story about a woman's decision that she "deserves a better life." Tears all around; some repeated statements — YOU fornicated ME — angrily declaimed, and a poem by a latecomer, a fastidious Korean man in a green *chima*, yellow Chucks, and a red CHVRCHES T-shirt.

He reads this poem:

> Your dad beat on you,
> You hate him, you are mad
> Your boss reamed you
> Your friends clowned you
> Your girl left you
> You are so mad you are seeing red
> But are you mad or is it dread?
> That they are right and you are bad,
> That scratch that anger and *Bam!*
> You are sad.

He gets a polite wave of applause, though I distinctly hear the words "an embarrassment" and "how awful" as the saint, who has just explained my entire life, steps off the stage, walks through the room and out the door.

As a moto-dyke is reading a sexy poem about her girl-friend busting a nut in "brown papery panties stained with your shining gunk," I get up and follow the wondrous poet.

He is standing on the street, bathed in white light.

"I like your poem," I say. He smiles and disappears, leaving a pink lotus flower where he stood.

I pin it to my lapel and go back inside to read my poem — drunk off my ass, did I say, and crying like a huge pussy because life is so terrible and then there is grace.

NOW POP THAT PUSSY.

This is me giving Annabel instructions, having just had a pole installed in the bedroom.

Because I have been having some difficulties and cannot stomach Viagra, she goes along with the plan, going so far as to outfit herself in stripper lamé, a long white wig, and six-inch platforms with ankle straps.

She is very nimble on the pole and as she spins, easing off the straps of her ventilated one-piece, I feel all the blood rush to my groin.

Oh, this is such a good memory, I think, as I jam pillows over my face to block out the sunlight and sound.

I stood and she stayed in character, pushing me to the end of the bed and grinding against me until I almost came in my pants.

And then she unzipped me and lowered, so slowly, her Oriental-lily mouth over the tip of —

"Dad!"

I force my eyes open, cough, and say, "What?"

"I have your breakfast, let me in."

I run cold water over my penis until it curls up, put on my robe, and accept Christine's pretty ceramic tray of buttered toast, melon, coffee, juice, and a small potted cactus.

"I thought the cactus was more you than a cut flower," she says, and I smile, indulgently.

Close the door because I am excited again, about the needles of a cactus forced into the pollen-drenched center of a big swollen bloom.

When I was living on the street, my daughter had the pole removed and I am too embarrassed to ask why.

Spin faster, I think, and I can almost see my sweetheart, her knee crooked around the metal, her face rapturous for driving me so hard for her.

I use a pen to make a cross on the floor where the pole was, and write GOLGOTHA beside it, kneeling and praying: God, won't she ever come back.

NOW THAT MY daughter and I have reconnected, I spend a lot of time with her.

I follow her around in my drunken stupors, telling her stories and imploring her to join me for "some spirits or perhaps a nice cold ale?"

She is good-natured enough to pour herself a glass of juice and join me as I talk about the film and Annabel, pausing occasionally to ask how she is feeling, if the baby has kicked, then interrupting her short, happy replies.

"The film could be my comeback—no, my *arrival*. Ash is already fielding offers from big directors, and I have done so many sensational photo shoots, I feel like a slightly older Bradley Cooper—no, better than that. I mean, he's so *bland*."

Then, "When I have more awards than I can hold, when I am so famous I can't walk down the street, she'll love me again, right?"

Christine takes my hand.

"Sure, Dad," she says.

"Sometimes," I say, "I wake up and I am holding her pillow and I think it's her and when I realize it's not, I fall apart."

"I think you should try to meet a nice lady, and start fresh," she says.

"I don't want a nice lady. I want my darling girl," I say, and the wailing resumes.

My daughter takes my hand and leads me to my room, tucks me in and kisses my forehead.

"Try to have nice dreams," she says, and I do.

Annabel is teaching tiny, limbless children to swim in the Caribbean Sea as I flake out on the shore, reclining on a sail-sized beach towel with a copy of *The Spanish Tragedy*.

She walks out of the water, pulling the children on a raft behind her.

In a sheer white bikini and pounds of wet, lucent hair, she is looking so good.

"Buzz, come swim with me," she says, and I jump up.

Leave the book open, right here: *Give me a kiss, I'll countercheck thy kiss.*

I don't mean it anymore. *Come home, baby*, I plead, wrestling the pillow until it explodes, crowning me with a jillion little feathers.

A new batch of tears fastens the feathers more: I turn the light on, grab a pen, and write SO LONELY and I COULD DIE on my hand.

I want to remember what these long, knifey nights are like.

I want to tell her, and have her make it better: she, the celestial creature who is always just out of reach and high, perched so high among the unnamed and transient stars.

I WRITE A poem for her every day, and have an assistant proofread and type it. He prints each one on fine Japanese paper, adding it to a corrugated binder embossed with a swelling sea.

I read some at the bookstore, where I have made several new friends, but they are too kind.

I suspect they are not listening so much as staring at me, at my big movie-star head, my costly accessories, and my well-packed jeans.

My suspicions are confirmed the day I read a deeply unpleasant piece about killing Annabel and dismembering her, lingering on the image of her flesh caught in the saw's teeth.

"That was beautiful," Sasha says. She is a burlesque dancer with an intriguing gap between her front teeth; she squeezes my arm as I sit back down.

"Did you like it when I cut her up?" I ask into her Camay-creamy neck. The reading is over, and I am pushing Sasha into the rear of the bookstore.

"Yes, I loved it," she says, combing my chest with her spangled nails and groaning when she feels my hard cock distend against her belly.

"And when I kissed her skull, what about that?"

I knead her underwired breasts, slip a finger inside her volcanically hot box.

"That was so good," she says, and kisses me.

A soft, hesitant kiss, filled with spearmint and unspoken questions.

I answer them.

"Never," I say. I turn on my heels and walk away, pecking at my face with my handkerchief and tucking in my shirt.

"Bastard," she says, her face wrecked, her clothes mauled.

"I'm not," I say. "I belong to someone else, that's all."

She cries: *O soave fanciulla*.

She is lovely in the moonlight, I think on my way to an

old tattoo parlor on Ventura, where I have PROPERTY OF ANNABEL inked on my lower back.

The cashier calls it a tramp stamp and laughs, showing off about an acre of pitted gums.

WHEN I HAVE finished the last poem — the violent one is not included — I look through the sixty-page manuscript.

I am sorry to have misrepresented myself, though. The saw-murder poem is a good rendering of my extremes, how far I might go on the wrong day.

The last poem is, instead, another entire alphabet. It is everything she taught me, from the Battle of Tsushima to Tchaikovsky's *Iolanta* and the vagaries of time travel in *Zarlah the Martian*.

I remove the poems from the binder and add them to my now-huge VALUABLES envelope — this is crayoned in seashell pink on its rumpled back.

I retrieve each item — including the Holy Spirit — and each poem, placing them one by one on the nice fire I have prepared in the living room.

When everything has imploded, I add the envelope and sit back with a stiff drink.

An occasional letter or word pops out: mostly mine, and most often "sweet" or "girl." Finally, "She doesn't need to see this."

My need, my large gaps of idle time: I had even made clay figures of us, hand in hand, that were bound to the manuscript.

These get thumped by my fist and swept into the trash.

I taught her things too, is my forlorn thought.

Then, *Oh! S'mores!*

I MEET WITH Crispin to finesse the way in which I talk to the media about the film.

He says, "Is it a Senecan tragedy? A revenge play? Yes. But it is more *Elizabethan* than Jacobean or Caroline: the *Hamlet* through-line is the loudest. And then there's Kubrick and Kray, and our revenge on them. In any event, the screen is littered with bodies in the last act."

I remember doing a run of revenge plays and stepping over corpses in the end.

"Are you ready to be a superstar again?" Crispin asks, twitching and rubbing his nose at our dainty table at La Bruschetta.

"I don't care anymore," I say, realizing, grimly, that this is true.

"You don't want all these bastards to eat shit, after writing you off for so long? This is *vindication*," he says.

"No," I say. "I once thought that was important. I once thought that so many things were important. And I don't want to sound ungrateful," I say, while making a little gnocchi log cabin with my fork, "but I'd trade everything that has happened or that could happen for another day in my bed at the Elsinore with Annabel, drinking warm Almondage and holding her tight, breathing in all the ambrosia of the world—"

"Hey," Crispin says, standing up and smacking my back as I sputter and cough, drowning in tears, "everything will be all right."

Which is the song she played for me, and so I go off like a foghorn and he stays standing beside me, dunking a napkin into my water and using it to soothe my big, miserable face.

FIVE

PARNELL AND ANNABEL, HOLLYWOOD, 2018
THE REAL GLORY

EVERYTHING IS BETTER than all right, as it turns out.

I win an Academy Award, as does the film, as does Crispin. I take Christine as my date, but so many models attach themselves to me that I am called the "Millennial Hef" on the red carpet.

I had an invitation sent to Annabel, but it was returned to me.

But I see her, I am certain, standing silvery on the gallery and gone, in a blink.

I thank Paramount, Hercamone, Crispin, the cast and crew, my daughter and her husband, my friends, agent, lawyer, manager, trainers, and "Mac from food services, for all of those crazy salads."

Finally, I thank "the one who got away."

I sleep with the heavy gold statuette and marvel: my anger has long since evanesced, and I am content as I can be.

I have a proper star unveiled on the Walk of Fame and more press about my talent, my genius even, than I will need for several lifetimes.

When I meet my people for lunch, legendary stars stop at my table, and I am "Wilde" to them now. They ask me to play golf, attend screenings and intimate dinners at their homes, on islands, in space.

Everyone seems to have forgotten what a broken-down wreck I was, and I'd like to forget as well.

I have been knocked to the floor and have returned to my feet.

Je vais à la gloire!

I dream that I am a debonair Belgian in a foulard scarf and top hat. That I am alone with my girl again, a dream that smells like red flowers, cured by the sun, their pusher.

I TAKE A ceramics class and make Annabel a tiny pink teacup with her name written in calligraphy on the side, send it to her and pray that she will accept my message of amity.

She hammers it into fine dust and has one of her birds return it to me.

"I'm done," I write on a scrap of paper that I roll up and slide into a tube, attaching it to the bird's leg.

I open the window and she flies away. I drink moonshine from a jug, and when it leaks all over me, I am taken aback by tears, more tears.

"I feel so bad," I say quietly, not wanting to seem ungrateful, but I know, at last, that it is hopeless, and I can't see any way out of the dark.

"Hold me," I say to the one dress she forgot to pack. It still flutters in her closet, exuding smoke and perfume and her pear syrup–sweet skin, and I wrap the arms over my shoulders and sway as the world slowly chimes *for all you lonely people out there*; my old radio soothes me as we cling fast through the night.

I START READING again, referring to a list Annabel made me a while ago.

I read a book, cross it off the list, and start the next: I have ten more to go.

I am rereading many of them, which I intend to keep to myself.

I don't talk about what I read to anyone. When the book is done, I am done with it.

But when I am in the middle, I can get quite absorbed, in a way I suspect is childish and not *comme il faut*.

When Annabel, for example, reread *Lord of the Flies* for a paper about boy-hooligans, she laughed and remarked that Golding's thesis is like "Foucault for Dummies."

I had no answer: I pantomimed a mouth full of peanut-butter sandwich.

I read the same book and run away from home.

I run and I run until I find an empty house that is being renovated, then sit in its roofless living room, crying and unpacking my paper bag, which contains animal crackers, a bottle of rye, a warm sweater, a flashlight, and a picture of Annabel in a pink, heart-shaped frame.

I curl up on my side and write WHY on the dusty floor, and when I wake up there are quite a lot of bats and they muster, then swarm me, rubbing their sticky business ends all over my face.

I yawp so loudly it triggers an alarm.

In the doorway, between the scaffolds: two armed guards and my girlfriend in a flesh-brown wrap, wringing her long, shapely hands.

"What happened?" she says, and I go to her mutely and hand her the book.

She quickly charms the cops into leaving us alone, takes me home, and throws the book on the fire.

"It's just emotional chiselling," she says as I lie down with my head in her lap.

I know what she means and am so grateful I pull her face down for a kiss that lasts and lasts. We give this kiss a chance to show us what it can do, and man, does this kiss sell!

Before we know it, we are actually hanging from the many-paned Tiffany lamp, locked together precariously but tightly, oh my blessed Virgin, my girl's pussy is so tight, it feels like an assassin's hand in a kid leather glove.

She fucks me with the space inside her that is not a vacancy but an inverted long, thick shape and I feel a series of small, acute spasms and spirals tear from me like the skin of an orange.

I let go at last with a sound like a menagerie in the woods where at least fifty animals are cooped up and free at the same time.

In the sound of the bars bending and breaking beneath my mouth, *Your body, your body*, I importune —

What is it?

Her body is the way out, past every enclosure ever made, past the heavens, nirvana, God's parlor, where there is always a lit fire, several small chairs, and the tinkling music of drowsy giraffes, wearing bells.

IN BETWEEN SUCH febrile memories, I do more media, learn conversational Amharic, sign on for three hot projects, and become a licensed pilot. I make plans to travel to various screenings around the world, make a rainbow cake, promote the crazy-hit film on late-night talk shows, and become very good at knitting.

And I find by the trash in the garage a Hermès bag and, inside it, Annabel's old magazine clippings and a short script written by her called *UltraviolenceToo*.

In it, Annabel visits girls in hospitals. Some are rape victims. Some have had their genitals mutilated by their families, and some are abused.

The exhaust of burning flesh: bones snapped like wet sticks, Annabel a girl herself somehow.

They follow her to Central Park and lie in wait. The image of Sid, in shadow, emerges, and they attack like the Confederate army, howling like banshees as Alex DeLarge did in his stolen motor car.

(Kubrick's iconic signifier of the romantic, read: the heroically doomed, maniac South.)

And they take him apart to his boutonniere.

It is in Annabel's mouth as she leads the girls forward, blood-painted and fattened, into a golden circle the Lakota Sioux call *the moon when the plums are scarlet*. The color of her skin is its reflection always, I think with a shiver.

"A full, Corn Moon," she has written, below which her girls drink and grow black stretchers and ribs between their shoulder blades to bat-terrorize the city.

As I read, I apprehend her. She is dark clover honey; Roman stones, old pennies, and phenocryst tablets.

Hoc est corpus meum, she has written by hand at the script's end. I carry this perfect film inside and call Crispin, who buys it and intends to make it with her along the line.

I clap throughout the night, alarming Charles and Christine; see Annabel's undead girls banging at the window, baring their teeth, and tell them that she is majestic, isn't she?

My daughter makes me go to bed and cannot wrest away the screenplay, even though it is torn in two and smells like garbage; it is the barge I ride to sleep below an empurpled mainsail and spinnaker broadened by the wind's frequent, intemperate kisses.

LAMPREY SENDS ME an envelope addressed to me in Kray's hand—discovered, he said, by Vivienne, whose health is very poor.

I want to tell her I am sorry, but I can no longer apologize or explain.

"My dear boy," the weak, barely legible writing begins.

> I am so pleased that you avenged the girl. I saw how you were living, and I was ashamed.
>
> And then I saw her, Annabel, and knew that if you could win her and protect her, you would be safe.
>
> To live or die, it scarcely matters.
>
> Please remember the one good day.
>
> Then curse my devil's soul forever,
>
> Lamont

THE GOOD DAY.

We flew to Los Angeles to meet with the promoters: he was in fine form. He wore Ray-Bans and an I <3 LA T-shirt; he urged me to do the same.

Later he was magnetized to the Santa Monica Pier. He won me an enormous pink elephant and we rode the Ferris wheel, marvelling: *So this is America. Beautiful, beautiful America!*

He squeezed my shoulder swiftly; his "I'm sorry" flew with the edacious gulls.

I forgot the day, kept the elephant.

Annabel lifted it up once from the sofa, taking in its bald patches and missing button eye.

"Hello, Peanut," she said.

I said, "He won it for me."

She said nothing, she is too intuitive. But she squeezed me as I squeeze this letter, knowing it is nothing really, and wrong also, but *damn you.*

It is a salve made by fallen angels, I think, crushing the letter without imprecation, and goodbye, I say goodbye at last.

ONE APRIL MORNING, the twenty-seventh, I am making Christine's baby an orange sweater with a raven in its center when she goes into labor.

I join her and Charles on the race to the hospital.

She has a beautiful, tiny girl she names Patrice, after my real, or first, name.

I fill her room with life-sized stuffed animals and baskets of fruit and candy, and I hold the baby, amazed at how easily she fits in my hand.

I wander down the hall and see a woman in a trashed gown, her hair in snakes, holding a bloody blue bundle.

Annabel.

I STAND IN the doorway.

A short, rotund doctor with a "Dr. Flank" pin on his coat is at her side, squeezing her hand and saying, to my astonishment, "We made it, Anna."

"We did," she says, raising her boy to her face and saying, "Didn't we, Buzz?"

The doctor raises an eyebrow at this name, but says nothing.

They both look up and see me.

"Christ, you're Parnell Wilde!" Dr. Flank says, standing up abruptly.

"I am," I say, moving in a trance toward my son.

"Parnell, this is Claude," she says, miserably. "The father. Um, maybe you've seen his dog Munchkin in some of my videos?"

"The Munch!" Claude says.

I stop, see a dull diamond ring on her finger, catch up.

"I'm the adoptive father," he says, lowering his voice. "The bio-dad was a real piece of work, apparently. Hey, how about a picture?"

"Could I talk to Parnell alone?" she says, and he complies, dejectedly returning his phone to his scrubs.

"I'm not barren, like I thought," she says.

"Clearly," I say. Coolly, but my chest feels like it's trapped under a flame tank.

"But there were complications. That terrible abortion, the miscarriage." She blushes. "I never told you, you didn't want—Anyways, I'm staying here for a while, until the bleeding stops," she says, and I nod, restively. "It was terrifying, actually. I had a pulmonary embolism during the C-section and was pronounced dead. In the middle of the pandemonium, my baby cried and woke me," she says, kissing his plush head.

"Dead?" How could I not have known? "The breaking of so great a thing should make a greater crack," I say. "Should have shook lions into civil streets and—"

"Citizens to their dens," she says. "You're quoting *Antony and Cleopatra*? But you never—I mean, you hate reading." She opens and closes her mouth. "I never did understand you," she says. "Or know when you were telling the truth."

"I never lie about anything that matters, I never would."

"I loved the movie," she says, her eyes not meeting mine.

"It was your idea, wasn't it?" she says. "To use my work."

I don't answer.

"I sold him your screenplay," I say. "Call him, and—"

"No. That part of my life is over," she says.

I reach for my son and she holds him tighter.

"Don't," she says.

I look at him closely, trying to memorize him.

"Annabel," I say. "I was afraid you wouldn't love me back, because you knew me. I was afraid you'd leave me. And you did."

She watches me, says nothing.

I flash on my old car jammed at an intersection that is alive with rage, and me, pounding on the dash in tears and pleading.

Just as some seven-foot-tall beast started walking toward me with a tire iron, the car burst into life and I soared off.

"You are the best thing that ever happened to me," I say, idling in the doorway, and then I leave her, clutching our perfect child with the lupine eyes and tuft of honey-colored hair.

I stall, trying to take in all of her.

Her curved, chancel-gold arms cradling the boy, the glorious love suffusing her beautiful face, her long neck craning to graze the baby's pleats of sugary skin.

"I love you," I say to them both, and leave.

All kinds of alarms go off. I guess she is trying to stand and follow me but it's too late.

I get into the elevator, descend, and hit the street.

"You handsome," a homeless lady says, and I kneel at her feet, slipping the flashy jewel I have kept in my pocket for months on her ring finger.

"Be mine," I say.

She says yes and stumbles away. I walk into the garage and depress the remote.

I follow the chirp and drive home.

I did it, I think.

I text a couple of friends, throw my phone on the floor. Opening my desk, I grab some paper and write for a while, curse when I can't find envelopes, find envelopes.

I dog-ear a book of poems where I have highlighted this:

> Ô pâle Ophélia! belle comme la neige!
> Oui tu mourus, enfant, par un fleuve emporté!

I am barefoot and dressed in a tuxedo, brushing my hair in the mirror.

I am very tired.

I see Darkling in mid-air, her muzzle quivering. I hear a rabbit creeping below the blushing cups of long, rolling poppies.

Aching with desire, I freeze. Poised above her, I can just make out the sweet twitch of her hindquarters.

Then she is gone.

The rest resides silently inside her, the fleet fragrance of what she offered and what I, infatuated and starving, senselessly let go.

Quickly, before I have to give it much thought one way or the other, I pull a gun from the drawer and blow my brains out.

EPILOGUE

ANNABEL IN ELSINORE, 2019
WHEREIN I DRAW MY BREATH IN PAIN
TO TELL HIS STORY

PARNELL LIKED HIS dad's music, a lot of jazz and Sinatra, mostly.

"It's my only memory of the sallow little prick," he said.

"Send in the Clowns," which I found torrentially lame, was his favorite. He liked the live version, with the melancholy talking bridge.

These days, I find myself playing it all the time.

My husband comes home later and later to our pretty split-level ranch house in Los Feliz.

I think he is seeing someone else. I have let myself go.

I spray SHOUT on his lapels to erase the lipstick skids I find there.

Me here at last and you—

I AM ON my own again this weekend, and want to make an event of it, not take pills and oversleep or conjure the past.

Last night, I dreamed Parnell and I were together again, walking on the beach. We made a lopsided sandcastle by the pinking light of the stars for the white jackrabbit he had presented me with, a blood-red stripe running down his back.

The bunny hands me a flask of cold water, and I drink, gratefully.

When he hops away, I see the writing on the flask.

EAT ME, it says, and Parnell is beside me, decomposing, on the bed, extending his ghoulish arm, and I love him so, I open my mouth and close my eyes.

He is gone and I am alone in my Wonderland apartment, listening to Nina Simone, writing, "I think I may be falling for HIM, who could be very good for me. He is sort of pathetic, but so kind. He brought me daisies from the park in a cone of newspaper. He looked so shy and scared, I was deeply touched."

THE NEXT MORNING, I drive to the Pacific Palisades with my hand under my skirt and am smitten with a memory that makes me pull over onto a side street filled with steel gates and a frill of palm trees.

After we had sex the first time, I was insatiable, of course.

He was still sort of a mess: paunchy and dishevelled, his face so crumpled with gratitude it both put me off and tugged at my heart.

To me, he was Marlon Brando in *Last Tango*: broken but powerful, his looks failing in the peculiar, gaudy manner of faded tulips.

One day, I woke him by kissing his feet, his knees, his soft downy balls.

He lifted me above him and ate my pussy as I watched the veins in his big arms pop out, and when I started to beg for mercy, he lowered me on top of him and let me take over, reaching under his pillow and handing me a small riding crop.

This is one way he saved me: sex was always scary to me, and bad, as if I were injected with Novocain from the neck down.

When I slept with Will, I always flashed on my rape, which excited and, more forcefully, nauseated me. So I would empty my mind and make grocery lists as he labored above me, wheezing, "You like this?"

But when Parnell and I first touched, I felt it between my legs.

And when we fucked, I flashed back to the devil he played and, in many ways, was.

Parnell let me master that creature, and win, in turn, an informal award for the most UTIs at the women's clinic that year.

Now, on the rare time my husband touches me, he bores into me when I am dry and rigid, wondering, "You're so tight, your baby-slit is so tight."

This kind of talk excites him to orgasm, and leads me, every time, to despair in the mud room off the kitchen of the enormity of my loss.

I flash on Parnell, big and wet beneath me, jerk my hand out of my pussy, and drive: I am still opening and closing, jammed in the lonely perfume of my sugar, he called it my sugar, without his briny salt.

IT IS GETTING dark when I get to the hill leading to a strip of beach, the sea.

Very quickly I did let myself go, giving away my entire wardrobe, dressing in old Gap painter's pants and Parnell's oversized sweaters, minimal makeup, the army boots he couldn't stand.

But *underneath*, hidden, I am waxed pinewood, nails buffed; my hair still a waist-length champagne breaker, tucked into the knit watch cap I once stripped off for him.

I have on a Strumpet & Pink black quilted bra with white ribbons attached to each square, skimpy white underwear, cut high, beribboned and reverse-quilted also, a red bunny tail on a black square on the rear.

And I have made up my face to perfection, pulled on the one outfit I put aside.

I am in a clinging scarlet silk slip dress, sea-blue silk heels, the rope of pearls, diamond earrings, and a tiara he messengered to me in New York, *light up your candles for me.*

Crossing the street clutching a pink chiffon wrap, I had forgotten what it was like: car jams, barbarous howls, all that shouting: *"Mami, ven aquí!"*

Fall has returned: I am twenty-three.

My baby has been dead for almost seven months. He lived five days before an embolism burst in his brain, devouring my darling boy's entire life in seconds.

Parnell's funeral was standing-room-only, but you have never seen a smaller ceremony than our child's.

Just me and the — as it turns out — cruel man I married, holding hands as a minister recited: *He will wipe away every tear from their eyes, and death shall be no more, neither shall there be mourning, nor crying, nor pain anymore, for the former things have passed away.*

I carry his ashes with me at all times.

"Buzz, look at the pretty waves," I say, kicking off my shoes. "And see—"

I SKIPPED THE funeral and spent the whole day locked in the bathroom, dry-eyed and vomiting.

Why didn't I forgive him?

I killed him.

Later that night, Christine comes to see me. My husband is working, the house is still.

She is carrying her baby in a sling against her chest, a plump pink creature with dozy eyes.

"This is Patrice," she says.

"I'm sorry," I say.

"Me too," she says. "He's missing everything."

"The animals," I say, and she tells me that she and Rabi have divided them.

"Did he leave you a note?" I ask.

"He did," she says, and smiles, her eyes clouded and kind. "Here," she says, and hands me an envelope addressed to *Duchess Wrath*. She apologizes: it is sprayed with blood. "Thank you for making my father a better man," she says, hugs me, and leaves.

Trembling, I open the letter.

Annabel,

I see you, desperately hiding your beauty from the sun dogs flanking your face. How parhelion-blind you made us all, my *belleza sagrada*.

Please show yourself.

And stop saying that you killed me. I killed myself.

And others.

I am attaching *Vindicta* with reservations. Read the details, or don't, but know that you have been avenged.

I delighted in all of it.

You never let me apologize, and I understand. The things I said and did are unforgivable.

Rape, for me, acted as an unstoppable force meeting my immovable soul.

I never loved anyone before you.

You saw the little bit of good in me that Kray could not spoil, and you saved me.

Because of this, it is your name that will have fallen from my mouth as I lay dying.

You were right to leave me: I might have hurt the child.

Even if I have changed, as others tell me, I can no longer carry the repulsive weight of what I have done.

Or live without you.

Thank you for loving and caring for me.

Because of you, I will be remembered for the best work of my life; because of you, this work murders the horrible Sid and his ultimately hateful ultraviolence.

And me. I'm no good and you know that too.

But wasn't I almost. In those perfect moments, suspended as Darkling, above us — intoxicating, dangerous, the field of you and me.

Kiss my baby, kiss —

Parnell

I CRY, AT last. Then I cannot stop.

HALF OF PARNELL'S assets plus the back end of the film leave me extremely wealthy.

The money, which my husband is unaware of, sits in the bank, multiplying.

I make a will of my own, which decrees that this money will be divided among charities for victims of sexual assault, for battered women, for sick babies and tortured animals, and for a well-appointed home, called Pannabel's, for former stars down on their luck.

My filmmaking days are finished for good.

Once, I had wanted to make an *Ultraviolence* sequel to vindicate myself as a survivor and as an artist.

Incredibly, he and his stylish director avenged me on their own — with my own voice and images woven in, like the silken threads of Kamal Haasan's *Aalavandhan*.

I rarely filmed Buzz, preferring to savor our moments together unmitigated, but three days after he died, I posted a video of his ascension called *Jealous God*, which was coded to disappear within the hour.

I found the antique ceramic doll at Little Paris on La Brea, a boy in a moth-eaten linen dress who looked like my baby.

Stuffed him in a trunk until I had hired three frowning Chinese women and dressed them in flowing red gowns.

"This color, it's forbidden," they said, explaining their funeral traditions.

"The child will become a ghost," another said, and laughed joylessly. "Well, that's what our ancestors think."

"Good," I said, and they rehearsed, then nailed the number.

I could not stand to see another coffin: the women are filmed placing a pink cloth over his face (more frowns) and a light-blue cloth over his body.

After burning real money in the flames of three white candles, Jia, Bo, and Ling wrap my baby in a tabloid cover with this blazon: "More Grief for Parnell Wilde's Ex!"

Then tear away their robes to reveal fitted gold lamé suits and sing, swaying, "You're the Only One."

God enters the room in the form of a white swan and He takes my beautiful son for he is *too good*, because He envies him; the girls rend their garments and wail as I freeze, unable to stop shooting.

"A jealous God," says Ling — who is married to a scholar of the Torah, a *hakham* — her voice ringing with compassion. She turns off the camera and signals to the others, who hold me and we sway.

Jealous God is viewed with admiration and disgust: I begin to read the comments, and stop.

I am almost finished.

THE LAST VIDEO, which appeared on YouTube, is an unnamed portrait of Parnell I filmed while he was sleeping in our bed, as the sun rose and our song played sweetly: "Everything Will Be Alright."

I sing as I post it and feel a thrill—some of the old savage energy between us.

This time, I pay attention to the rush of comments.

The first says: "You killed him, bitch."

The last: "Want to make a million dollars at home? I did."

Somewhere in the middle: "I always wanted to feel what you did for each other. So much love. I'm sorry."

There is grace.

I am lying safely in his broad arms with Tubby, and the night is just starting to shake down, a big blue-black blanket that shelters us, its moth holes letting in points of starlight.

"I love you," I say, and he doesn't answer, just holds me.

Dr. Jain once said, out of nowhere, "His silence is eloquent, isn't it?"

I shook my head. But yes, it was. He loved me, wordlessly—

Adoration, bliss, concupiscence, dear, my dearest heart, *everything everything*.

My old white man and me, a skinny black girl.

Unlike my mom and dad, we fit, and when we didn't, we banged the pieces together in a divine cheat.

I destroyed the *Vindicta* file quickly, after anxiously noting the words "Two cops, one docent, a barfly, my own son, and—"

I couldn't finish this but held it papoose-close, cursed and thanked him.

I have read his letter so many times, it tears at the creases. It is stained with my crying: squid-sprays of mascara, saline bombs.

And I read it as I walk farther into the water.

Let the water bear it away.

"I miss you," I say. "Everything bad and good; your hands,

swollen with crime, as tender and sacred to me as gentle, furious Christ."

I have buried the Rimbaud book in the sand, and swallowed the pink sapphire and turquoise — our birthstones — he left in a, also buried, velvet pouch.

The water is warm and soft: it does not resist me as I press forward.

"I never loved anyone either," I tell him, "except my mother."

"And you, desperately, and our son," whose paper bag of ashes I am hanging on to.

I managed to snatch some of Parnell's as well, before they were interred, and I have smudged my sleepless eyes with them: *sweet prince!*

I was chicken too, especially in the end — and so cruel!

"I wanted to hurt you, like you hurt me," I say. "Not lose you. I would have come back, how could you not have known that?"

I know how, of course.

But I want another chance.

"Please forgive me?" I say, as an unusually large pekoe-colored wave rises and knocks me down, pulling my child from me, drawing him into the depths.

"And love me always?" I ask feverishly.

"As I am, larded all with sweet flowers," I sing, like a mad girl.

I stand, and another wave pulls me down until I am sinking, sleepily, my lungs filled with joy.

Above, I hear *flights of angels* singing him — singing us — to our rest.

It is him I hear most clearly, answering what I have asked and longed for, as my heart slowly stops.

He says yes, he says yes!

ACKNOWLEDGEMENTS

MY BELOVED DOG, Francis, then dying, lay near me, patient as always, as I finished this book. In the course of rereading it, in his great absence, I see that the story's love and pain are his and mine. I never could thank him enough for his constancy and goodness: for his *noble heart*.

I thank my father, Douglas Crosbie, an early and strong advocate of the book's title, who inspires me always, whose wit and counsel I miss every day of my life.

My mother, Heather Crosbie, read an early draft with her usual intellectual and emotional skill. David McGimpsey read and remarked, very well, on a draft also: I thank them both for their insights, patience, and kindness.

At House of Anansi I thank Sarah MacLachlan, truly and always, and my editor, Noah Richler, above all, for his instruction and edification: I am most grateful for his unwavering belief in *Chicken*. I thank Maria Golikova, managing editor, for her hard work and insight, and ace publicist Laura Meyer, who is an animal-lover, a dumpling connoisseur, and someone to aspire to in every way. Thanks, too, to

344 | LYNN CROSBIE

Lorissa Sengara, a deadeye, and Stuart Ross, a great editor and friend. And last and in no way least, Alysia Shewchuk created a beautiful cover out of thin air. I am very grateful for her vision.

Thanks to Helen Floros and the Ontario Arts Council for assistance tendered. To Lola Landekic for her powerful work. And to Carol Dalziel, best friend of my youth, who is the inspiration for my heroine, Annabel.

I give thanks to my talented friends Chase Dylan, Sarah Faber, Jeff Kirby, Neil Schwartzman, and Jim Shedden, with particular gratitude to the very gifted Sara Peters and Billy and Margaux Williamson.

My blue groom, Robert Siek: I love and thank you for your good heart and hot talent.

Steph Cilia VanderMeulen, who lost her dog Lucy not long after Frank died. You have been my lifeline. Emma Richler also: you understand all too well.

I met Malcolm McDowell at the appalling Fan Expo in Toronto (run by very nice people), and he was both horrid and charming. I thank him for embracing my hands and calling me "Darling."

Thanks finally to the Malcolm McDowell fangirls, my Insta friends (you are all gorgeous and crazy): Ariel, Emily, and Karin.

If I have forgotten anyone, and one always does, I thank you anyway, with love.

A number of movies, songs and books are alluded to, drawn from, or recast here:

The chapter heads include fragments from "Everything Will Be Alright," by the Killers. Although the song is only named here, it is meant to be Annabel and Parnell's song and, as such, is critical to the book, and is much admired by me. The headings also include some Nadsat from the novel *A Clockwork Orange*. *The War in Heaven* is the title of an excellent book of short fiction by Kent Nussey, and it refers to the brawl detailed in John Milton's *Paradise Lost*. It is Rocky Balboa who says, quite rightly, that the world will beat you to your knees and keep you there (the actual speech is far longer and infinitely more complex.) It is Hamlet's, and Annabel Wrath's, broken hearts that are *noble*, and the epilogue is drawn from the play (*Hamlet*) as well.

I was strongly influenced by the following as I conceived of the book: Marlon Brando's memoir, *Songs My Mother Taught Me*, Anthony Burgess's *A Clockwork Orange*, James Kirkwood's *P.S. Your Cat Is Dead*, Stanley Kubrick's *A Clockwork Orange* (and the glorious Malcolm McDowell), Richard Price's *The Breaks*, William Shakespeare's *Hamlet* (and all of the revenge tragedies cited herein), and Scott Walker's song "Duchess."

Finally. I am indebted to The Velvet Underground (and their wine and roses), Joni Mitchell's "Lady of the Canyon," Ted Hughes's notion of sitting "godless" before the telephone and "beautiful America." Rainer Maria Rilke's *Duino Elegies*, the Comte de Lautréamont's *Les Chants de Maldoror*, Julio Iglesias, and Warren Zevon and Loudon Wainwright III, for the heartbreakers "Keep Me in Your Heart" and "Daughter," respectively.

Christopher Marlowe's *Doctor Faustus*, John Milton's Paradise Lost, Zora Neale Hurston's *Their Eyes Were Watching God* (Parnell's memory is Hurston's women's memory, to a T).

John Lydon, for his idea, explicated in his memoir (with

the same title,) that *anger is an energy*. My dad read Richard Ellmann's Oscar Wilde biography a long time ago, and *the boys are behind me one hundred percent* is one of his paraphrases from the same.

Brian De Palma's magnum opus *Scarface* appears, a snatch of Tony's crass, astonishing dinner monologue regarding the cruelty of (male) ageing: "You're fifty. *You got a bag for a belly.* You got tits, you need a bra . . ."

Nathanael West's *The Day of the Locust* offers the following verity: *Few things are sadder than the truly monstrous; Hamlet* is cited several times. See if you can find it, and let me know.

Ben Jonson speaks of this, *No clime breeds better matter for your whore*, in *The Alchemist*.

I make a reference to Jacques Brel's *"Ne me quitte pas,"* to Hank Williams' falling tears and "Lovesick Blues," to R. Kelly's "Your Body's Callin," to "How Great Thou Art," performed by Elvis Presley.

I recall Theodore Roethke's sad geranium and pure despair; Rimbaud's "Ophélie," Isadora Duncan's unreal last words (*Je vais à la gloire!*) and Lana Del Rey's "Ultraviolence" (of course).

One of Parnell's suits is made by Hans Gruber's (fictional) tailor in *Die Hard*, The Pearl Poet's poem "Pearl" is cited/altered here, and Jean Genet and the Friendly Giant are lovingly noted/alluded to.

Muse of Mad Eros Jack White's "Love Is Blindness" appears, Disco Jesus (and the Doom Patrol) is the name of a great Toronto-based band, circa 1988, fronted by Joel Wasson; Joy Division creep in, *frightened by the sun*, as does a sliver of Erín Moure's diction (I am thinking of her use of the nominative case in *Furious*).

It is the great Lord Byron who *awoke one morning and found (himself) famous* after the publication of "Childe Harold's Pilgrimage" in 1812.

Yves Montand, in *Let's Make Love* (1960), snaps that *L'incident est clos!* The wonderful Beach Boys play at some point, and George Eliot's *The Mill on the Floss* is evoked.

John Berryman's *Dream Songs* are invoked, meaning the author's "axe" (likely Kafka's, borrowed for sinister purposes).

AUTHOR'S NOTE

CHICKEN IS A revenge tragedy, steeped in those very plays, and it is a comeback story.

It is, additionally a *roman à clef*, based on both Alexander DeLarge (from *A Clockwork Orange*, the film) and Malcolm McDowell himself, who was, when I began the book, starring in horrid commercials and making the fan expo scene.

It must be noted that unlike Parnell Wilde, McDowell has never hit the skids and is, by all accounts, a kind, clean, and sober family man; he is extremely wealthy and, I am happy to say, doing marvelously well with *Mozart in the Jungle*, a sort of artistic sequel to *Clockwork*.

Other stars make appearances. I will leave it to you to guess who they are.

I am a great admirer of Stanley Kubrick as well (it must be noted that Kubrick bears absolutely no resemblance to Lamont Kray) for his understanding that *Militiae species amor est*.

Writing while immersed in his starry horrorshow was a great pleasure.

I leave off with the quotation from the book and the film I had McDowell inscribe on a vintage *Clockwork* poster. He did so, cursing and complaining as Alex might: *It was gorgeousness and gorgeosity made flesh.*

Courtesy of the author

Poet, essayist, and novelist LYNN CROSBIE was born and raised in Montreal. An award-winning journalist and cultural critic, she has written about fashion, sports, art, and celebrity. She has a Ph.D. in English literature and a background in visual studies, and she teaches at the University of Toronto. Her volumes of poetry and prose include *Queen Rat*, *Dorothy L'Amour*, and *Liar*. She is the author of the controversial book *Paul's Case*, about the Paul Bernardo–Karla Homolka murders, as well as the novels *Life Is About Losing Everything* and *Where Did You Sleep Last Night*, a Trillium Book Award finalist. Her most recent collection of poems is about her father, entitled *The Corpses of the Future*.

TELL THE WORLD
THIS BOOK WAS

| Good | Bad | So-so |